Virginia chuckled and blew her dark curly bangs upward, then kissed Ruby on the cheek, thankful she had finally gotten shoes on her daughter's wiggly feet.

"Is Sister Crystal Grace coming to see me today?" Ruby asked.

"No, I think she's resting. A close friend of hers passed away."

"Mrs. Bryant."

Virginia cocked her head sideways. "How did you know that?"

"Everly told me." Ruby giggled. Then her teeny face turned serious, and her lips pursed tightly. "I know a secret," she whispered, her sapphire eyes sparkling.

Virginia put the tip of her nose to the tip of Ruby's. "Yeah, kiddo? What is it?"

"I'm not really an airplane," Ruby whispered. "I'm an angel." She grinned to show tiny white perfect teeth. Then she covered her mouth with both hands.

"Yes, you definitely are." Virginia picked her up, twirled her around, and placed her on the floor. "And you're going to be a hungry angel if we don't get you some chow before your class." She put Ruby's pink rain jacket on her, and then pulled on her own. "It's raining hard today. We'd better button you up. I don't want you to get a cold."

"I won't, Mommy."

Virginia held Ruby's hand as they walked to the car. Her tiny hand was so warm. She loved her so dearly.

"School buses carry lots of kids, don't they?" Ruby remarked.

"Yes, darling."

"Kids that need to grow up and do important stuff someday."

Virginia met her eyes. "Yeah. Why ya askin'?" She belted her into the carseat.

"Just thinking about the bus and all the kids, and how I gotta do the good thing."

# BY SHELLY GAIL MORRIS

*Ordinary Women—Not!*

*Saving Dandy James*

Sandy,
I hope you love
my stories.
Shelly Gail Morris

# SHELLY GAIL MORRIS

# TALL TALES of MYSTIC RIDGE

ZUMAYA EMBRACES          AUSTIN TX

2023

TALL TALES OF MYSTIC RIDGE

© 2023 by Shelly Gail Morris

ISBN 978-1-61271-359-5

Cover Design by GetCovers.com

"Zumaya Embraces" and the dove logo are trademarks of Zumaya Publications LLC, Austin TX, https://www.zumayapublications.com

# TABLE OF CONTENTS

# DEDICATED...

*to all the wonderful people
involved in animal rescue*

# EVERLY VISITS

THE HUGE MAHOGANY DOOR CREAKED AS EMMA WALKED ONTO her front porch. Feeling grateful, she took a deep breath of the warm Tennessee air. She detected the slight scent of cinnamon.

Her new home was everything she had ever wished for. The nearly fifty-year-old two-story house had a large wrap-around porch. Window boxes filled with pink petunias added cheerful spots of color to the white cedar siding. Black shutters were just the right touch of Victorian elegance.

She picked up a brass watering can and walked down the three steps to the narrow cobblestone sidewalk then tiptoed barefoot through thick green grass to the water spigot. After she filled the can, she watered the green ferns that hung from each corner of the porch, and the geraniums in ceramic pots on each side of the front doors. She set down the empty can and put her hands on her hips as a warm breeze drifted through her long brown hair. This was always how she had envisioned summertime. Life seemed perfect here in Mystic Ridge.

Well, almost.

It had only been three days since she and her husband Caleb had moved in, and already several of their neighbors had brought over delicious pies, cookies, and muffins—literally a warm welcome. People had told her the residents of Mystic Ridge were eccentric and unusual, but she found them kind and gracious. They treated her like she belonged here, like family. She had everything a woman could possibly want.

Yet a lump formed in her throat. Some things would always be unattainable. She had to accept it. Wrapping her arms around her waist, she went back inside.

Sighing, she leaned against the door. The sitting room on her left was full of brown boxes. In the larger family room on her right, Caleb's favorite worn-out recliner and big-screen television had purposefully been placed in the middle of the floor. She cringed. They did not exactly fit into the antique setting of the room.

She had three months to perfect her decorating, and it would not be easy. It was June, and in September she would begin her teaching job at Smoky Valley Elementary School. She looked forward to it. She loved teaching. Knowing she could make a difference in a child's life gave her a real sense of accomplishment.

She sat down in the recliner and watched the lace draperies floating in the delicate breeze. Sometimes, she would dream of a little girl with Caleb's brown eyes and her long flowing hair, but the doctors had assured her it could not happen. When she and Caleb were all settled, they were going to look into adoption. A child would complete her life, and she couldn't help but yearn for one.

The sound of banging interrupted her thoughts. Caleb was upstairs, noisily removing cracked paint from the master bedroom walls.

"Honey, someone's walking over," he shouted.

She rose and rushed to the front door. Once again, the hinges creaked as she opened it. A man she estimated to be in his sixties was climbing the steps.

"Hello," she greeted him.

"Hi, I'm Owen Bryant," he said, extending his hand.

She shook it. "I'm Emma Parsons. My husband Caleb is upstairs making a few repairs."

"Welcome to the neighborhood. Are you new to Mystic Ridge?"

"Yes, we're from Macon, Georgia. My husband's a geologist, and he's here to study the Early Precambrian rocks."

"Oh, well, we've got plenty of rocks here in ol' Tennessee." He chuckled.

"I'm going to teach second grade at Smoky Valley Elementary," she told him.

"That's just wonderful. Welcome. Expect great things from this here community. We all look out for one another. Mystic Ridge seems to bring out the best in folks, despite our supernatural reputation. My mama, Violet, lives in the house directly across the street." He pointed toward a burgundy Victorian home with alabaster shutters.

"I don't mean to trouble you, but I live about thirty minutes away in Knoxville. Mama will be ninety-four on her next birthday and still insists on living alone. So stubborn. The folks who used to live in your house always kept an eye on her, but they hit it big in the lottery and moved to Florida. Father Harrison stops by once a week. But would you mind watching out for the place?"

"I'd be glad to," Emma said.

"She's fine, and totally self-sufficient. There's a working security system, when she doesn't turn it off." He scoffed. "She also has an emergency necklace that will alert me if she needs me. Her groceries are delivered, and I have a service for the yard. I'd just sleep better with a real set of eyes on the place. You don't have to do a thing, really. Just call me if you notice anything out of the ordinary." He handed her a card containing several phone numbers.

She took it.

"I look forward to meeting her."

"That's dandy. Let me warn you, though, she's a pistol—sweet as molasses, but a sure-fire pistol." He grinned and shook his head, nodded and then shook his head again. "I hate to leave her, but she refuses to move. She's got a lot of crazy ideas these days. But I can't deny her intuition. She's got a real connection to the Man Upstairs, if you know what I mean."

Emma felt herself grinning.

"Well, call me day or night if you spy anything unusual. I'd like to introduce you, but I've got an appointment in town. Thank you so much."

"I'm happy to do it," Emma said sincerely.

He turned and hurried down the steps, and then stopped and looked back at her.

"I really think you two will get on charmingly."

Emma was pleased at the thought. "I know we will." She didn't have any friends yet and was excited about befriending someone with a connection to the Man Upstairs.

Owen Bryant dashed across the street, climbed in his car, waved, and sped away.

She gazed down at the card. It was sweet that he still looked after his mama. She decided now was as good a time as any to go meet her. The house was stunning, and she'd love to get a peek inside.

She leaned in the door and shouted to Caleb, "I'll be back in a minute. I'm just gonna run across the street."

She closed the door firmly and headed for the Victorian house. As she approached it, she could see a woman through the window. She was laughing and seemed to be waltzing around the room, her vintage apparel flowing behind her. Emma chewed her lower lip. What had she gotten herself into?

When she reached the door, she saw an old door knocker with a cursive *VB* on it. Her heartbeat sped up. She knocked, and after a few seconds, the door slowly opened with the same creak she was growing accustomed to from her own door.

A small woman with white puffy hair and stunning sapphire eyes grinned up at her. "Good day!" she squeaked.

Emma instantly liked her. The woman was petite and frail, yet clearly giddy and excited at the prospect of a guest. She wore a pink-and-blue floral dress, and a fluffy white boa was draped around her neck. Tiny white lace gloves covered her hands, and a pink rose was tucked behind one ear.

"Can I help you, sweetheart?" she asked in a tender voice.

Emma looked down at her own attire. Her jogging suit suddenly seemed oddly inappropriate.

"Hello, I'm Emma Parsons," she finally managed. "I'm your new neighbor. I just moved in across the street." She pointed. "I wanted to come and say hello."

The woman stepped aside. "Oh, do come in. Come in, please. It is so wonderful to meet you. My son just left. I was enjoying some tea. I'm Violet, Violet Bryant. I wasn't expecting visitors." She took deliberate steps. "But I'm so glad you came. So glad. We love visitors. Emma—what a lovely name." She gazed toward the window. "Whenever I meet someone new, I seek the reason our paths have crossed.

Most encounters have a real purpose, you know. Everly agrees. I think soon I shall know why we have met."

Emma was in awe of the elderly woman's youthful energy.

"So," Violet continued, "welcome to Mystic Ridge. Is everything going smoothly? I've heard moving is a lot of work. You're going to love it here. Mystic Ridge has quite the ambrosial reputation. I suppose you've heard of my friend Sister Crystal Grace?"

Emma shook her head.

"Oh, you must have a seat. I insist. It's a long sordid tale of loss, and then joy!" Her eyes sparkled.

She motioned to a red velvet couch, and Emma sat. Violet settled in a teal brocade-upholstered rocking chair and wound her gloved hands together.

"Oh, where should I begin? A very long time ago, when we were just girls, Crystal left her duties at the washbucket and went exploring up the ridge. Later, she told me she was summoned by a higher power. I don't know about that."

Violet's eyes grew wide, and her tone serious. "Anyway, she got lost. The whole town searched for her for weeks, including me. It was so awful. National television aired our plight. Quite the scandal." She crossed her tiny arms. "But after a candlelight vigil, she showed back up, fit as a fiddle, healthy and unscathed. It was remarkable—some said it was a miracle. She had amnesia and was vague about any memories. Personally, I found her smarter, braver, keen and sensible." She adjusted the boa around her neck dramatically. "Her family was just thankful to the heavens for her return. The whole town celebrated."

Emma smiled. "I love happy endings."

"On her eighteenth birthday she entered the Sisters of Southern Mercy Convent and became a nun. It's very close by, and I just adore her visits. She brings me homemade grape jam. I'll share some with you. We see quite a lot of her. She's close with Everly, too."

"We went by a park near the base of the mountains," Emma began. "I think it was Crystal Caverns Park."

"Yes," Violet said. "It's named after her. They give tours and offer hiking up the ridge and into a few of the caves."

"I must take a tour."

"Oh, yes. Quite exciting. I will introduce you to her. I think she will like you." She paused. "Everly thinks she will, too."

Emma wondered who this Everly person was, but she focused on her surroundings.

"Your home is stunning." There were paintings on every wall, and each had its own dainty spotlight. A painting of Jesus caught her eye. She rose and walked to it.

Violet stood and moved beside her. "That's a reproduction of *Christ Blessing Little Children*, by Charles Lock Eastlake, from eighteen-thirty-nine. It's my very favorite. And see this little figure in the back, almost hidden by her shawl?" She pointed. "I always joke that it's my friend Sister Crystal Grace, because it looks just like her, and she plays along and says that Charles was bossy and grated on her nerves while she posed for him." She laughed and placed her gloved hand on her stomach. "She just loves to tickle my funny bone. Whoever heard of a time-traveling nun?"

Emma chuckled and studied the painting; it was mesmerizing and seemed to float on the wall. She felt that the characters represented feelings of deep love and true adoration. She'd never experienced anything like it.

"It's quite heavenly."

"I know," Violet whispered. "Reaches right into your soul."

The room was filled with porcelain trinkets and glass figurines. She noticed four porcelain white kitten figurines, their eyes jeweled. There was a tiny gold Egyptian pyramid, and a lifelike owl, also. The entire home had an ethereal glow and smelled of vanilla and fresh flowers. Dozens of family photos filled the tables.

"You rest yourself, and I will be right back," Violet said, and slowly made her way from the room.

Emma sat down, feeling like she had traveled back in time herself. Violet returned after a while with a tray containing a small teapot and two porcelain teacups.

Emma stood. "I'll do that. Please, let me." She took the tray.

"Aren't you a sweetheart." Violet accepted the offer and sat down. "My hands aren't as steady as they used to be."

Emma put the tray on a mahogany coffee table and poured a cup for Violet and one for herself. She returned to the soft couch. When she took a sip, the sweet honey flavor relaxed her.

"This is delicious."

"Thank you. Everly taught me to use a touch of honey and cinnamon in my tea."

Violet pressed her lips together thoughtfully. "The neighborhood has really changed. I remember when I first moved in—I think Dwight Eisenhower was in the White House, but I can't be sure. My husband Gene was so proud of this place."

She sipped tea. "My favorite movie, *The Search for Bridey Murphy*, was on at the picture show. If I remember correctly, I saw it three times. Teresa Wright starred in the movie, but I think Vivian Leigh would have been a better choice. Did you see that picture?"

Emma thought for a moment. "No, I don't think I've ever seen that one, but Vivian Leigh was such a talented actress."

Violet waved her boa. "Without saying, without saying, marvelous, simply marvelous. I haven't been to a picture show in years. My son has tried to take me, but I prefer remembering my old favorites. Did you meet my son?

"I did," Emma replied. "A pleasure."

"Handsome devil. Everly and I were just talking about Owen. He's starting to show his age, you know. He's a dear boy, just a dear. But he's not so little anymore. Do you have any children?"

"No," Emma said, and then found herself revealing a secret she hardly ever divulged to anyone. "I'm sad to say that I can't have children."

Violet's brows creased. She sipped her tea thoughtfully. "Doctors don't know everything."

Emma poured herself another cup, embarrassed that she'd shared something so personal. Violet smiled at her, relieving her awkwardness.

"Now, exactly what divine intervention brought you to us here in Mystic Ridge?"

"My husband Caleb recently finished his masters in geology." She chuckled. "He's obsessed with rocks and gems and crystals and dating them. His employer asked if we'd consider moving here. We came up to have a look around and saw the home across the street. The realtor was in the yard putting a sign up. She let us go inside, and we knew we had to have it. We placed an offer, and Caleb agreed to relocate, all on the same day. We both felt it was meant to be our home, and we didn't even look at any others."

"My, my, I'm so pleased. That's wonderful. How long have you been married?"

"Five years. While we were here, I applied for a teaching job."

"Oh, a teacher, a teacher. Did you hear that, Everly?" Violet said as she clapped her gloved hands together.

Emma looked around the room, wondering about this person Violet kept talking to. Then she remembered Violet's previous comment.

"Oh, yes, yes, I'm starting at Smoky Valley Elementary in September. I teach second grade."

Violet stood. "That's splendid, just splendid. Let me get us something special."

She slowly but purposefully stood and headed off for the kitchen. Emma could hear her tiny voice as she talked to someone. Her voice was soft, but her tone was serious.

"I think this is the answer to our prayers. She seems genuinely nice, and smart, too, and she's beautiful to boot. It's a divine opportunity for you, darling. This is it. This is what we've been waiting for."

Emma wondered if someone else was in the kitchen, but she only heard Violet's voice.

Violet reappeared in the doorway with a silver tray of pink petit fours. "These are simply delicious, even if I do say so myself. They take an entire day to prepare if you do it properly." She placed the tray on the coffee table near the tea.

Emma tried one. It melted in her mouth. "Oh, my, yummy! You must give me the recipe."

Violet held up a finger. "Only if you promise to come visit me again very soon. I want to know all about you."

"You've got a deal," Emma agreed.

They spent the entire afternoon discussing treasured recipes, flowers that grew well in the area, and neighbors who had come and gone. Emma found that she hung on every word Violet said. She thoroughly enjoyed the day, and she thought Violet had as well. She felt grateful she had met such an intriguing, almost inspiring woman. Violet was proud of her life experiences and the relationships she treasured. She was also sharp as a tack.

They said their goodbyes as the sun began to set, and Emma returned home to the overwhelming job of unpacking. Violet filled her thoughts. She went over their conversation again and again. There was something unique about her elderly neighbor, something peculiar. She wanted to know more about her and this Everly person.

That evening, as Emma and Caleb relaxed on the front porch, she told him about Violet; but she had difficulty verbalizing the strange connection she felt to her. He was pleased she had made a new friend. As the sounds of crickets and frogs filled the night, Emma felt as if she was exactly where she was supposed to be. It was calming. But she also felt there was something on her horizon, something in her future, something unusual, and only Violet had the answers.

At eight o'clock she watched Violet's lights go out. She stared at the home, longing to visit again as soon as possible.

❦

When Emma woke, she found a note from Caleb—he had gone to the hardware store to buy a few painting supplies. She hoped it was more than a few.

She showered and put on a robe. Boxes waited to be unpacked in almost every room, but all she could think about was paying another visit to Violet. She remembered a recipe her aunt had given her. It was for Georgia pecan banana bread. Excited, she set about making it, but as she prepared the bread, she felt oddly nervous.

She whipped together two loaves in no time. While it was cooling, she went upstairs to search for the perfect outfit to wear. She knew she was behaving irrationally, but for some reason, all she cared about today was impressing Violet. She desperately wanted her neighbor to like her.

As she dug through suitcases and boxes looking for an appropriate outfit, she heard Caleb downstairs.

"Honey, I have a surprise for you," he shouted. "Come here, hurry."

Emma hurried down. Caleb was holding a large brown box. She peered into it. A large white cat with emerald eyes looked back at her. Then, a tiny white kitten appeared under the cat's paw, and another one after that.

"Didn't you have a white cat when you were a child?" he asked.

"Yes." She nodded. "This sweet mama looks exactly like her. Oh, Caleb, they are so adorable and calm. Where did you find them?"

"When I came out of the hardware store the box was right beside my truck door. They looked up at me, and I was smitten. I couldn't just leave them."

"Someone knew you were a big softie. You did the right thing." She kissed him over and over until his face turned a bright shade of scarlet. "I love you so much."

Caleb had a huge heart; it was one of the things she loved most about him. He had compassion for all living creatures. And this was the most incredible housewarming gift she could have ever imagined. She caressed the mother cat, and then the kittens.

"We have plenty of room. Here, give them to me, and you go find a blanket."

He handed her the box and dashed away. "We're a family now," he bellowed.

She chuckled.

After a few minutes, he returned with a blanket and placed it in the box as Emma positioned the kitties on top. They found a warm corner in the kitchen with just a touch of sunshine. The mother and kittens snuggled close and fell fast asleep.

Emma hugged Caleb as she watched them. "They are just the sweetest. We'll need some food, litter, and a bowl for food and water."

"I know. I know. I'll run back up to the store." He kissed her on the cheek. "I forgot dropcloths, too, and paint thinner. I don't know where my head was." He grabbed his keys and disappeared.

Emma watched the animals. They stretched out and purred, content in their new surroundings. It was as if they belonged here. She felt it, too.

Suddenly, she had an idea. Maybe Violet would enjoy seeing them. Her mind raced. Yes, that was a novel idea. She needed a reason to show up at Violet's door.

This would work. Eagerness consumed her.

She located the perfect ensemble—a purple sundress with lace and flowers around the neckline. She dabbed a bit of cologne on her wrists and pulled her hair into a neat bun. After she was satisfied with her appearance, she skipped through the house and into the kitchen. She whistled a cheerful tune as she sliced a loaf of banana bread and wrapped it. Caleb arrived home just in time.

She rushed to greet him. "Honey, I really want you to meet Violet. How about if we take the kitties over? I know she'd enjoy seeing them."

He put his bags on the kitchen counter and smiled at her. "You think so?"

She nodded excitedly.

"Okay." He took in her neat appearance. "I can see this unpacking and remodeling thing is going to be a long, long process. It's all good, though. I do love our new home..." He paused, "...and you."

She kissed his cheek, then opened the door and followed him down the front steps.

"It's odd, really. I feel a strange anticipation when I'm with Violet. It's like I'm waiting for her to tell me something very important. I want her to like me.

I can't explain it."

He chuckled. "You spruced up, lookin' good." He lifted the box. "I've been thinking of names—gemstone names, crystal names."

"Oh, good." Emma peeked at the momma, concerned she might be wary. But she was licking her babies trustingly.

"Hold that box tightly. Be careful."

They proceeded across the street. When Emma knocked on Violet's door, she thought she heard music.

The door creaked open, and Violet tilted her head sideways and smiled at the couple.

"Hello, Emma, my new friend. It's so nice to see you. Is this your husband?"

"Yes. Violet, I would like you to meet Caleb."

Since he was holding the box, he nodded politely. "Pleased to meet you."

Violet blushed. "Look, Everly. He's very handsome."

Caleb looked behind her. The cat and kittens began to squirm.

Violet squinted at him. "What do we have here?"

He placed the box on the ground.

Emma spoke up. "Caleb found a sweet mother cat this morning, and two kittens. Someone left them right beside his truck."

"An unusual welcome," Violet commented. "But quite typical."

"I had a white cat when I was a child," Emma told her. "These three are all white."

"Really?" she drawled, tapping her chin. "Childhood memories come to life."

Emma continued. "We're going to keep all three. I'll have them altered before they can reproduce, and I'll keep them indoors. They won't bother you. I thought you might like to meet them."

Violet peered into the box. "Oh, like a powder puff or freshly fallen snow. Simply lovely." Her eyes filled with moisture as she began petting them. "I bet Sterling is the culprit. He's a big old pristine alabaster male that lives at the senior home. They say his sapphire eyes are hypnotic. He's been there since I was little."

Caleb glanced at Emma.

"They're precious, just precious," Violet said. "Caleb, you are too kind, too kind. Pardon me just one moment, please." She swiftly shut the door.

Caleb shrugged. "What's that all about?" he asked.

"Shhhhhh," Emma instructed. She needed to hear Violet's voice. She absolutely had to hear what she was saying. She placed her ear near the door and listened intently.

"Everly, Everly," Violet was saying, "he's a dear man, and she's a charmer. Think about it. I implore you. I'm not going to be around forever. Your time is running out. They're lovely people."

Suddenly, the door swung open, and Violet grinned. Emma straightened up and smiled nervously.

"I brought you some banana bread." She held it out.

"Well, you must come in, and we will enjoy it together."

Emma turned to Caleb. "You take the kitties back home—they've had a long day. I'll be there in a little while."

"Okay. It was nice to meet you, Ms. Violet," he said. "You gals have a good afternoon." He lifted the box and headed back across the street. Emma blew him a kiss and followed Violet inside.

She handed Violet the bread and studied her as she walked toward the kitchen. Never in her entire life had she been so curious about anyone. She just had to know all about her and this Everly person.

She sat on the same red velvet couch she had occupied the previous day. Gazing around the room, she was again in awe of this woman who managed so well all by herself. A few minutes later, Violet came in with the bread on a silver tray.

Her arms shook.

Emma rose. "Please, let me help you." She took the tray and placed it on the coffee table.

"There's tea in the kitchen, if you wouldn't mind fetching it, my dear. I'm a bit tired today." Violet sat down. Emma handed her a ruffled pillow and a small blanket that were lying nearby.

"Please, you rest! I'll get the tea."

She went into the kitchen and found the water still warming on the stove. She located the teapot and filled it inside when the kettle came to a boil. As she looked for cups, she noticed several bottles of medication. Each one was full. Was Violet not taking her prescriptions? Maybe she should call Owen. Yes, she would.

She found some cups and returned to the living room, setting the tea beside the bread. She could tell Violet had spied her worried expression.

"I'm fine, really," she said, guessing the cause. "Those pills make me groggy. I still have a few things to take care of. All that old medicine can't help me. I don't expect to live forever. Why would anyone want to?"

Emma wasn't sure how to respond. She poured Violet a cup of tea, handed it to her, and sat back down.

Violet's thin lips curved upward. "Actually, I'm looking forward to my journey. I have so many old friends and loved ones to visit. I'll see my Lily again."

Emma felt a wave of panic. The thought of Violet dying after she'd just met her was unbearable.

"Don't worry about me, sweet child. Everly has told me all about everything."

Emma's heart skipped a beat. She seized the opportunity. "Violet, who is Everly?"

"Oh, she's my traveling companion. She's been here with me for a few years now. Young Everly came to ease my fears and accompany me to heaven, but my heart just keeps on beating. We've had a grand time together, sharing stories. The funny thing is that I think things have really taken an unusual turn." She leaned close to Emma. "Don't tell anyone, but I think I ease her fears."

Emma nodded, completely confused by what she was hearing.

"You see, Everly is a scared soul. She lived on the western frontier in the eighteen-hundreds. It was a filthy, lawless place. There were constant attacks and wars—no one was safe. As a result, her family was always on the move, and the poor thing never had a real home. She spent months in rickety covered wagons, battling storms, heat, cold and hunger. Her family joined with another family for safety's sake, and she fell in love and was engaged to be married.

Her new beau brought her joy, but it was very brief. She fell ill, and her life ended tragically. It was an extremely oppressive existence. Her fears are completely founded." Violet shook her head. "I've been teaching her all about modern life. She's very intrigued by it all."

Emma was speechless and uneasy. She reached for a piece of banana bread and began to nibble it.

"She loves stories. I read to her every day. She likes you, you know." Violet added nonchalantly, helping herself to a piece of bread. They ate in silence for a moment.

Violet put her tea and bread down, clasped her hands in her lap, and sat a bit taller. She examined Emma closely, her eyes narrowed. She placed a hand on her chest, turned and gazed out the window.

"I've felt like it was my time to go for years. I've been ready. But something has kept me here. I think it is my love for Everly, maybe my longing to see her live a peaceful, happy life. She deserves it. I've prayed about it for many hours. Love has kept us here, both of us." She stared deep into Emma's eyes.

"Come here, please."

Emma put her tea and bread down and went to kneel beside her. Violet took hold of her hands.

"It's you, my dear. I've been waiting for you. We've been waiting for you. Everly needs you. It's her turn."

Emma stared into Violet's serious blue eyes. She didn't know what to say. She was utterly confused.

Those eyes pleaded with her. She felt an unexplainable desire to accept what she was hearing, even though she did not understand. Upsetting Violet was the last thing she wanted to do.

She nodded in agreement.

A gracious smile slowly spread across Violet's face. Her small body slumped as she relaxed.

"I'm so relieved. I can't tell you how long I've worried about her. I couldn't leave her all alone. Things will work out now..." She hesitated. "...now that you're here. It's like a weight has been lifted off my shoulders and my heart. One never knows what the future holds." She released Emma's hands, took a deep breath, her small chest rising and then lowering. "I'm suddenly very tired, my child. Would you help me to bed?"

She stood, and Emma helped her to a small room just behind the kitchen. It was furnished in soft white and yellow and had gold paisley wallpaper. A walker was shoved into the corner, buried under blankets and throw pillows.

As Violet went into the bathroom to change, Emma took the dishes into the kitchen then returned to the bedroom. She found Violet in a long white gown with lace around the neckline and wrists.

She grinned. "You look like an angel."

Violet chuckled. "I was thinking the same thing about you."

Accepting Emma's help, she climbed into bed, and Emma covered her with a pastel patchwork quilt that lay nearby. Violet looked up at her. "Windows of time can be gracious here in Mystic Ridge. I'm so pleased you're the one. You're going to get along splendidly. You both possess so much compassion.

She can teach you a lot about embroidery, and she loves to sing. She loves sparkly things and is obsessed with emeralds. She's an eager learner. Thank you from the bottom of my heart. Take good care of her." A lone tear crept down her cheek. "I'm so very grateful. Goodnight, my dear." Her eyelids fluttered, and then closed.

Emma was terribly confused and concerned. Violet seemed so exhausted and had spoken so strangely. Maybe that was her nature, but Emma's mind swirled with possibilities and scenarios. Violet needed to see a doctor.

She washed all the dishes and carefully dried them. She wiped down the counters and dusted and straightened all of Violet's precious knick-knacks. Before she left, she peeked into Violet's room and watched her sleeping. She looked peaceful.

She made sure all the doors were locked and crossed the street to her home.

That evening, Emma called Owen. She thought he should know that his mother had not been taking her medications, and that she seemed very fatigued. She also told him Violet seemed to think she had an invisible friend named Everly. He said he had heard talk of Everly for years, but it was all harmless. He thanked her for her concern, promised to ask Dr. Abernathy for a home visit, and vowed to stop by himself early the following day.

⌇⌇⌇

As Emma lay in her bed that night, she was confused by all the things Violet had said, and about her own fascination with Everly. The box containing the mother cat and kittens was on the floor beside her. Their presence gave her comfort.

She watched them as they cleaned each other, cuddled, and purred. There was something so comforting about a mother and her babies. She petted them gently.

She remembered Violet's earnest expression as she spoke of Everly, the eighteen hundreds, and Everly's fascination with modern life. Violet had spoken so matter-of-factly, like it was normal to have friends from the Nineteenth Century. Maybe Everly had been a character from a book. What if Everly was a spirit who lived in the house? She did believe in spirits and ghosts, she always had. Maybe having an imaginary friend made Violet feel less alone. And that was okay.

But why would Violet say she'd been waiting for Emma? What was she supposed to do? It was beyond puzzling.

She tossed and turned for hours, and then finally succumbed to sleep.

⟨≈⟩

The next morning, Emma stretched and went down to the laundry room to get the kitties a warm sheet from the dryer. As she strolled through the hallway to the stairs, she looked out the window and saw Owen's car in Violet's driveway. To her horror, she also saw an ambulance. She ran outside in her pajamas, Caleb behind her. She stopped on the front porch, trembling. She felt Caleb place a jacket around her shoulders.

They crossed the street together as the ambulance doors closed. Owen appeared at the front door of the house.

"What happened? Is Violet okay?" Emma said in anguish.

He hung his head. "Just after I got here this morning, she passed."

Emma's knees wobbled, and Caleb grabbed her tightly around her waist.

"Oh, no. Not now! She said she had plans for me," Emma cried. "I need to talk to her. I really do."

Owen hung his head. "I'm so sorry. She was in no pain, I assure you. And in her last moments, she spoke of you. She had a box of items all ready for you. Hang on." He went inside and returned with a large cardboard box. "Here. It's marked Everly, but she specifically told me to give it to you. It was her last request."

Caleb took the box as Emma began sobbing. "Thank you," she managed.

Poor Violet. Her new friend was gone, and she still had so many unanswered questions. Now she would never understand what plans Violet had for her.

She looked at Owen. "I'm so sorry for your loss, Owen. She was an incredible woman, and even though I only knew her a few days, I'll never, ever forget her."

Owen smiled weakly. "She was one of a kind."

"Is there anything we can do?" Emma asked.

"Sister Mary Jean Stevenson and Sister Crystal Grace are on their way. They've taken control of most of the details. Mama had relayed all of her wishes to them."

Caleb patted him on the shoulder. "We're here for you. Please, let us know when the service will be."

"Will do." Owen turned and went back inside the house.

Caleb escorted Emma home. She cried openly and walked straight upstairs to the bedroom. Caleb followed with the large box. He placed it on the floor near the window. She sat on the edge of the bed and stared at it.

"I'll be right back," he said, and dashed from the room.

Emma felt drained. Why, oh, why had this happened? Violet was her only friend.

Caleb returned with a bottle of water and handed it to her. "I guess it was her time. I'm glad we got to know her."

The momma cat jumped in Emma's lap and nuzzled her chin. She petted her as her mind swirled.

"Me, too. If we'd moved in a few days later, I might never have even met her."

The thought was almost painful.

"You lay down for a while." He kissed her on the forehead and left the room.

She situated the cat on her pillow and felt calm come over her. The kittens chased each other under the bed. She rose and walked to the box Violet had given her and peered inside it. She lifted out the painting of *Christ Blessing Little Children.*

"Oh, my," she breathed.

It was magnificent.

*Thank you, my friend.* She took it to a corner of the room and leaned it against the wall. It looked perfect. It evoked peaceful feelings inside her. They would hang it today.

Returning to the box, she saw a worn book titled *The Wonderful Wizard of Oz* by L. Frank Baum. She took it out. There was a VHS tape of *The Sound of Music.* There were several Little House on the Prairie books, and a couple of Nancy Drew titles, and two cookbooks. She vowed to read every word. She touched each one, honored that Violet had shared her favorite things with her.

She lifted out two lace handkerchiefs that were folded neatly, and a pair of pearl-embroidered gloves—dainty, shimmering.

A flat black velvet box was the final item. Her knees felt shaky. She sat down on the floor and took it out. She slowly opened it and revealed a spectacular emerald necklace with three stunning stones and a thick silver chain. To her, it looked like a piece that would adorn the neck of an Egyptian pharaoh.

The lush green hue seemed to glow against the dark background. Dangle earrings with substantial round stones were secured in the middle. The jewelry was mesmerizing, haunting. She felt that these pieces had an ancient story, a tale she would never know.

Exhaling, she closed her eyes. This necklace had a past, and a future—a future that somehow involved her.

An uneasy churning knotted her stomach, and she felt a slight cool breeze swirl around her. She opened her eyes.

"Thank you, Violet. Thank you so much. I will treasure these things forever."

She put the items back in the box. The kittens halted their romping and regarded her curiously.

Suddenly, Emma felt odd, as if she had pried through someone else's belongings. *Everly's* belongings. She thought about that poor young girl, living and dying so many centuries ago. It didn't seem fair that she had suffered so much and died so young. A lone tear cascaded down her cheek. If only Violet could have lived longer. She longed to know more about Everly.

She rose and looked out the window at Violet's house. Deep sadness panged in her chest. She missed her.

She went back to the box and took out a few of the books and tucked the box underneath the bed. She couldn't believe Violet was really gone.

❧

*Three months later*

Caleb was up on the roof repairing gutters when Emma swung her car into the driveway. She rushed to the side of the house.

"Caleb, Caleb!" she shouted. "Get down here! I have news. It's Everly, I just know it."

Caleb carefully climbed down the ladder. "Calm down. Calm down. What's 'Everly'?" He held her shoulders and gazed deeply into her eyes. "Are you okay?"

"Of course." She wrapped her arms around his neck and kissed him repeatedly.

"You're never going to believe it." She couldn't contain her joy. "I went to the doctor today. I was gaining weight, and I thought I felt something—something inside me." She released him and threw her hands up in the air. "I'm pregnant!"

"But..."

"Yes, it's a miracle. And everything is fine, truly. My uterus looks perfect, and my blood work is superb. Everything is wonderful. I'm right on track. I feel tired, yet energetic. I even heard the baby's heartbeat, I swear." She couldn't contain her excitement. "I was as shocked as you."

Caleb picked her up and twirled her around in circles. Then he carefully placed her on her feet. "Are you sure? Really sure?"

"Yes, you're going to be a daddy!" She laughed. "And I'm going to be a momma."

"This is incredible. I...I can't believe it." He ran his fingers through his hair.

"I gotta get a little basketball hoop, and one of those tiny baseball mitts."

Emma laughed and shook her head. "Darling, it's a girl."

Caleb tilted his head sideways. "It's so early. Did they do a sonogram?

"No."

"Then how do you know?"

A slow, thoughtful smile tipped the corners of her mouth.

"It's her turn."

# THE INVISIBLE GIRL

"SISTER CRYSTAL GRACE, I'VE BEEN SO WORRIED ABOUT YOU," Sophie said as she squeezed the telephone. "I know you were close to Violet Bryant." Still no response. "She was a charming woman and a pillar of the community. She will be greatly missed. Darling, are you okay?"

"I'm all right," Sister Crystal Grace replied. "I will see her again. Time is almost irrelevant. The Lord does not promise us an endless life on this earth. Everlasting life exists only in heaven."

"You're correct, as usual." Sophie cleared her throat. "We all know you need some time to mourn, but everyone misses you terribly. *I* miss you."

"I'm old, Sophie, older than Violet was."

"Well, you look amazing. The Lord blessed you with good genes."

"That is very problematic for me." Sister Crystal Grace paused. "Regular women show their age. My DNA has been altered somehow. Dear Violet had many theories on the matter. She was my sounding board. I could bounce ideas off her—and Everly. They were always so helpful, my true friends."

"Everly?" Sophie questioned, confused by many of the things she was hearing. "Your DNA?"

Sister Crystal Grace continued. "I try hard to keep things running smoothly in Mystic Ridge. I really do. But every action has a reaction, a repercussion. It's so difficult to keep up." Her voice sounded labored.

"Are you pacing, Sister?"

"Yes, I'm in the vineyards, pruning vines. I just can't settle today." Her voice faded.

"You don't sound like yourself," Sophie remarked. "Maybe you should sit down. Is your wheelchair nearby?"

"I even went back and tried to help Everly and her family." Sister Crystal Grace groaned. "Her father was tenacious, and ornery, and wouldn't listen to a word I said. He completely dismissed me. He even called me a vagabond."

Sophie tapped her fingernails on her large wooden farmhouse table, a pile of sewing before her. Poor Sister Crystal Grace was distraught. Nothing she said made any sense.

"A vagabond...that's unusual."

Sister Crystal exhaled loudly. "Everly was astute for her age. She appreciated my effort and tried to understand my warnings. But I couldn't change her fate."

Sophie began cutting the thread at the hem of Joey's jeans. "I would love to meet her."

"And Poovie," Sister Crystal Grace continued hopelessly. "I tried, all those years ago, I did try to warn her. She got a glimpse of things no one wants to know. It's not healthy to know one's future. It affected her. It changed the course of her life. Poovie has a wealth of strength and courage, as does her family. I won't intervene again. There's nothing else I can do for her."

"I adore Poovie's newspaper column and her Instagram and Facebook and her podcasts. She posted a photo of a caramel-peach pecan pie last weekend. I absolutely have to make it."

"It's all so unfortunate," Sister Crystal Grace whispered.

"Is Poovie all right? Is she in danger?"

Sister Crystal Grace made a few puffing noises. "It's just fate," she blurted. "I can't control it, as much as I try. Admittedly, I brought Mariah and Daisy here. I know it was selfish, but I need them so, so desperately. I'm too old to handle everything on my own anymore.

"I've struggled to think it all through. Mariah is wise, yet so wary. She needs more faith in herself. Daisy is a clever spirit, and she's really coming into her own. My mission will require them both. I didn't want Ruby to be alone, like I was. She's still so little. She needs a confidant, and Daisy is perfect." She exhaled loudly. "Ruby can mentor Evelyn someday."

Sophie felt like she was hearing about folks from another dimension. She lifted her warm tea and listened intently. Sister Crystal Grace continued, as if she were reassuring herself.

"Josephine must find Cade. It's imperative. He's going to be a stellar resident of Mystic Ridge. His future and his past are riveting."

"Pardon me, Sister. I'm super-duper confused," Sophie managed.

Silence floated between them.

"Don't try to process any of this, Sophie, I'm just rambling and running on and thinking out loud. Keeping everyone straight can put me in quite a tizzy. I'm just an old soul, and I've been under a lot of stress lately. Don't process, Sophie, it makes your nose feel dry and itchy."

Sophie sneezed and juggled her phone. "I'm so sorry, Sister Crystal Grace. Where are my manners? What were we talking about?"

"You, love. You said you were struggling."

"Oh, yes," Sophie said. "Me. I'm losing my mind. Seriously, losing it."

"I doubt that, darling."

"I'm so glad you called. I've been unable to explain it to anyone. No one on earth would understand. I keep having these freaky daydreams about running away and joining the circus." She perched the telephone between her shoulder and her chin. "Actually..." She hesitated. "...my contemplation has almost become an obsession. What I mean is that this fantastic world of people has moved into the depths of my mind. I can't stop thinking about them. They're with me all the time." A beep sounded on her phone. "Oh, bother, it's Burt."

Sister Crystal Grace spoke softly. "Living up on the mountain and homeschooling all those children must be difficult. But I've always found it's good to listen to your inner voice."

"Even if it's wacky?"

"Well, have Burt give you a physical and check your blood pressure, just to be sure." She chuckled. "But keep listening. It could be very significant, Sophie. Trust me. Bye, dear. I know you'll do the right thing."

When the line went dead, Sophie clicked over. "Hey," she drawled, as she pulled the last thread out of Joey's jeans.

"Did you get all the transcriptions done?" Burt asked.

"Yes. I did it while Deanne was working on her ABCs."

"Great. I'm going to take Dr. Kent to dinner tonight. He's from the state university hospital and was passing through on his way to visit his brother in Alabama. I won't be too late."

"Okay," Sophie said, relieved. She closed her eyes, placed her elbows on the table, and rested her head in her hands. She closed her eyes. The energetic sound of applause filled her mind.

*The auditorium was jam-packed. The air was thick with anticipation. She watched Pyotr as he made his way to the center ring on the twenty-foot stilts. His wife had passed away a few months earlier, and he was emotionally unstable. It was nerve-wracking to watch him.*

*Tonight, though, he seemed to be moving swiftly. Thank goodness—last night he'd almost toppled over several times. If Daryl, the ringmaster, found out that Pyotr was drinking, he would deport him back to Russia in a second flat.*

*Sophie relaxed. This evening Pyotr was graceful in all his enormity, wowing the crowd with his poise and agility.*

Interrupting her vision, Burt continued, "This weekend I want to clear the leaves and pine straw from around the cabin. Will you help me?"

"Sure," she answered without really having heard or caring about the question.

"Caitlin can watch Deanne. Get some masking tape the next time you go into town, please."

"Sure." The smell of sawdust, peanuts, popcorn, and cotton candy tickled her nose.

"Oh, my mom called from Florida. She said she ran into your sister at the bank. She said Nell looked fit as a fiddle, and that she was dating a banker who just purchased his own houseboat."

"Really?" Sophie said, opening her eyes. The vision of Pyotr vanished. She'd spoken with Nell just a week ago, and she hadn't mentioned anything about a new boyfriend or a boat. "That's fine."

"Fine?" Burt repeated. "What's your problem?"

"Nothing. I'd better go. I need to start dinner and help the kids with their homework, and I'm still patching a few tears in their jeans."

"Allright," Burt said. "I love you."

"Love you, too." She pushed the end button and laid the phone on the table. She struggled to recall the last time she'd been on a boat—three, maybe four years ago.

A slow smile gradually formed on her lips. Tiny Bob could dive from a forty-foot plank into a five-foot tank of water, right on the money, every time. She could always depend on him to make her laugh. Even when he wasn't in the center ring he was performing. At every meal he tried out his magic tricks and stunts. He could do amazing feats with mashed potatoes. Even though he had a disability, he made the best of his condition and received more applause in one afternoon than most people would experience in an entire lifetime.

She shook her thoughts away, carefully pulled the thread through the fabric for the last time and tied a knot. Keeping Joey, Caitlyn, and Deanne looking good was a fulltime job.

"I don't get this," Joey whined as he leaned over his algebra book in the family room.

"Because you're an idiot," Caitlyn sneered.

"Stop," Sophie commanded, and raised a hand, cutting off Joey as he opened his mouth to retaliate. "Caitlyn, say you're sorry."

Caitlyn held up her cell phone. "I only have two bars, our service here sucks. Bruce called on the landline, and Joey told him I was out hiking. Joey's a liar, and he's ruining my life."

"Joey, that was extremely rude. No video games tonight."

"I did you a favor. Bruce is gross. No one appreciates me." He smirked. "Well, I don't have any decent video games anyway."

Deanne strolled into the room. "I want a little sister," she announced. "I'll be six soon. I could teach her to dance and sing, and I promise I will share my toys."

Sophie took in the sight of Deanne cuddling a small baby doll she'd meticulously covered in bandages. A pang of sadness touched her heart.

"Oh, she's not really sick," Deanne proclaimed. "Daddy could fix Isabella right up."

"That's a beautiful name," Sophie said, touching her daughter's soft cheek. "But I don't think I'll be having another baby. It's already a zoo around here."

"A circus is more like it," Caitlyn piped up.

Sophie felt the air leave her lungs, and she suddenly had to cough. Had her daughter really said *circus*? She covered her mouth with her hands and tried to clear her airways. Finally, after several minutes, she could breathe freely again, but now her stomach ached.

It reminded her of the miscarriage she'd suffered almost a year ago. Not a day went by that she didn't miss the child she had lost. She was never able to verbally work through it or mourn the loss. She kept thinking she was over it, but the pain lingered, and the loss was still with her. Even though her home was chaotic and messy, she always felt like someone was missing. It hurt more than she could put into words. She'd miss that baby forever.

"You okay, Mommy?" Deanne asked. "Have you got asthma?"

"How do you know about asthma?"

Deanne put her hands on her hips. "I know about a lot of things. My daddy is the famous Doctor Burt Abernathy."

Sophie chuckled. "Oh, I know, allright. I helped put him through medical school in beautiful Tampa, Florida, where I'm from."

Deanne pouted. "Don't you like living in the mountains?"

Sophie thought for a few seconds. After so many years, she should have adjusted to the change of scenery, but occasionally she missed the warm temperatures and the salty air.

"The ridge is lovely, the view is astounding, it's just different from where I grew up."

"Oh," Deanne said, pacified. "I'm gonna be a doctor like Daddy. I'll take care of everyone in Mystic Ridge, just like he does. When are we gonna eat?"

"Soon."

Sophie stood up and gazed out the window. Majestic mountains stretched all around them, and their home felt like a lodge, rustic and homey. Her chin quivered as she thought about her answer to Deanne's question.

After all that school and hard work, Burt had chosen to move to Nowheresville and be a smalltown doctor, a local hero, basking in the praise of his friends and neighbors. Saving the rural folks had become his mission in life, and he was dedicated. She was proud of him.

Still, she felt as if she had become transparent. *She* was invisible. She would never take center-ring. Her talent was to love and support everyone else. The edges of her mouth curved. That really wasn't such a bad skill.

Dinner was the issue at hand, and she hadn't found the strength to venture down the mountain to the market. She'd been transcribing Burt's medical notes for hours and going through the events that led up to the Civil War with Caitlyn and Joey. Between teaching the different grades of schoolwork, doing the laundry, mopping the kitchen floor, picking up messes and vacuuming, she hadn't made it out all week.

"Your father won't be home until late. How about I thaw out some peaches and warm up some chicken tenders and corn?"

"Eww," Caitlyn groaned.

"Nasty," Joey added.

Sophie placed her hands on her hips. "My dinners are delicious. I made cornbread and homemade beef stew yesterday, and you guys ate it in seconds flat and disappeared like the amazing Rayfini. No one even mentioned the fact that it was terrific, but today everyone wants to complain about a quick and easy meal."

She stomped across the kitchen and put the scissors away. She took a bag of peaches out of the freezer, placed frozen chicken pieces onto a baking sheet and put it in the oven. She added water to a pot and put five ears of corn into it. She turned on the burner, carried the newly mended clothing to the laundry room, and closed the door.

Tears glazed her eyes, and she quickly wiped them away. Why was she on edge? They were just kids being kids. She was ridiculous to take their comments so personally. It was absurd. Normally, their silliness just floated off her, but recently she'd become sensitive. Maybe her hormones were out of whack.

She rubbed her face with the palms of her hands. Her skin felt dry.

The heavenly sound of Louie's piccolo surrounded her, and she relaxed. The melody embraced her like a welcome, sympathetic friend. Leaning against the washing machine, she envisioned the three rings, ready for the evening's performance. Wearing his crimson-and-gold tuxedo, Daryl the ringmaster would waltz into the center ring at any moment. He'd hold his hands out by his sides, bold and impossible to resist. The crowd would roar with anticipation, and the animals would line up. The dancers would don their flamboyant outfits and get in order. Right on schedule, the show would commence. It would be magnificent. Her salvation, her joy!

"Mom, Mom!" Deanne shouted from the other side of the door. "Something's burning."

Sophie flung the door open and raced to the stove. The water had boiled down to practically nothing, and the corn was scorching on the bottom of the pan. She urgently moved it to the sink and added water. The landline rang, and Caitlin raced across the room.

Joey slammed his book shut. "I ain't doin' this no more. It's pointless."

"When are we gonna eat?" Deanne asked. "I'm so hungry."

"Can I go to the movies tonight?" Caitlin asked. "Everyone's going. I'll drive super carefully."

"That's a joke," Joey blurted.

Sophie found a blank spot on the wall and pictured Ming and Chin Ye, always calm, always cool. The Chinese brothers nodded their readiness and began taking minuscule steps across the tiny wire that stood between them and certain death. How could they be so brave? How could they take such an enormous risk with their lives, night after night, day after day? She stood frozen. Oh, how she admired their courage and dedication. Especially since, when they were teenagers, their father had taken one perilous step and fallen to his death right before their very eyes, and those of an audience of more than four thousand.

A tear rolled down Sophie's cheek as the pain of the tragedy consumed her.

Suddenly, the smoke alarm began blaring, halting her thoughts and everyone's voices.

"Send in the clowns," she screamed. "Franco, Serguei, Zibayar, where are you?"

≈≈

Burt handed Sophie a cup of warm green tea and crossed his arms tightly. Taking a small sip, she avoided eye contact. Their automatic fire notification system had worked like a charm. The fire truck had pulled up in their long gravel driveway just as she tossed the burnt chicken out the front door. Three handsome firemen had been relieved to discover everything was okay. Sophie apologized profusely and felt utterly ridiculous and embarrassed. Caitlyn, Joey, and Deanne had thoroughly enjoyed the chaos.

Sophie melted into the chair. Her kids were just like the children who attended the circus, easily entertained. Young folks were always enamored with Ivan. He was burly and fearless as he ventured into a cage with two Bengal tigers day after day. And it really was dangerous; everyone in the circus knew it.

The poor animals spent way too much time being caged. They desperately needed to run and forage through wide-open spaces, but instead a minuscule man commanded them. Sadly, everyone accepted the fact that one day Ivan would be mauled and brutally killed by one of his pets. It was just a matter of time, and it made the spectacle even more terrifying.

"Sophie, talk to me." Burt snapped his fingers. "Who's Franco and Ivan? You were mumbling about a Guennadi, too. Who are these people? What's the deal? The kids are really concerned about you."

She digested his sentence and met his curious stare.

"But you're not?" she asked.

He shrugged his shoulders. "What's the problem with you? We're making ends meet and saving a little for a vacation. The kids are great. We've paid off all my medical school loans. My practice is booming. Why are you making things difficult?"

"Difficult," she repeated. "I've never been difficult. I go along with everything. And I can't explain this phenomenon. I don't have a choice in what I witness. There's an alternate world in my head." She paused and gazed down at her lap. "It's an odd world of people who provide me with a wide array of conflicting emotions. Guennadi, the director, makes me angry and defensive, because he treats everyone with little or no respect. He's always yelling and demanding more and more from everyone. Jesus, they already do everything that they can." She clenched her fists.

"And sometimes I watch Renada, the stunning acrobat, and I find myself beaming with pride. She trains practically every day and has more talent than any of her siblings. She's so dedicated. I just hope she's not hooking up with Amando—he's not right for her. He's flighty, penniless, and he'll never commit. She can do much better."

Burt sat down beside her; a panicked expression etched on his brow. "What on earth are you talking about?"

Sophie's shoulders began to tremble. "See, I knew you wouldn't understand."

"Did you meet these folks on the internet?" he asked.

"Oh, no."

"Then how do you know them?"

Sophie's chin rose a notch. "I think I'm one of them. I'm the Invisible Girl," she proclaimed proudly.

Burt covered his mouth with his hand. "Oh, my God. You've completely lost your mind." He stood. "I don't know how I didn't see this coming. Is it the miscarriage? I know you took it hard. I did, too. We haven't really addressed what happened. I've been so busy. I'm sorry. I'm going to the pharmacy right this minute to fill a prescription for you."

"No," Sophie protested. "I won't take it."

"Not another word," he said through his teeth.

Sophie rose and put her hands on her hips. "Don't speak to me like that."

Burt ran a hand through his hair. "Okay, you're right. I apologize."

"I don't take orders from you or the director, Guennadi. I'm special."

Burt regarded her with raised eyebrows. "Yes, you are. I don't know what to do here. Let me hold you."

Sophie held up a hand and shook her head. "No. I'm not a child. That won't change anything. I'm fine—just leave me alone."

"I can't do that. You're not fine. You're losing it. You've been cooped up for too long. You've created imaginary characters for emotional support. I'm a doctor, let me help you. Or at least let me take you to Dr. Baker in Chattanooga. She's a psychiatrist. Maybe she can talk to you about what's going on."

"Nothing's going on. These people call to me. They share their lives with me. They want me to be a part of it."

Burt took her shoulders in his hands and gazed deeply into her eyes. "Darling, something is definitely going on here. Saturday, I want to drive you to see Dr. Baker. Caitlyn can babysit. I can't let you fall apart this way. I can't. I love you."

Sophie began to sob. "They're real. They are," she cried. "They need me; I feel it deep in my soul. They're reaching out to me —somehow!"

Burt took her into his arms and held her tightly to his chest. "I know. I know, dear. We'll work this out, I promise. Don't worry. Please don't cry. Everything will be okay."

<hr>

Sophie opened her eyes a bit when she realized the car was no longer moving. Unfortunately, they were traveling to meet Dr. Baker in Chattanooga. Burt had insisted, and even convinced the doctor to come in on a Saturday. She'd had to go, but she dreaded it. How would she explain this phenomenon?

She examined Burt's profile. He was slumped over the steering wheel, staring ahead as if in shock.

"Are we at the doctor's office?" She looked around, and saw they were pulled over on the shoulder of the expressway. He didn't speak, just pointed to a billboard. She focused on the enormous, colorful sign.

# CIRCUS CLASSICAL
## MAKES ITS FORAY INTO YOUR AREA
### *Don't Miss This Amazing Spectacle*
### *With Once-in-A-Lifetime Performances*
### FEATURING

### *Ivan the Tiger Trainer*
### *The Kichang Twins*
### Masters of the High Wire

# AND

*Franco*

The World's Most Amusing Entertainer

*Directed by the One and Only*

## GUENNADI

"I knew it," she heard herself saying. "It's them. They're real."
She read the performance times. "They're waiting for me. We have
to go. We must."

Burt started the engine. "This is insane, Sophie, insane." He
cautiously pulled back onto the expressway. "But I'm sorry I ever
doubted you."

"It's allright, honey. Today's first performance starts soon."

"Where am I going?"

"The Omni Vista Arena. Get moving. Hurry up."

"I've got to call Dr. Baker's office and cancel your appointment."

She grabbed his cell phone. "I'll do it."

"This is too weird, even with all the supernatural tall tales
about Mystic Ridge. I've never heard of anything like this. Are
you sure you didn't just read about these folks on Facebook?"

"No. I already told you. I know things about them that would
never be posted on the internet. I know what they eat, and what
kinds of pajamas they wear. I know who's dating who. I know
which performers have an attitude, and which ones are home-
sick. I need to get there. They're calling me. There's something
urgent."

Burt placed his hand on her knee. "There's no medical explanation for all of this." He glanced at her quickly. "I love you,
Sophie. And I'm sorry if I've been neglecting you. My family
comes first."

"I know. Now step on it."

&#10070;&#10070;

They hurriedly paid full admission price, although the matinee
performance was almost over. As they rushed inside, Sophie
felt her knees begin to tremble. The familiar aromas of popcorn
and sawdust and animals surrounded her.

"I'm here," she whispered softly. "I'm here."

The cheerful music was exactly the way she'd heard it in her daydreams. It was frightening yet thrilling. Her breath came quickly as her heart pounded fiercely in her chest.

"Let's go to our seats," Burt said as they stood in the aisle looking down at the rings. A magician was performing tricks with a dwarf.

"That's Rayfini and Tiny Bob," she told him. "I want to walk around. I need to get down on the floor, near the performers."

"I'm sure the ushers won't let us anywhere near them."

She gazed around. "I don't see any ushers. After everyone was seated, they probably cut out."

She walked all the way down the aisle as Rajess and his three Australian longhaired ponies ran into the second ring. There was a small rail that blocked the track surrounding the rings.

She kissed Burt on the cheek. "Don't freak out. I'll be right back," she said as she tossed her leg over the rail and climbed down.

"But..." he protested with a worried expression, which melted into a trusting smile. "Be careful. I'll wait right here."

"Will do."

Bending over so she wouldn't be noticed, she made her way around the track to an opening where Stefan was wheeling out his cart of African monkeys. He smiled as if he'd been expecting her.

"Good day." He nodded.

"Yes," she mustered. Her body was sweating profusely as she neared whatever it was that had compelled her to this point. She backed against the wall to avoid bumping into Pandira and her box of poodles. Pandira also flashed a familiar grin.

She moved to a large hallway and watched as the frenzied crowd of circus performers whirled around her. The pulse of the atmosphere was familiar and real and coursed through her. Her body began to sway, and she wasn't sure if it was elation or confusion.

Then, suddenly, everyone stopped moving. The spinning scenario abruptly ceased. All eyes were on her, and no one spoke. An eerie silence descended. She stood frozen, waiting for something, unsure of what it was.

Out of the corner of her eye, she saw a tiny girl in a wheel-chair approaching. She faced her. The girl wore a faded pink-and-ivory dress with a tattered tulle tutu. Lace framed her small face and arms. She wore tights, and black lace-up shoes adorned her tiny feet. Her long, messy hair was strawberry blond. A stuffed animal lay in her lap—a white kitten. She looked like a porcelain doll from an antique shop, but she was real. Very real.

Everyone watched as the child stopped in front of her. Sophie knelt to meet her gaze.

"You're here. You came," the child exclaimed.

Sophie grasped her hands. "Yes, I'm here."

"Gypsy Taniqua said you'd come. She said you'd see every-thing with our eyes. She said you would know us and under-stand us."

"I have been seeing all kinds of amazing things." Realization coursed through her, and her eyes grew wide. "You're the Invisi-ble Girl," she said softly. "Not me."

"Yes. I'm Isabella. I'm four." She held up four fingers.

Sophie urgently gathered Isabella in her arms and hugged her tightly. A sweet sugary smell radiated from her. Holding her felt so right, so destined. *Why? Why am I here?*

She moved the child to arm's-length. "Are you okay?"

"I need a mommy," Isabella whispered. "I never had a pop. My mommy died from 'monia, and now I'm all alone. Aunt Pandi-ra and Taniqua watch after me, but I don't feel good so much, and they have lots of stuff to do."

Sophie inspected the girl. "Why are you in this chair? Is it your legs?"

Isabella shrugged. "I don't know. I'm sick lots. I can't breathe sometimes."

Sophie noticed all the animal hair on the tutu, and the dirt smudges on her tights. "It might just be allergies."

Isabella shrugged, her green eyes brimming with tears. "I can't do any tricks. Aunt Pandira says my talent is hugging. But I think I get in the way." She caressed the stuffed kitten in her lap. "Did you lose your girl?"

Sophie gasped, startled at the question. Only Burt and Sis-ter Crystal Grace knew about her miscarriage. She exhaled. She'd never known if it was a girl or a boy.

Isabella looked up at her, her expression serious. "Do you want me?" she asked, her chin quivering with emotion. "I heard you were a great mommy. I picked you all by myself. You're pretty." Her brows rose hopefully.

"You picked me?" Sophie was so very confused, yet immensely flattered. "I don't know if I can just take you. There are interviews, papers and procedures..."

Suddenly, a dark-skinned woman wearing a gold-sequined veil approached them. "Madam Sophie, I am Pandira, Isabella's aunt and legal guardian. I have everything right here. She is a United States citizen. We've signed and notarized each important document. You can be her custodial guardian to start with, and if everything is pleasing to you both, you can file adoption papers."

Sophie rose and took the papers. She glanced at the pitiful child once more and felt a deep, unexplainable connection to her. She loved her already!

"I'll file for adoption immediately. How can I get in touch with you?"

Pandira flashed a joyful, yet tearful smile. She pointed to an email address and phone number on one of the pages. "We only want the best for Isabella. We all cherish her dearly. But she requires qualified care, and a good mother and father. We see much love in your heart. We are so deeply grateful to you. You've answered our prayers."

Sophie touched Pandira's jeweled arm and nodded. One after another, all the performers kissed and hugged Isabella. Sophie cried openly, as did everyone, including Isabella.

Ivan handed Sophie a tiny suitcase. After the last hug had been bestowed, sound returned to the arena. The performers scattered to their places. Three mini-cars sped past them.

Sophie caressed Isabella's frail shoulder and ran a hand through her long, disheveled hair. "Sweetie, I promise to take very good care of you. Burt is going to adore you. You're coming home to our circus now."

Isabella sat up a speck taller in her wheelchair, wiped her tears away, and flashed a tiny, dazzling smile. "I'll never be the invisible girl again."

Sophie kissed her on the cheek. "No, you won't."

# HER GARDEN

SALLY JACOBS KNELT BESIDE THE ROOM-SIZED SQUARE OF BLACK dirt. Her lips tightened as she remembered all the time she'd spent breaking up the soil and carefully planting a few rows of Brussels sprouts, one row of carrots and another row of lettuce, and many, many rows of crimson pansies. It had been four weeks, and nothing—not one sprout.

Everyone had told her this area of Tennessee was not known for the quality of its soil. Mystic Ridge wasn't famous for growing much at all, except rocks, and people with cryptic stories and imaginary visions. She'd lived here her whole life, though, and nothing eerie or paranormal had ever happened to her.

Her shoulders slumped. She simply longed for flowers and color and, truthfully, the lift she hoped they would bring. She felt blue.

It had been a difficult few weeks. She missed her friend Violet Bryant terribly. Violet's passing had been such a shock. One week they'd shared coffee and pecan rolls, and the next week she was gone. Sally's heart ached. Such a thoughtful and sweet woman.

Since the funeral, she'd felt restless. She needed something radiant. Were a few flowers and veggies too much to hope for?

"Come on, dirt—do your thing," she commanded.

Her thoughts drifted to Sister Crystal Grace. She was probably devastated— she and Violet had been friends for practically ever! They'd grown up together. She had seen Sister Crystal Grace at a distance at the funeral, but it had been so crowded she hadn't gotten to speak to her. She hoped she was all right.

Although it was a town secret, a lot of people knew Sister Crystal Grace went into deep, coma-like sleeps from which she couldn't be awakened. Sometimes they lasted for hours, occasionally days. When she woke, she was always malnourished and dehydrated but lucid. The sisters had brought in several doctors, and none could make heads or tails of her condition.

Once, she was out for so many days they had a doctor administer intravenous fluids and nutrients. When she woke, she insisted it was just her soul recouping. She refused extensive tests and in-depth medical care. She insisted she was fine. Without her consent, there was little the sisters could do.

The poor thing was probably going to be out for days over Violet's passing.

Sally gazed toward her house and saw her reflection in the sliding glass door. Of course, she was thankful to be healthy and to have a delightful family. But she was just so annoyingly boring and predictable and safe. Maybe that was her lot in life. Success was not her strong suit.

"Mommy, Mommy, I'm hungry," A shrill voice rang out as her daughter Polly approached.

"Honey, you just had some animal crackers. You're fine," Sally replied, trying not to sound irritated.

She looked back at the dirt and stood up. Sometimes all her efforts seemed pointless, useless, a big fat waste of time. She heard the phone ringing inside the house. It rang and rang. She rolled her eyes, knowing her sixteen-year-old son Nathan was lounging on the sofa, obviously too "busy" to answer it. Land lines were so yesterday, he insisted.

"Mommy, I want to use my new markers. Show me again how to draw a butterfly," Polly demanded.

"Okay, let's go inside."

As they began the short walk back to the house, she cursed herself for wasting so much time on the stupid garden. What had she been hoping to accomplish? She did have other important things to do, like vacuum, grocery shop, trim the hedges—and draw butterflies, she thought sarcastically. Sometimes, being a stay-at-home mom felt futile and completely unproductive.

She was distracted from her negative thoughts by Nathan thundering out of the house, his huge nose ring sparkling in the sunlight. She had made it quite clear she did not find it attractive. Today, she would just ignore it.

"Mom, I think there's a message from Grandma's neighbor on the machine. I gotta get to the car wash, and afterwards I'm gonna stop by the football game."

"Don't be too late. We have church in the morning."

"Maybe. I'll see you later," he called out as he got into the car and drove away.

Sally wrapped her arms around her midsection. He was always so busy these days. Sometimes, it felt like everything she said to him went in one ear and out the other.

As she suddenly remembered the message, she stopped breathing, and panic consumed her. She ran into the house with Polly close behind.

≈≋

Two hours later, Sally sat alert and determined behind the steering wheel, headed to Villa Rica, Georgia. Her mind raced. She'd left the house so quickly, but she thought she had taken care of everything. She prayed she had. Picturing her mother, injured, just spurned her on.

The poor thing had fallen down the stairs and broken her leg. Her mother insisted she was okay, but her voice had been slurred, and she'd sounded confused. Sally was worried, and the neighbor who'd taken her mom to the emergency room seemed very concerned.

She knew her mom was getting older, but it was still a shock to hear that she'd fallen.

Cellphone beside her, she stayed focused on the road and sang along with a hippie radio station. Then, she began a mental list of things to take care of when she arrived. Mom was stubborn, and she feared it wouldn't be easy. She'd have to handle the situation delicately. Mom was also proud and would never consent to being taken care of by anyone.

Her mind drifted to her own home and family. How were they going to fare without her? She took care of so many details in everyone's lives. She kept things running smoothly. She chewed her lower lip. Had she taught them anything at all, or doted on them too much? Would they be okay, or would it be chaos? Could she handle all the new responsibilities that might be thrown in her lap?

She squeezed the steering wheel, that familiar uncertainty churning in her stomach. Doubtful, very doubtful.

⋙⋘

Five days had flown by since Sally had arrived at her mother's home. Now, she was back in the car, singing show tunes, cellphone perched in the cupholder. The black pavement stretched out in front of her, and she felt a bit energized.

She thought about all the things she had done. She had visited the grocery store, the maid service, the pharmacist, and even lawn care providers and laundry services. She had drawn up a schedule for each service. She had spelled out their individual responsibilities, and the times and dates their services would be expected. Mom had a detailed, written agenda of who was handling what, their phone numbers and email addresses. She prayed she had handled all the obstacles her mother might face. Mom could walk on her cast, but it was quite cumbersome.

A smile pursed her lips as she recalled rummaging through all the many boxes in the house. There was much more clutter than she'd remembered. So many items had to be moved so Mom could get around. She grinned as she glanced at all the treasures in her back seat. No way could she part with her childhood goodies. It was amazing her mother had saved so much.

It was nice remembering the old times. She recalled Mom's nostalgic smile as they'd shared uninterrupted discussions about love, marriage, children, and all the little things in life they rarely had time to discuss. It had been heartwarming to rekindle their close bond, and nice to see her mother so peaceful.

Sally had enjoyed the visit and the time they spent reminiscing. She tried to feel a sense of accomplishment, but it was her duty to care for her mother. She'd just done what any daughter would do. When Mom had hugged her and said she was proud of her, Sally had been stunned. Why? she wondered now.

As the car sped forward, she pondered the idea. She had never done anything special at all. Why on earth would her mother be proud?

She pulled into her driveway just past dinnertime, parked, and took a deep breath. She entered the foyer and inhaled the sweet lavender scent of home. It was nice.

Polly spotted her first. "Mommy's home!" she shrieked, throwing her arms around Sally's waist.

Nathan rushed down the stairs and grabbed her suitcase. "Hey, Mom, let me carry that. Guess what! I gave my boss a list of what I'm going to concentrate on for the next six months, and he gave me a raise. Just like that. Hashtag washing cars rocks. I didn't even have to ask." He smiled proudly.

Sally followed him up the stairs. "Nathan, that is simply wonderful. Hashtag impressed mama. Lists are the best. I couldn't get through one day without my lists."

When they reached her room, she sat down on the messy bed. It felt soft, like home. The gray-striped sheets that matched the dust ruffle looked inviting and homey.

Her husband Vern tiptoed into the room carrying an oversized coffee mug. "Here, honey, I brought you a surprise. It's a decaf-cappuccino, steaming hot, like you always make for me, but this one is just for you."

"Wow." She was genuinely surprised. She took it out of his clumsy hands. "I guess you can teach an old dog new tricks," she teased.

Nathan laughed, "Hashtag barista dad."

"Mommy, Mommy." Polly ran into the room waving a piece of paper. "Look! I drew a butterfly all by myself, just like you taught me. Ms. Emma said it was terrific. Look, it's the same color as the ones in your garden." She handed Sally the picture. "Butterflies love gardens."

Sally looked at the colorful picture, and her eyebrows rose. Carrying her coffee, she walked to the window and peered down at the garden plot.

"There were butterflies?"

"Uh-huh, this morning," Polly explained.

The orange glow of sunset covered the sky, but she could still see the perfectly aligned rows of sprouts from one side to the other. Her eyes welled with tears. She could not believe it. She had finally accomplished something, minor as it may be. Flowers were growing. Lettuce was sprouting.

Lightning bugs floated through the air, illuminating her achievement, congratulating her. The garden was thriving. Their cat Ivory raced back and forth, enjoying the spectacle, almost glowing. The scene was so lovely it warmed her soul.

As she turned to tell her family, she stopped. She spotted her reflection in the mirror and grinned. She looked happy. Truthfully, she *was* happy.

She studied Vern. He had the warm expression of a contented man. Polly was flapping her arms with pride over her picture. Nathan appeared so grown-up and responsible, and the nose ring was gone.

Glancing back at the dainty sprouts, she wiped the moisture from her eyes. Strangely, she felt triumphant. Mystic Ridge soil had decided to cooperate after all. Or maybe it was the fact she'd insisted. She stifled a laugh. Her garden was growing all around her!

# COOKIES

VIRGINIA PETITT WAVED TO THE BOYS AS THEY CLIMBED INTO their dirt-covered jeep.

"Go straight to school, guys. No smoothie stops. Pete, don't forget to pay your library fees. Gus, find out if you can serve your detention on Saturday." Groaning, she urgently closed the front door. "Oh, those poor teachers. Okay, find your shoes, Ruby, we don't want to be late for dance class. Where are you, kiddo?"

The blond four-year-old raced in, arms out by her sides. "I'm flying. I'm flying," she shouted as she raced from one side of the room to the other.

Virginia took a deep breath. The child had more energy than the electric company.

"Watch me fly. Watch me fly," Ruby sang.

"Yes, yes, you are wicked fast, but if we want to eat a bagel before your class, we need to go now. Mountain Bagels can get very busy." As Ruby darted by, Virginia grabbed her by the wrist. "I got ya, little airplane."

Ruby stopped and tapped her chin. "Yeah, I'm an airplane. I go way, way up high."

Virginia picked her up and set her on the kitchen counter. Ruby squirmed as her mother attempted to put her shoes on. She could be a handful at times, but mostly, she was delightful.

It had been a total surprise when Virginia found out she was pregnant with Ruby. She'd had a twelve-year-old son and a thirteen-year-old son—she'd planned her first two pregnancies down to the month. She'd wanted two children, close in age, and she'd gotten exactly that. Gus and Pete had been more than enough to keep her busy.

So, eight years later, her third pregnancy had been a real surprise. It had been so long since she had cared for a baby. She'd been stunned but thrilled by the unplanned addition.

Ruby's birth had been completely painless, and the infant had hardly ever cried or fussed. The entire family had celebrated her arrival. And in contrast to the rest of the Mediterranean-complexioned family, she was pale with blue eyes.

Virginia was Greek, and although Brian had light-green eyes, they couldn't find anyone in their immediate family who had blue eyes. Everyone marveled over Ruby's uniqueness.

As she grew, they discovered she possessed a rare generous spirit. She was extremely easygoing and loving, not self-centered like most children, and had no problems sharing her favorite toys. She was never demanding and slept peacefully. She seemed to understand what went on around her, even at a very young age. When Virginia and Brian explained things to her, she understood.

She was energetic, though, and Virginia often ended up chasing after her. Keeping hold of her tiny hand was a challenge. Ruby always wanted to go places and meet people. Sometimes it seemed like she had an agenda, and they were all struggling to keep up. They did joke about the possibility that maybe she was saving up all of her trouble for her teenage years.

The entire family felt a close bond with Ruby. The boys were very protective of her and doted on her. Brian gave her a big hug each and every night first thing when he returned from work. Even their two golden retrievers would regularly seek her out and rest comfortably by her side. Virginia's Facebook was full of cuddly photos of Ruby and the dogs.

When someone was having a bad day, Ruby seemed to sense it. She would do her best to shower that person with affection. She had an unparalleled empathy for others. Her presence was always comforting.

Virginia chuckled and blew her dark curly bangs upward, then kissed Ruby on the cheek, thankful she had finally gotten shoes on her daughter's wiggly feet.

"Is Sister Crystal Grace coming to see me today?" Ruby asked.

"No, I think she's resting. A close friend of hers passed away."

"Mrs. Bryant."

Virginia cocked her head sideways. "How did you know that?"

"Everly told me." Ruby giggled. Then her teeny face turned serious, and her lips pursed tightly. "I know a secret," she whispered, her sapphire eyes sparkling.

Virginia put the tip of her nose to the tip of Ruby's. "Yeah, kiddo? What is it?"

"I'm not really an airplane," Ruby whispered. "I'm an angel." She grinned to show tiny white perfect teeth. Then she covered her mouth with both hands.

"Yes, you definitely are." Virginia picked her up, twirled her around, and placed her on the floor. "And you're going to be a hungry angel if we don't get you some chow before your class." She put Ruby's pink rain jacket on her, and then pulled on her own. "It's raining hard today. We'd better button you up. I don't want you to get a cold."

"I won't, Mommy."

Virginia held Ruby's hand as they walked to the car. Her tiny hand was so warm. She loved her so dearly.

"School buses carry lots of kids, don't they?" Ruby remarked.

"Yes, darling."

"Kids that need to grow up and do important stuff someday."

Virginia met her eyes. "Yeah. Why ya askin'?" She belted her into the carseat.

"Just thinking about the bus and all the kids, and how I gotta do the good thing."

"Honey, what are you talking about? The boys don't ride the bus anymore. Gus drives."

"I know," Ruby said.

Virginia shook her head in confusion and scooted behind the steering wheel. "Don't worry yourself."

She pulled out of their driveway and drove cautiously through the storm. When they reached Mountain Bagels, they exited and ran through the downpour to the entrance.

"Wow, it's really coming down. You're soaked," Virginia proclaimed.

"No, I'm okay," Ruby replied. "Flowers need the rain, Mama."

"They do," she agreed.

They entered, and Virginia took off their jackets and hung them on a hook near the door.

"Oooh, cookies," Ruby squealed as she spotted them in a clear display case. "I want a cookie. I want a cookie." She darted to the case and pressed her nose against the glass.

Virginia hurried over. She couldn't deny that this shop had the best cookies in the entire town. They were provided by a local baker, Maura Cooper.

"If you eat a good breakfast, I'll buy a bag of the mini-chocolate chip for later. You can have some after your dance class." She tilted her head sideways and tried to look stern. "*After* dance class."

"Okay, Mommy." Ruby looked at the tiles on the floor. "Hopscotch!" she exclaimed as she began jumping from tile to tile.

Several customers laughed.

Virginia chuckled. "Mommy's getting in line." She held her hand out. "Come and stand with me." Ruby hopped over to her. The line was long—there were seven people in front of them. Virginia groaned softly.

"What's wrong?" Ruby asked.

"Oh, nothing, honey. It's just that there are a lot of people here, and I don't want to be late. I think you guys start a tap song today."

Ruby pulled free and hopped forward and backwards. "We need to be here," she said without looking up.

"You think so?" Virginia asked her.

"Yup. Don't forget my cookies."

Virginia tried to be calm, but the long line was moving so slowly. Everyone was ordering complicated coffee drinks. This place was for bagels, not gourmet coffee. She crossed her arms. Ruby continued to hop around with a few ballet moves mixed in.

Virginia tried not to show her annoyance when she finally ordered. She paid and carefully carried the tray away from the counter. Her heart sank when she noticed there were no seats.

Ruby seemed to read her mind. "There's a table over there." She pointed.

Virginia spotted it. There were three empty chairs, but one was occupied by a woman wearing gym shorts and a tank top. She was soaked.

"Someone is already sitting there."

Ruby rushed over to the table. "Come on, Mommy. This is where we should sit."

Virginia hurried behind her. "Ruby, no."

The woman looked up and smiled. "Please, have a seat. I'm about finished."

Virginia approached the table and recognized Cora Homer, the owner of the local cheese shop. "I'm so sorry. I don't want to interrupt your breakfast."

"No, that's fine."

Ruby sat right next to Cora and scooted very close. "What's your name?"

Virginia cringed.

"I'm Cora." She looked at Virginia. "I mean, Ms. Homer."

"That's right," Ruby nodded.

Virginia placed the food in front of Ruby and pointed. The three of them ate in silence for a few moments.

"I love your cheese shop," Virginia said.

"I thought I recognized you." Ms. Homer smiled. "I'm getting a new shipment from Moldova this afternoon."

Virginia nodded. "I'll have to come by. I need some real feta for my spanakopita."

Ruby stared at Ms. Homer, eyes never leaving the woman's profile. She even leaned in her direction. Virginia was beginning to get embarrassed.

"How's your breakfast, Ruby?"

Ruby didn't seem to hear her. Virginia reached across the table and touched her arm. "Darling?"

Ruby remained focused on Ms. Homer. "Why are you running in the rain?"

"I need to run every day," she answered. "It makes me feel good to get some exercise."

"You shouldn't run in the rain," Ruby told her. She put her bagel down and faced her mother. "Can I have a cookie now?"

"Eat your breakfast and finish your milk. The cookies are for after dance class, remember?"

Ruby nodded and took a sip of her milk.

Ms. Homer crumpled up her trash as she finished eating.

"You can't go," Ruby said in a small, frightened voice. "It's not safe for you to run in the rain." She paused. "You might get hurt. *They* might get hurt."

Ms. Homer rose. "I'll be just fine, don't you worry."

"No, no, you can't go," Ruby cried.

Virginia touched Ruby's hand. "Honey, it's just drizzling now. She'll be all right."

Ms. Homer took her garbage to the trash can.

Ruby stood up in her chair and purposely knocked over her milk.

"No. No. She can't." The white liquid quickly covered her food and seeped all over the table.

"Oh, crap." Virginia exclaimed. "Calm down, Ruby. Calm down, right now. Don't move. It's headed for your dress. I'll get some napkins." She hurried over to the counter.

Ms. Homer returned to the table to help out. She lifted the bag of cookies and began moving Virginia's food out of the way.

Ruby grabbed her wrist. "Please, don't run home," she pleaded. "I have to stop you."

Ms. Homer pressed her lips together. "I run in all kinds of weather. I've been running all my life. It's no biggie."

Ruby squeezed Ms. Homer's wrist, closed her eyes, and then squeezed again.

Ms. Homer's eyes flickered, and her body jerked.

⌘

Cora Homer saw herself lying on the sidewalk as the rain beat down on her lifeless body. Blood seeped from her nose and ears. An overturned school bus lay inches away, and she could hear children screaming. The horn of the bus blared nonstop, and the sound of sirens approaching stung her ear....

She gasped, her lungs suddenly void of air. The vivid images caused her heartbeat to become erratic. Her knees weakened, and her body swayed. She tried to focus on Ruby's face, praying the horrific scene would disappear.

Suddenly, the girl's eyes opened. The images vanished, and Cora rejoiced in the heavenly sapphire gaze that met hers. Air returned to her chest. She was relieved, yet she still couldn't move or speak.

⚜

Virginia approached the table, groaning, her hands full of napkins. "What has gotten into you, Miss Ruby? I've never seen you act this way." She wiped up the spilled milk, shaking her head and mumbling about the cost of good dance lessons.

"I ne-ne...I need to sit down," Ms. Homer stuttered as Ruby released her. She melted into her chair. "I won't run home. I won't."

"Cora, please accept my apologies. I don't know what's gotten into her," Virginia exclaimed.

"I'm sorry," Ruby murmured as she gently retrieved the bag of cookies from Ms. Homer's trembling hand.

Virginia got nose-to-nose with Ruby. "Look, it's okay, kiddo. But don't do it again. I'm not gonna lie, you freaked me out a little. No more tantrums. Got it?"

"I got it." Ruby grinned. "And all the kids will be okay." Her face lit up.

Virginia scrutinized her. "Did I miss something?"

Ruby slowly inched a cookie out of the red-and-white-checked bag. "Nope. Did you hear that there's a new teacher at school? She's gonna have a baby girl."

Virginia crossed her arms and tilted her head, aware Ruby was trying to distract her. Ruby pointed a small finger at Ms. Homer and took a nibble of a cookie.

"Can we give her a ride home?"

Virginia checked her watch and looked at Ms. Homer. She was slumped in her chair, staring out the window, almost in a daze. Her skin was ghostly pale, and her hands were shaking.

"Yeah, I guess we should." Virginia inhaled and exhaled deeply. "Yes. Let's do that. Some things are just more important than dancing."

"Like cookies," Ruby shouted with glee, her eyes wide as she held up the bag.

"Yeah, like cookies," Virginia agreed.

# MAKEOVER TIME

ROSALIE STOOD IN FRONT OF THE MIRROR AND COMBED HER extremely long hair. It was brown and thick, with natural auburn highlights, and hung all the way to her waistline. After the perfect shine appeared, she swiftly braided it and bound the bottom with a tan rubber band and a strip of ivory lace. She studied her reflection. A pang of confusion jarred her. Why did she insist on this ancient vintage hairstyle? Why was she attached to this stupid braid?

Everyone encouraged her to cut it, but she just couldn't do it. It was like her security blanket. It represented who she was. It was a part of her. Weren't people from Mystic Ridge supposed to be unusual? Squinting, she tried to picture herself with a different style. Her shoulders slumped, and her stomach churned. She couldn't.

Today was a novel day. Her younger sister Nancy had made her an appointment at Mountain Beauty Boutique. So, why was she nervous? Getting a makeover was supposed to be fun. Most women loved taking time out for themselves, but it made her feel weirdly stressed. She inhaled and exhaled. Maybe it was time— time for a real makeover. Time for a new Rosalie.

Before she could begin to thoroughly panic, the doorbell sounded; and the twins made a dash for the door. She raced out of the bathroom, following closely behind them. Sometimes they were a bit clumsy. She didn't want any morning accidents. Not today. She cautiously opened the front door.

Nancy stood grinning. "Hello, silly girl. Whaz up?"

Rosalie gazed at her sister's pink-tinted hair and emerald-colored bangs. There was a new tattoo on her neck, a lifelike owl. Hmmm. *Why an owl?* she wondered.

Her sister was quite the original.

Nancy was Mystic Ridge's only massage therapist, but she didn't stay very busy. She spent a lot of time photographing wildlife and selling essential oils. She also did energy work on those people who needed a boost. While Rosalie was practical and cautious, Nancy was eccentric and flighty. The two sisters were practically polar opposites. Rosalie was in awe of Nancy's confidence and bravado.

"New ink?" she asked her.

"Yep. This dang owl has been following me for quite a while. I thought I'd add him to my persona."

"Following you?" Rosalie repeated.

"Yeah. Freaky, right? He's everywhere I go, but he seems harmless." She tilted her head sideways. "It's badass, right?" She pointed to it.

"Right." Rosalie struggled to sound convincing.

The twins hugged Nancy's legs tightly and pulled at her camouflage backpack.

"Girl power to the rescue," she bellowed, entering the house. She kicked off her furry boots, sat down, and kissed the girls. "My, my, two birthdays, and they think they can wrestle me to the ground." She looked up at Rosalie. "They're growing so fast. They'll need their own reality show soon. So, are you ready for your day of leisure?"

Rosalie shrugged, "I guess."

Nancy rose and stroked Rosalie's long, silky braid. "Sis, it's beautiful and unique, just like you, but every once in a while, you need to rediscover yourself. I love you. You are very fab, but you look like you just escaped from the Sisters of Southern Mercy Convent." She paused. "I mean that in a good way—sort of.

"But at least think about cutting it? Or you could bleach it platinum blonde, very *Frozen*." She giggled. "Wouldn't purple be epic? Just go and bask in the glory of self-indulgence. Get your nails done, and get a facial. Wax your brows. They can even give makeup tips. You deserve some relaxation. Plus, you've had that gift card for over a year. Those things do expire. The girls will be fine."

She pulled off her backpack. "I brought my iPad, portable speakers, and energy stones. Good vibes are flowing. We're starting their dancing lessons today. It's never too early to get your groove on. Now, go, get out of here." She snapped her fingers and brought her hands to her hips. "Go, silly girl, and don't come back until you're a new woman!"

Rosalie handed her a list with lunch foods, nap times, and the phone number of the Mystic police and fire departments. Feeling reluctant and unsure, she kissed the girls and ventured out.

As she drove, she giggled to herself. The past three years *had* been confusing. Her nickname "Silly Girl" fit her perfectly. Once a true believer in women's intuition, she'd found out the hard way that it was nothing but nonsense. The entire time she'd been pregnant she was sure she was having a boy—not just sure, she had been positive. She'd declined a sonogram several times. Her doctor had just laughed.

Violet Bryant said she was a visionary. Sister Crystal Grace had touched her belly but kept her opinions to herself. Dolly Porter and Poovie Lamay insisted that a woman always knows!

Yes, she had told everyone it was a big baby boy, and she had purchased only blue clothing and blankets. Her intuition was so definite that all of her family and friends had believed her as well. Every single gift she had received was for a boy. When she gave birth to a tiny girl, and then another one, she was utterly shocked.

She'd felt a little foolish—no, a lot foolish. Everyone had a good laugh. She had been teased for weeks, especially as she tried to exchange all the blue clothing. Oh, the embarrassment.

And someday the girls would hear the zany story as well. She dreaded that. Crazy stories hovered over Mystic Ridge. The town was almost famous for them, and she fit right in, in a ridiculous way.

Nancy had given her the nickname "Silly Girl", and everyone embraced it. She turned on the radio. Whenever she was alone, she always began to ponder the memory. Why had she felt that way? And after two years, why couldn't she let it go?

As she drove toward the spa, she continued to question herself. All her life, even as a small girl, she had pictured herself with a little boy. When she and Nancy were kids, Nancy always pretended to be a pop star, while she always carried her cat around, pretending it was a baby boy.

Her brows creased as she remembered the day after the girls had been born. Amidst all the congratulations, she had spiked a fever. An infection had spread from her incision, and she would not ever be able to have more children. It had been a painful realization that she would never have the boy she had dreamt of. She thanked God every day for the girls. She was blessed, she knew that. And she was grateful, too. She loved them with all her heart, but for some reason there was an empty spot in her soul that she couldn't explain to anyone, not even herself.

As she listened to relaxing classical music, Rosalie abruptly realized she had driven the wrong direction. The salon was located near the mall, and she was nowhere near there. She glanced at the clock and realized she was already ten minutes late for her appointment.

She stopped at a red light and just felt tired—mentally tired. She spied Cora Homer jogging past in a neon-yellow vest and bright orange shorts. She waved, and as she lowered her hand, she spied Enchanting Treasures. There was a portion of a white picket fence outside and an old worn school desk, windowpanes, rusted buckets, and a vintage bicycle. The wooden "Open" sign was very old, and hung inside the store next to a faded American flag. The soft lighting inside gave it a welcoming glow. It beckoned her to come in and explore.

Her stomach fluttered, and goose bumps rose on her arms. Her appointment was forgotten; she knew she had to go inside.

As she entered the shop, an elderly woman with a kind smile greeted her from behind an ornate mahogany desk.

"Hello, honey, I'm Millie. Can I help you find anything today?"

Rosalie waved a hand. "Oh, no. I'm just looking quickly. Quickly looking," she replied in a foreign, shaky voice. What was wrong with her? "Browsing."

Millie nodded. "You make yourself at home. There are a lot of things you'll want to see. I'll be right here on my laptop if you need me."

"Thanks." Rosalie relaxed. She suddenly felt comforted by all the old items.

The room was extremely crowded. She could barely walk. There were glass bottles in every shape and size, and old tables with scratches from unknown people. There were needlepoint pillows and pictures, hats and jewelry, boots and candles, teacups, and dishes. A rusted Bubba's Honky-Tonk sign perched against an old chrome car bumper. The shop was perfectly warm and smelled wonderfully musty with a tiny hint of vanilla.

She carefully touched plates, iron buckets, silver bowls, lace handkerchiefs, silver spoons, quilts, and many other unique items. She felt a familiar presence here. These were personal items, which people had treasured. They carried grand stories and had seen different times and interesting places. It all seemed so intimate. But she also felt an odd belonging, an unexplainable hominess.

Ever so slowly, she made her way through the tranquil room. She noticed an alabaster cat leisurely cleaning itself as it spread out on an emerald-upholstered high-back chair. It looked almost like porcelain. She touched its soft head as she walked past. It had a small pink collar with a silver heart that read *Wendy*.

"Hello, friend," she whispered. It purred, and a wave of calm seemed to flood through her.

As she reached the back of the store, she noticed a tiny corner booth that was illuminated by a softly lit hanging chandelier. The area was almost glowing. It called to her. She entered the booth and saw a grandiose sapphire gown on a lifesize mannequin. It had an extremely high neck with a small black cameo pinned to the front. White pearls made a square shape across the chest area. The sleeves puffed out near the shoulders and then came back in at the elbow. The bottom seemed to stand out as if a petticoat were underneath. A velvet sash was draped around the waistline. Pink beads circled the hemline.

As she embraced the vision, she could not breathe. It was so lavish. Yet, it seemed familiar. There was something curious about this gown. She couldn't take another step. It seemed to invite her closer.

She shouted to the front of the store, "Excuse me, can I try this on?"

Millie hurried to join her, stopped, and studied Rosalie. "Yes, yes, I think you should." She carefully removed the perfectly preserved gown, then faced Rosalie and presented it with her arms stretched out in a rather formal manner.

As Rosalie took the gown, a wave of déjà-vu engulfed her. She steadied her feet. The dress was heavy, but soft and lush and, oh, so delicate. It smelled like lavender.

Millie motioned for Rosalie to follow her. Carrying the dress like a helpless child, she trailed the older woman to a teeny dressing room with an enormous vintage mirror inside. It was enclosed by a burgundy velvet window panel. Rosalie stepped inside.

"If you need any assistance, I'm just a holler away," Millie told her.

"Thank you," Rosalie heard herself whisper.

As she pulled the panel closed, she felt nervous and frightened, but elated at the same time. Her heart thundered. She quickly undressed and cautiously put on the antique gown. The neckline was perfect. The hemline was right where it should be. Rosalie stared dumbfounded at her reflection. She felt immobile.

"Do you need any help with buttons?" Millie inquired.

Rosalie slipped the panel open. "Please."

As Millie buttoned her up, she could barely breathe. The fit was exact.

Millie tied the sash. "It's perfect. Fits you like a glove. I'll be right back with the shoes." She hurried away.

Rosalie stood staring at her reflection. *Is that me?* she wondered.

The cat moved to the base of the mirror and surveyed her.

"Here, darling." Millie handed her a pair of shoes. "You take your precious time. Wendy is quite infatuated with you." She pointed to the cat and walked away.

Rosalie's brows creased. There was no way the shoes would fit. She sat down and stared at them. The cat's green eyes widened. Suddenly, she knew the shoes would, indeed, fit. It terrified her, but she had to know for sure.

With shaking fingers, she placed a delicate blue slipper on each foot. They had been worn many, many times. They had walked on cobblestone streets, squeaky wooden floors, green grass, and muddy paths. She could see the steps. She could see the dainty shoes in motion.

Standing, she gazed in the mirror. She moved her long braid to the side of her neck. She looked somehow ghostly, and her body began trembling. She looked unbelievably but totally familiar. Something very mysterious was happening. She couldn't blink her eyes because the blissful vision might disappear. Maybe this was a dream.

She glanced down at her cell phone perched against her purse. No. This was happening.

The cat rubbed against her, and she felt her nerves calm. This vision was real, and the vision was her. She stood unmoving, taking in her own presence, remembering music and laughter, rain and sunshine, crisp leaves and chilly evenings. She felt mystified, and grateful.

The sound of a phone ringing somewhere in the distance jolted her back to reality. She wasn't sure how long she had been standing there, but suddenly, she had to see what else was in that area of the store. She swallowed hard. Was there something else there, something of importance to her? There must be.

The cat exited the fitting room, and she felt compelled to follow it back to the softly lit corner.

As she peered around, her eyes darted to a medium-sized portrait that glowed on the wall. The gold frame was scraped and splintered. A thick layer of dust covered it, but she could make out tiny green eyes in the portrait. Her heart thundered. She knew those eyes. She rushed over and urgently cleaned it with the sleeve of her dress. A gasp escaped her.

There, in the alabaster glow of a crystal lamp, she saw a painting of herself. She was wearing this exact blue dress. Her hair hung long at her side, braided exactly as it was now. A little boy about three years old, wearing white socks, blue knickers, a white shirt, and a black bow tie, was sitting on her lap. Her arms were placed lovingly around his waist.

His familiar sapphire eyes melted her heart. She remembered that he didn't like to sit still for anything. He was so full of energy. Chuckling, she remembered him balking and complaining as the artist had worked. It had taken so long. Tears cascaded down her face. It was him, the little boy of her dreams. There was also a small white kitten perched near their ankles. She noticed that the portrait was dated 1902. Her heart seemed to stop beating, her knees buckled, and she slowly crumbled to the floor.

❦

When Rosalie awoke there was a soft pillow beneath her head and an icepack on her forehead. She was still wearing the dress, and it was arranged perfectly around her. The cat was staring down at her, looking concerned. She felt exhausted.

Millie was sitting in a rocking chair smiling at her. "Ah, you're awake. Thank heavens. My dear, are you okay?"

Unsure, Rosalie could not answer. She turned her head toward the painting and beheld the vision again. There he was, the rambunctious little boy she missed so much. A slow smile spread across her lips. He was perfect. He was adorable. How could she have ever forgotten his sweet face?

For several minutes, she just lay there, tears of recollection seeping from her eyes. She adored every detail of the wondrous painting and the memories she had of its creation. She concentrated hard but couldn't remember much else about that life. She knew it had been a good life, and that this precious boy had brought her immense joy. She wiped away the moisture on her face and sat up. The details didn't matter. Her soul remembered him. He had been real. And although she was wearing a vintage dress, lying on the floor of an antique shop, she realized that maybe she was not so silly after all.

She stood up in the familiar gown and slippers and felt rejuvenated.

Millie grinned at her. "So, you've come for your things, have you?"

Rosalie nodded.

"Sister Crystal Grace told me one day you'd find your way here."

Rosalie's jaw dropped.

❦

For several hours, Rosalie sifted through the items in the booth. She saw herself playing the piano, laughing, singing, and entertaining. She found a lace handbag, two hats that she could clearly picture herself wearing, and an opal ring she knew she'd worn. But their finances were tight. The twins were going to need new carseats soon, and she couldn't afford to spend very much. Plus, she didn't feel it would be right to bring too much of her old life home to this one. She couldn't obsess over this discovery. She was a busy mother with a vivacious family.

These would be her special possessions, her bond with her past. It was a gift, finding the painting of the boy she loved so much. He had been a presence in her mind for a long time, maybe forever. She knew he would always be in her heart, and she had a real treasure, and the knowledge that her love was real.

She looked in the mirror, and even though she looked the same, she was different, very different. It was like her soul had experienced a makeover. Now, she had confirmation of a love she'd felt for so long. And wonderfully, she felt she could be at peace. She could enjoy her own life to the fullest. She was free to change her hair or anything she wished. She would not remain stuck in the past, needing answers.

This discovery freed her. There were no more confusing feelings inside her. She would go to the salon. She would get several inches of her hair cut and maybe some highlights, maybe some bangs. She felt enlightened and empowered.

Now she understood why so many people frequented antique shops. Her mother had always told her that amazing things happened in Mystic Ridge, but she'd never understood—until now.

Rosalie approached Millie carrying the dress and the portrait. "Thank you so much for your help. You've been so compassionate and understanding. How much do I owe you?"

Millie rubbed Rosalie's cheek. "Not a dime, honey. They're your things. Be content with the secret you've discovered."

"I will. Thank you." Grateful, Rosalie wiped her wet cheeks and realized she was weeping again, tears of joy.

The cat jumped up on the counter and meowed. Rosalie petted her. "Thank you, Wendy. You were very helpful."

"She's the best," Millie added. "She just showed up here a few years ago and ran into the shop on a windy day. She made herself at home and refuses to go into a carrier to come home with me. She wants to be here. Sometimes she looks out the window for hours, like she's waiting on someone. She's assisted several of my customers."

"She's so exquisite and helpful," Rosalie chuckled.

Millie wrapped the dress is white tissue paper and placed it in a large flat box. She wrapped the portrait in brown paper and taped the paper over the aged golden edges. As she completed her task, her eyes met Rosalie's.

"I'm so glad you came by."

"Me, too." She carefully lifted her treasures. "Does this happen very often?"

Millie rubbed her chin thoughtfully. "Sometimes..." She paused. "Sometimes, you just have to be open-minded and really see what's on your path, and where you are led."

Rosalie nodded.

"I get a magical ringside seat," Millie chuckled. "You have a blessed day."

Rosalie smiled. "I already have."

# SPECIAL MOMENTS

P ATSY LOADED THE LAST OF THE BREAKFAST DISHES INTO THE dishwasher. She noticed dirt on the kitchen floor. Tobias, her husband, had tracked it in.

Every morning he had to rush out and check on his tomato plants. Had a gust of wind blown them over? Had the rabbits found them? Had the tomatoes turned red? Were they ready to eat?

He constantly fussed over his potted tomato plants—he had six buckets strategically placed throughout the filtered sunlight in their back yard. They couldn't eat them all even if they tried. But Tobias had been a good man and a caring husband for forty years. She could live with a little dirt in her kitchen.

She put away the morning paper and decided to dust and vacuum. Wearing her soft fuzzy robe and slippers, she took out a pink feather duster and began dusting her many trinkets. She had lots of ceramic cats and dogs that resembled beloved pets she'd had in the past. She picked up a glass kitty statue that resembled Coconut. It seemed like just yesterday the kids had come home with that malnourished kitten. She'd spent weeks nursing it back to health, and then years with him at the foot of her bed. He'd brought a lot of joy to everyone in the family, but especially her. They'd had a connection.

He was buried near the oak swing in their back yard, his grave marked with a white rosebush.

She also had candles and teacups and family pictures that gathered dust regularly, and that was okay with her. She felt comfortable and content. Each day was relaxed and uneventful, just the way she liked it.

At sixty-seven years of age, she had really begun to appreciate all the special moments in her life. She noticed a Bubba's Honky-Tonk shot glass and giggled. Such good times. She ran the duster over it. Reminiscing was her favorite thing to do. It was soothing.

Each day she tried to really notice all the things she was thankful for. Her husband and two children were tops on her list. Louise was twenty-eight and engaged to be married in June; her fiancé Charlie was a loan officer at the Mystic Affairs Community Bank. They were a high-energy couple, always jogging, hiking, volunteering, and traveling. Patsy found them a tad exhausting. And the wedding planning had more details than she could have ever imagined. But Louise had a good head on her shoulders and was usually open to compromise.

Her son Doug was happily married to Maura, a lovely woman who had a passion for baking. She baked from her home and delivered her treats all over town. The local bagel shop couldn't keep the ones she provided them in stock. The whole town knew about Maura's cookies, and her cupcakes were quickly gaining a delicious reputation as well. Patsy loved her daughter-in-law's visits, and the cookies she always brought. If her business ever got too busy for Maura to handle, Patsy planned to be her first employee. The thought of baking sweets all day sounded simply divine.

She was so thankful that both her children were settled.

Tobias had cut back his work schedule to three days a week, and it was nice having him around the house more.

When a young, energetic new teacher named Emma was hired at Smoky Valley Elementary, Patsy knew it was her cue to leave. The children would be in good hands. Retirement was calling. She had been teaching for more than thirty-five years. It was time to move on.

Yet, she still longed for meaning in her life. She still wanted to feel useful and needed. Of course, she was needed by her daughter, and possibly her daughter-in-law. She felt her face melt into a smile. Spending time with her family was exactly what she wanted to do.

Very carefully, she dusted her family pictures. Then she picked up her most beloved book—*Soaring Wings*, the biography of Amelia Earheart. The book had belonged to her mother. They had read it together when Patsy was taken ill as a teenager. Her mother had barely left her side, and read the pages out loud. As Patsy healed, they discussed Amelia's courage. Back then, it was unheard-of for a woman to be so brave. They had also discussed what a tragedy it was for Amelia to be lost forever.

Reading the story had been a bonding time for the two women, and Patsy would treasure the book, and the memories it held, forever.

Amelia Earheart would always be one of her heroes. She had written a paper on her in high school. It was still pressed in the back of the book. She flipped through the pages. If only Amelia had had a guardian angel to guide her home safely. She dusted the treasure, and then carefully laid it back on the table.

She put her duster away and took out the vacuum. As she pushed the heavy machine around the family room, she began sweating. The warmth quickly moved up to her face, and she could feel perspiration on her cheeks. She turned it off and sat down. Hot flashes still plagued her. She would talk to her doctor about them—again.

Tobias came in from his tomato-plant inspection. "Hiya, honey. I got eight more buds coming through. We'll have enough tomatoes for a whole bucket of salsa." He inspected her. "Are you okay?"

"I'm just a little warm."

"Can I get you some lemonade?"

"That would be nice."

He scurried to the kitchen.

Patsy took a few deep breaths, trying to cool down. She turned on the television. *I Love Lucy* was on. Tobias returned with her drink.

"Tobias, remember this show. Oh, how it used to make us laugh." She thought for a moment. "We had a puppy named Lucy, remember?"

"Yeah, I remember her. She chewed up my favorite hiking boots." He sat down beside her and began watching the show. "Are you feeling better now?"

Patsy nodded and held his hand. They watched together, occasionally giggling out loud.

A commercial came on for the Mystic Mall. She couldn't remember the last time she'd been there. She turned to Tobias.

"I think I'll go over there today and have a look around."

"What do you want to do that for?"

She stood up and stretched, feeling much better. "I may look at the women's golfwear and the dishes. Louise will be registering soon. There might be a sale."

Tobias watched her with raised eyebrows. She tossed up her hands up.

"I don't know. I just feel like going. Violet always said to listen to your inner voice. My inner voice says, 'Go to the mall, old woman.'" She chuckled.

Tobias shook his head. "We're on a budget now. Don't buy anything that's not a necessity."

Patsy rolled her eyes, put the vacuum away, and went to get ready.

≈≈≈

As Patsy entered the mall, she realized she had not been there in a very long time. The floors and ceiling were different than she remembered. Fancy tile and marble had replaced the old hardwood floors. It was also bigger than she remembered. She probably would not be able to get from one end to the other, which was okay.

It was early, and the stores were just opening. She spotted a couple sitting on a bench, openly embracing. She tried not to stare, but something about them piqued her curiosity. Her body felt warm again, and a few beads of perspiration formed on her brow, so she stopped walking and took several deep breaths as she watched them.

The boy looked to be twenty-something. His hair was dyed black, and he wore ill-fitting, dirty clothes. He was unshaven, and smoked some kind of electronic cigarette as he kissed the girl at the same time. Yuck. The poor thing.

Patsy felt a bit disgusted, but she just couldn't stop staring. She ducked into a nearby card shop so she could watch them without being noticed. Her heart beat quickly. She wanted to get a better look at the girl.

After a bit, she got a clear view of her. She was about seventeen, with reddish-blond shoulder-length hair. She was not much taller than five feet. She had the most adorable freckles on top of her nose, and her cheeks were rosy. Her clothes were filthy, too, and Patsy wondered where she'd been sleeping.

Although the girl was smiling, Patsy had a very strong feeling she was miserable. Her heart ached for her.

"May I help you?" a saleswoman asked, startling Patsy.

"Oh, yes. I would like to look at your wedding invitations," she managed.

"We have several styles—follow me," the woman instructed.

Patsy spent the next twenty minutes looking at invitations. After the enthusiastic woman calmed down, Patsy found an opportunity to get away.

"I'll have to bring my daughter back this weekend. Thank you so much for your help." She hurried from the store.

Her heart sank when she noticed that the couple was gone. She looked in every direction but didn't see them anywhere. She swallowed the lump that formed in her throat. Why was she so emotional? Why was she so worried? What was going to happen to that sweet young girl?

She shook her head. She was acting silly. It was none of her business. They were gone. The moment had passed. It was rather ridiculous for a woman of her age to be obsessing over complete strangers.

She clutched her handbag, lifted her chin, and made her way to the sporting goods shop. She tried on a couple of women's golf hats, but her heart just wasn't in it. She picked one out anyway. She knew Tobias would like it, so she purchased it.

As she was paying, she heard a loud commotion outside the store, in the mall area. She finished swiftly and hurried out. Her mouth dropped open when she saw the grungy boy in handcuffs. He was being escorted by mall security officers. *Where is the girl?* She looked in every direction, but there was no sign of her. Patsy didn't need a hot flash to know she absolutely had to find her.

As she began walking, she gazed inside stores on both sides of the mall. She became frantic, but it was a huge mall. The girl might be hiding—all alone. *I must find her.* She walked fast. The girl needed her. She could feel it in her old bones. Her mind raced with scenarios.

Abruptly, she halted. *Stop, woman. Think. Where would a young girl go, a girl who was all alone and afraid?*

She noticed a Mystic Pet Palooza ahead, and knew it was a distinct possibility. She hurried there and looked around at the entrance. She ventured to the back of the store, and her heart leapt when she spotted the girl gazing into an aquarium. *Thank heavens.*

Patsy slowly crept up beside her. Then the girl walked to a kitten adoption window, and stared at the cages of cats. Again, Patsy crept up beside her. Dried tears stained the girl's cheeks, and she appeared exhausted as she swayed close to the glass. Patsy decided she had to seize the opportunity.

"Those two little white ones are just precious." She pointed.

The girl gasped, and then her eyes met Patsy's, and she seemed to calm down. She nodded.

"Would you like to hold one? I could ask."

She nodded again, her lower lip trembling.

Patsy snapped her fingers urgently toward a store clerk. "Excuse me, sir. Could we please hold one of the tiny white kittens?"

A teenager with dark straight hair hurried over. He surveyed them for a second and then said excitedly, "Heck yeah, we have a bonding room. You can sit and all. We just cleaned it this morning."

Perfect.

"That sounds lovely." Patsy glanced at his name tag. "Thank you, Jason."

They went into a closet-sized room and sat down. Patsy noticed the dirt under the girl's fingernails and the thinness of her cheeks.

Jason arrived with a kitten. "This little dude is the coolest. He saw you in the window and wanted to meet you badly."

Patsy pointed to the girl, and he handed the kitten to her. She immediately cradled it to her chest and closed her eyes.

"I'll let you know when we're done," Patsy told him, unable to take her eyes off the girl as she cuddled the kitten so closely. "Thank you."

"No problem. Chill as long as you want. I gotta fill water bowls." He smiled and left.

The kitten squirmed and wiggled in the girl's arms, licked her chin for a few seconds, then closed its eyes and began to purr. Patsy sat quietly. Patience was a virtue she had always possessed.

Without opening her eyes, the girl whispered softly, "I'm so tired."

Suddenly, Patsy realized the girl was much younger than she had first thought—not seventeen, possibly only fifteen, or even fourteen. The kitten rubbed against her chin, and the girl moved her head from side to side in a comforting fashion. Patsy felt her eyes well with tears and she forced them away.

"Let me help you," she whispered.

"Me? Why would you want to help me?" Her eyes opened. "I've been a little shit."

Patsy touched her shoulder. "We all make mistakes, and we all deserve forgiveness."

The child sat in silence, thinking, stroking the kitten. Patsy waited. Ten or fifteen minutes went by.

Jason came back in. "What's up, gals? Wanna take the little dude home?"

The girl handed him the kitten. "I can't," she whispered.

He looked at Patsy and shifted from one foot to another, and then cradled the kitten in his arms.

"It's all good. He says he likes you a lot."

He glanced at the girl. She rubbed her eyes urgently.

He met Patsy's gaze. "I'll take the little guy back for lunch. Think it over."

"I can't," the girl sobbed.

Patsy stood, and the girl followed suit.

"Well, no rush. Shop a bit. Y'all have a good one," Jason said, and left with the kitten.

Patsy put an arm around the girl. "Can I buy you a sandwich, honey?"

She nodded.

Patsy led her back into the mall and to a sandwich counter. She pointed to the menu and listened to the tiny voice as the child ordered a small turkey sub. Patsy interrupted and insisted they make it a large sandwich, and added chips and a drink and a cookie to boot. Then, she ordered her own meal.

They found a table and began eating in silence. As the girl wolfed down her food, Patsy was startled—the poor thing was practically starving. When they'd finished, Patsy wrapped up all the leftovers and put them back in the bag. An awkward silence floated between them, and again Patsy waited.

"Thank you," the girl said.

"You are very welcome," she paused. "Where are you from?"

"Chattanooga." She stared at her lap.

Patsy chose her words carefully, not wanting to scare her away. "Would you like to tell me your story, dear?"

The girl tucked her dirty hair behind her ears and finally looked up at Patsy. "It's really dumb. Derrick said he loved me and my parents hated him, for real. We ran away. I thought it would be so dope. It's been about seven months, living here and there and every-freaking-where. It wasn't an adventure, it was gross." She ran her hands down the sides of her face. "We were in Knoxville for a while. Then I read a brochure about Mystic Ridge. It said everyone was welcome. It said it was a window to destiny. It talked about mountain views and baking contests, and a journey home. I just had to come here.

"We hitchhiked and rode with a trucker. He said there was a famous nun here?"

Patsy giggled. "Yes, there is. I've met her a few times, she's quite amazing, but her life has not been an easy one. It's a long tale. She disappeared as a child. The details are still sketchy. Now, she won't talk about it at all. My advice would be not to get lost in the caverns."

A few moments of silence passed, and slow, thick tears began cascading down the girl's cheeks.

"Would you like to go home?" Patsy asked her.

She wiped her eyes with the back of her hand. "I dunno."

Patsy lifted her chin and looked deeply into her eyes. "Darling, did your folks mistreat you? Did they hurt you?"

"No, they just wouldn't let me see Derrick. But he loved me so much. He said he needed me." She paused. "My friend Crystal said he was a player, a loser. She begged me not to trust him. Crystal was a good friend. But I didn't listen to anyone."

"First love can be all-consuming and incredibly confusing."

"I'm an idiot, and I'll never love anyone again."

"Now, now! You don't want to end up like Lucinda Smith, nasty and bitter. Don't give up on love altogether. There's a lot of love in this here world. I'll bet your parents just want you home."

She slumped in her chair. "I have a little brother. He's five." She wiped her eyes again. "I miss him so much."

"There's a special bond between siblings. Patsy held her hand. "Child, I don't even know your name."

A tiny smile pursed her lips. "I'm Amelia."

Patsy froze for a second. Like Amelia Earhart; and just like Amelia Earhart, this girl was lost. Was this actually happening?

She patted her chest softly. "I'm Patsy. Patsy Cooper," she managed and then smiled. "Amelia, it's perfectly lovely to meet you. I bet your little brother misses you so much. Do you have a phone?"

Amelia shook her head.

"Can I call your family for you, please?"

Amelia nodded.

Patsy took out her phone and listened as Amelia whispered the numbers. Then, she took Amelia by the hand. "Come with me. Let's get your hair a little wash and style, spruce you up."

She took her to a hair salon just a few yards down from the food court.

As Amelia eased her head into the shampoo bowl, Patsy scooted to the back of the salon and called the number. She explained who she was, and that Amelia was with her. The woman on the other end shrieked with joy and then broke out in thundering sobs. Patsy had never heard anyone so relieved and grateful. Together, they put together a plan to get Amelia safely home to her family, who loved her dearly. When the conversation ended Patsy felt so relieved. *Thank you, Lord.*

She returned and watched as Amelia's nervous smile eased into a relaxed grin. Her clenched hands slowly loosened. When she shook her strawberry-blond locks out in front of the mirror, her face was eager. It warmed Patsy's heart, in a good way. She hurried to the receptionist and paid.

Amelia stood. "Thank you so much, Ms. Patsy. My hair was so..." She hesitated. "...radically disgusting."

Patsy touched the soft fringed bottom of her long hair. "Well, it's stunning now. You're beautiful, dear. Come on. Let's get you some comfortable traveling clothes, maybe some of those leggings and warm boots."

"Really?" Amelia's eyes lit up. "Are you sure?"

"Yes, but we have to shop quickly. No dilly-dallying."

Amelia looked concerned. "What did my mom say?"

"She cried with joy, Amelia. She's sending a car here to get you and bring you home. She's gathering your family and preparing a huge meal. She's ecstatic. Honestly, I've never heard anyone so happy in all my life."

"I don't know what to say." Amelia squeezed her eyes shut then opened them again. "I'm scared."

Patsy hugged her. "Dear heart, you belong with your family. They want to take care of you. They love you unconditionally. You don't have to be scared anymore. Now, let's get shopping and toss those smelly rags you're wearing."

A broad smile spread across Amelia's face. "Oookay."

＊＊＊

After just thirty minutes or so Patsy had bought Amelia a pair of comfortable jeans with lace embroidery and a pink camouflage sweatshirt. Amelia thanked her over and over. Patsy checked her phone, awaiting a text from the driver Amelia's mother was sending. There was still a little time. Thank goodness.

She took Amelia by the hand. "We have one more thing to tend to. I don't want you traveling alone."

"It's not that far, Ms. Patsy. I'll be okay."

Patsy walked fast. "I don't want you to have second thoughts, or feel lonely, or have one ounce of anxiety. So, you're going to have a job on your journey."

"A job?"

Patsy pulled her into Mystic Pet Palooza and located Jason. "Excuse me, Jason. I'd like to adopt the white kitten we held earlier. We need a proper carrier and some food and a bowl.

Jason's eyes grew wide. "Awesome," he shouted, startling everyone within ten feet of them. "I kinda had a feeling. I'm the Adoption Coordinator for a reason." He stood a bit taller. "I have a knack of knowing which people were meant for which pet— and who to say no to. Sometimes the pets themselves tell me."

Patsy and Amelia exchanged a glance.

Jason continued in a businesslike tone, a hand on his rock-band t-shirt. "I think his sister will go to another lady very soon. I'll get everything he needs, and I'll throw in a squeaky mouse or two. Back in a minute."

Amelia shrieked with excitement. "Oh, my, Ms. Patsy. You think of everything."

Patsy nodded. "I asked your mother first, and she said it was fine. She liked the idea of you traveling with a teeny friend."

Amelia hugged Patsy tightly, resting her head on her shoulder. Patsy thought she might cry. The sweet thing deserved so much love.

"I won't make the same mistakes again, I promise," Amelia told her.

Patsy moved her to arm's length. "Everyone makes mistakes. This one is all over now. But we have to go." They hurried to the checkout line.

Patsy filled out a lengthy adoption contract in record time while Jason explained proper kitten care to Amelia. As she paid a cashier, she noticed how naïve Amelia looked in her trendy clothing, with her clean hair. It was definitely possible she wasn't even fifteen. Who knew what would have become of her?

Her smile was ecstatic as Jason handed her a blue carrier with the tiny kitten meowing inside. Patsy gathered the bags with the food and bowls and toys, and they left the checkout line.

Hopefully, Amelia would tell her parents what she had experienced. But this way, she could return with her head held high. She was giggling and sticking her fingers through the small openings in the front of the carrier.

Suddenly, Patsy's phone signaled that she had a text. She checked it; the driver was waiting at the front entrance of the mall.

"Your car is here."

Amelia took a deep breath, but she didn't speak.

Patsy took her hand. "Let's go, dear." Then, she smiled at Jason. "Thank you, Jason. You've been quite helpful."

"You beautiful babes are definitely welcome. Come again."

They rushed through the mall and out the front doors to where a black sedan waited by the curb. A woman wearing a professional-looking blue pantsuit stepped out. Patsy approached and confirmed she had been sent from Amelia's mother and had specific directions to deliver Amelia home safely. The woman was personable, and cooed and fussed over the kitten in the carrier.

Suddenly, Amelia faced Patsy. Her face was distorted and flushed. "What if they can't forgive me? What if they never forgive me?"

"Stay calm. I knew this would happen." She placed her hands on Amelia's shoulders. "Remember this—love can heal the deepest of wounds. Your mother said she was sorry she hadn't listened to you. She said she's going to do better. I can tell she adores you. She said you belong with the family who loves you, and I agree with her."

Amelia chewed on her lip, her brows furrowed, her eyes clouded.

Patsy continued. "You're all spruced up. You made a mistake, and it's over. It's time to get on with your life. Chin up! And this little kitten deserves a real home, and he's counting on you. It's a big responsibility."

Amelia started to cry.

Patsy hugged her tightly, and she could feel the thin body trembling. "Everything will be okay, Amelia. You have a bright future ahead of you. But make good choices. Think things through. I know you're a smart girl." She kissed her on the forehead.

Amelia looked up at her. "When I woke up this morning, I had no idea my day would end this way. I've been lost and confused for so long. You're an angel, a real-life angel."

Patsy shrugged. "Nah."

"Living on the road is nasty. It's horrible."

Guiding her toward the car, Patsy nodded.

The woman driver greeted them and opened the back door. Patsy placed the kitten carrier in the back seat and the bag with the food and bowl on the floorboard. She also put in the rest of her sandwich. The driver smiled, rounded the car, and took her place behind the wheel.

Amelia scooted in.

"Your mother has my number, and I expect a phone call tonight when you arrive home."

"I promise," Amelia said.

"And I'm on Facebook. I expect you to find me." She pointed a finger at her. "I expect to see lots of photos of that feline, and videos, too. I adore cat videos."

"I promise," Amelia said again. "I'll never forget you."

"And I will never forget you, either."

Patsy blew her a kiss and closed the door. As the sedan pulled away, she felt a surge of heat. Damned hot flashes. She saw a bench nearby and sat down. Her feet ached. The sedan weaved through the parking lot and then disappeared. Amelia would be okay. That little lost bird would find her way home.

It was almost dinnertime. Tobias was probably worried—she'd been gone the entire day. For the first time in quite a while, though, she felt a real sense of accomplishment, and her heart felt full. She savored the moment.

The orange glow of the sunset pierced the clouds and shone directly on her. Her entire body was illuminated by a heavenly hue. She shook her head and waved a hand in the air.

"I was happy to do it." Taking a deep breath, she crossed her hands in her lap. "Call me anytime."

# SKIN DEEP

**L**UCINDA CLIMBED OFF HER EXERCISE BIKE, ADMIRED HER RE-flection in the mirror and wiped the sweat from her brow. Staying beautiful was a pain in the butt, literally. She stared at the television as a young slim blond woman bit into a hot and steamy cinnamon roll.

"Delicious," the actress cooed.

"Bitch." Lucinda scowled and rubbed her flat stomach as she watched the sugary icing melting on the girl's lips. Her mouth watered. She hadn't eaten sweets in what seemed like forever. Women didn't really scarf down ten grams of fat first thing in the morning, did they? Maybe some of the Mystic chubs, but they probably regretted it two seconds later.

Her chin rose as the commercial ended. She had will power. She had the stuff, even if she wasn't a young thing anymore.

*Good Morning America* came back on. She lifted her cell phone. Working out was her special time, no interruptions allowed. It had rung three times, but she'd refused to answer it. Nothing could distract her from bettering herself. Her well-being came first.

Checking the caller ID, she saw that the first call was from her son Felix. She exhaled. He was attending college on an academic scholarship and worked part-time in the school bookstore, but he always needed more money. He never appreciated a dime he got, and spent his summers working as a camp counselor for a boy's club, a totally minimum-wage gig. He said he liked working with the kids, and life wasn't all about making the big dollar. He said he liked giving back. Ridiculous! The child was living in a fantasy world. What was his problem? He'd even had the gall to call her self-absorbed. He was ungrateful. Whatever it was this time, he could fend for himself.

She wet a washrag and ran it across her neck, her thoughts drifting to her inheritance. She loved it so much—just as if it were a real living person. Which was probably twisted as hell, but so be it. She loved having money. It gave her independence.

The second call had been from the nail salon, and the third from her masseuse, Nancy Connors. She'd return those later, at a more convenient time.

She walked through the foyer and stopped at an ornate brass-and-silver mirror. She studied her reflection. The facelift she'd had seven years ago was wearing off. Her neck appeared saggy and wrinkled, and her eyes looked hooded. Being fifty-two sucked ass. There was no way around it.

She strolled into the kitchen and poured a cup of premium-roast coffee. Mondays, she had the house all to herself. It was the best day of the week. Her paralegal job kept her busy, but the hours were somewhat flexible; and she loved having Mondays off. And although she hated to admit it, she relished her husband Simon's absence on Mondays. He was so fat and lazy, and seemed to take up so much space. It annoyed her to see him reading on his tablet, or munching on chips and watching sports on television. She constantly fluttered around him, trying to encourage him to tend to the gardening or take a turn on the treadmill. But he preferred to relax, talk on the phone, or play fetch with the damn cocker spaniel.

Simon was a high-powered attorney, and when he had on an expensive three-piece suit, she always found herself in awe of him. But when he was a gushy pushover, doling out money to charities or giving computers to the local schools, she thought he was an utter fool. Didn't he realize that people never learned a thing from receiving handouts?

She sifted through the mail and came upon an envelope from her daughter Loraine. Her lips tightened. They'd had no contact since Loraine had married that horrible dark-skinned boy named Philo Priscus. What kind of name was that, anyway? She had forbidden the marriage, and Loraine had blatantly disobeyed her. They hadn't attended or paid for a single thing, not even her dress. It infuriated her even further that Simon continued to stay in contact with their daughter and voiced his regret constantly. But what was done was done, and she refused to dwell on it.

Lucinda tore open the envelope and was shocked to find photographs of Loraine holding a baby.

"No," she shouted as her hands began to shake. "How could she?"

How long had it been since the wedding? She tapped her toe for a few minutes. Two years—it had been about two years. Anger seethed in her. She was a grandmother. No! She urgently began ripping up the picture until not a single image was visible.

She read the letter. Loraine was thanking Simon for stopping by the hospital and for the thoughtful gift.

Stopping by? What the hell? Thoughtful gift? That son of a bitch.

A light tapping on the front door distracted her rage. She stood motionless. Whatever it was, she wasn't interested. Her heart raced. How could he have betrayed her? She waited several minutes, and then dropped the letter and torn photograph into the trash. She raced toward the stairs, anxious to shower and get to Simon's office and cuss him out properly.

"Lucinda? Hey, there," Sister Mary Jean Stevenson yelled through the sidelight window beside the wrought iron door.

Lucinda cringed. It was the town do-gooder. She couldn't stand her. She gritted her teeth and approached but didn't open the door.

"I'm in a bit of a rush. I've got to get to my husband's office," she yelled.

Claire O'Donnell peeked through the opening as well. "We just need to talk to you for a minute. Don't be so paranoid. Get over yourself for one minute and open up."

Biting her lower lip, Lucinda pulled the large double doors open. "Good afternoon," she said coolly.

"Hi, dear," Sister Mary Jean said. "We just wanted to stop by and see if you could help us out. Muriel Hutchins, in the white colonial on the corner, lost her husband last fall." She shook her head sadly. "Well, she's really been in a pickle with the four kids and all."

Lucinda rolled her eyes, wishing they would just go away. They were always falling for someone's sob story. Maybe that psychic nun Sister Crystal Grace should have told Muriel what was about to happen. She could have planned ahead.

Claire lifted a box full of baby food jars. "Muriel's husband was a chemist, and he invented a result-oriented skin cream before he passed. It smooths out fine lines, diminishes dark spots, evens out skin tones, and takes years off your appearance. Muriel named it Skin Deep. We're helping her raise money for a patent. This is the most amazing stuff—ever. Mark my words. Sister Mary Jean and I have been using it for years."

Crossing her arms, Lucinda surveyed them. They were in their mid-thirties. What did they know about wrinkles and aging? They'd find out soon enough.

"So." Sister Mary Jean took charge of the conversation again. "We are selling these jars of Skin Deep for twenty dollars each. It's for a good cause, and it's such a top-notch product. Just knowing that you helped poor Muriel and her family will give your spirit that young, exuberant, generous feeling." She smiled, tilting her black-veiled head to one side.

Lucinda was unmoved. "I doubt that."

"Oh, I guarantee it," Claire insisted. "It's crazy-good stuff. How about a few jars for you and all your friends?"

"I'm sorry," Lucinda shook her head. "Full disclosure, times are tight here with Felix away at college. I send him money practically every day. I just can't afford to help out right now."

Claire exhaled and rolled her eyes, displaying her lack of surprise. Sister Mary Jean's shoulders slumped just a tad.

Lucinda struggled for words. "Are you two still looking for towels and blankets for that animal place? I may have a couple now. I've just been so busy. Busy, busy, busy—that's me."

"No, we've overstocked the local rescue and the animal control shelter," Claire told her in an irritated tone.

"Maybe next year," Sister Mary Jean added. "Well, thank you for your time, dear. Here." She held a baggie out to Lucinda.

"No!" Claire tried to stop her.

Sister Mary Jean smiled softly at Lucinda. "I'd like to give you a sample of Skin Deep."

Surprised, Lucinda took the clear bag containing about a tablespoon of gooey beige cream. "Thank you," she managed. "I really need to run, ladies. Have a good one."

The women frowned in tandem. She swiftly shut the door.

"Damn it," Lucinda muttered. Like she had time to help every lost soul that moved into the neighborhood or take geezers to the movies. This town was so full of weirdos. She had important shit to do. Sister Mary Jean and that Claire needed to get a life. Donating here, collecting there was a waste of time. Didn't they have anything better to do? Were they that desperate for acknowledgement? Pitiful.

She raced up the stairs. She'd never understand why Simon had been so set on moving here. He'd said it would make her happier. He'd said it was a good place to raise a family, and maybe she could finally get over her unplanned pregnancy, blowing her "one and done" plan.

Admittedly, she'd been bitter since she became pregnant with Felix. The second child had altered her entire life, and not in a good way. Once again, she'd had to put her career on hold. Raising two children was extremely difficult and not what she had wanted. Nothing seemed to work out for her.

Suddenly, she remembered the photo of Loraine and her baby, and the letter to Simon. Her annoyance turned back to anger. She stared at her enormous closet full of designer clothing, and her chin rose. She did have exquisite taste in clothing. That was her forte. A woman had to always look good, no matter what. Even if she was cussing out her pussy of a husband!

⌘

A week had passed, and life was not good. Lucinda and Simon had an argument practically every day. He would not apologize for reconnecting with Loraine. He wasn't even sorry. She just didn't understand. Their daughter had married that loser, and she was supposed to be okay with it?

It was the longest fight they'd had since the second time she'd become pregnant, all those years ago. It seemed odd, somehow, like they had traveled full circle. The house was empty, but they were back to arguing over the children.

And Simon was changing. He was softer than ever, and completely unapologetic. This damn town had changed him. He was almost proud to be a pathetic wimp. For the life of her, she couldn't understand it. She hated Mystic Ridge.

She turned off *Good Morning America* and got into the shower. She wasn't about to back down now. She'd meant every nasty word she'd said. Her children were self-centered and completely ungrateful for their privileged upbringing in Delaware. If only they had stayed in Delaware.

But Simon had insisted that after she'd sideswiped the school bus none of the townsfolk would forget her transgression. He didn't want the kids to get teased about it.

She scrubbed shampoo into her scalp. All kids got teased about one thing or another. And the damn bus had been sitting for over ten minutes. She'd had every right to go around it. It wasn't fair that she lost so much of her inheritance over a tiny driving infraction. She mourned that loss.

She should have insisted they stay in Delaware. She wasn't ashamed.

As she toweled her lean body off, she thought about Simon. He always got his damn way—about the baby, and the move. He didn't yell; he was just sneaky, and somehow convinced her to go along with his ideas. There was a reason he was a successful lawyer, and sometimes she hated his powers of persuasion. He adored Mystic Ridge, and he relished the silly town folks and the awful restaurants.

He thought Loraine and Felix were caring, mature, well-adjusted adults. What did he know? He couldn't even see that his suits were ill-fitting. He'd divulged that he'd bought Felix a vehicle. Unbelievable! They had been arguing about that since the day Felix turned sixteen. She insisted that he needed to earn his car. And now, after two years of college, Simon thought he had. He wasn't a father; he was Santa Claus!

But the worst betrayal of all was that Simon had been secretly seeing Loraine. He was without shame. He even seemed happy about it. He'd told her he'd lunched with Philo, and that the guy was successful and kind, and a hard worker. He declared that Philo had gotten a job at the biggest brokerage firm in Chattanooga and commuted every day. He declared he wanted to get to know Philo and be a good grandparent to Loraine's child. Who was he trying to impress?

Lucinda was livid, and each day her anger seemed to grow. She had spent all that money for Loraine to attend an Ivy League school, and now she was just playing house with a loser. All that girl did was whine about her depression. That's all she'd ever done—for years! She was so ungrateful that she'd never even taken the bar exam. *I can never forgive her for that. Never.*

She dried her hair. Her skin looked sullen and flaky and dry. She noticed the baggie containing that silly skin cream. Putting a hand on her hip, she decided to try it. She reached her fingers into the baggie and scooped out a blob. She smoothed it over her face and neck. It tingled nicely and smelled like sweet vanilla. No time to dwell on it. She got dressed, applied her makeup over the cream, and darted out the door.

Today she was going shopping. Arguing with Simon for so many days had left her a little down. She'd worked out very hard for the past week, and barely eaten a thing. She'd kept the house immaculate and had even found time to go online and balance her checking account. Even in stressful times she could keep it together. That's how educated women functioned; they didn't boo-hoo about sadness and depression. She felt pleased with herself, and damn it, she deserved a treat.

It was comforting keeping her finances separate from Simon's. When it came to money, he was not reliable. He would randomly donate to homeless shelters and soup kitchens. No way could she trust him. The interest accumulating on her inheritance was almost orgasmic. That brought her joy—a lot.

She drove to the Mystic Mall and rushed into the only pricey department store in Mystic Ridge. It was practically deserted. *Figures.* She browsed through the gold watches, and then sauntered to the statement handbag counter. They were all divine. A Brahmin purse caught her eye. Maybe. Then she browsed through the finer boutique area. Something sparkly might be nice.

Instead, she picked out several tailored skirts, a blazer, and a cashmere cardigan. A woman could not be respected in the workplace unless she looked successful. A professional wardrobe was a must. She spent a small fortune on her clothing, and that was her prerogative. She was proud of her attire. She looked smart, fashionable, and trendy at all times, no matter what.

Suddenly, she caught a glimpse of her reflection in the mirror and gasped. Her heart seemed to skip a beat. She looked like Loraine! She rushed closer to the mirror.

"Oh, my God," she gushed out loud. Her skin was radiant—smooth and supple, and young-looking. The dark circles under her eyes were gone. The chickenpox scar on her forehead had disappeared. The skin around her lips was full, and the smile lines were gone. The brown spots on her jawline had been replaced by tight, pale skin. The dry crusty patches around her nose had vanished. Her eyes looked bluer and more open than they had in years.

"Skin Deep," she muttered. *It's that goofy cream crap Sister Mary Jean gave me a week ago. Holy shit, it actually works.* She paid for her purchases and dashed from the store. She looked radiant. She had to show someone, anyone.

But no one came to mind. She didn't have any friends. The people at her office were jealous of her, they wouldn't care. So, the idiots at Simon's office would have to do. She took out her phone and snapped several selfies, then drove straight there.

When she entered the lobby, she expected to see Pearl Hathaway, Simon's cute but essentially plain secretary, but she was nowhere in sight. She charged into Simon's office, and he wasn't there, either. Damn.

Suddenly, she heard footsteps.

"Why, hello, lovely Lucinda. What brings you to our humble little institution?"

She knew that teasing tone. She ground her teeth. Calvin Carter, Simon's partner, always made her uncomfortable. He was African American, an ex-athlete and a first-rate lawyer. He constantly joked with her, and humor was not her strong suit. He was tall and broad, and constantly smirked at her, like he knew exactly what she was thinking.

She looked up at him and plastered on a tense smile. "Good afternoon, Calvin. I have to see Simon. I have to show him. I used a new skin cream."

"Now, that's news. Hang on, let me update my Twitter."

She crossed her arms tightly.

He chuckled and tilted his head sideways. "Lucinda, I'm just playin' with you, girl. You always look stunning."

"No. It's different this time. I was transformed. It was magic." She frowned as he laughed. "Stop. It really worked."

He stepped closer—too close. "I got nothin' but respect for you. You're the hottest woman in town, even at your age."

She scowled. "Leave me alone."

Just then Simon and Pearl Hathaway entered the office, arm-in-arm, laughing.

Lucinda's chin dropped. She stomped toward him. "Where have you been? And why are you touching that woman?"

Pearl frowned and brought her hands to her sides.

Lucinda snarled, "What on earth are you wearing, and how many kids do you have now?"

"I can't afford to throw my salary away on clothes, Lucinda. I'm divorced. I have real responsibilities," Pearl retorted. "And my family is my business."

Simon moved between them. "Calm down, ladies. All is well. I was just telling Pearl about a cat video I saw on Facebook. I thought maybe it came from someone here in town."

Pearl stood motionless. Calvin chuckled.

Lucinda shot Pearl a look of disgust. "You are a paid employee, right? Shouldn't you be working?"

"Leave her be," Simon insisted.

Pearl flashed a cocky smile and brought her hands to her hips.

Lucinda stood frozen. *He is defending her—that plain, mealy-mouthed Mother Goose!* Words would not come. She bolted from the room, down the hallway, and out to her car. Tears threatened in her eyes, but she would not cry, especially over freakin' Simon. If he was doing it with that little slut, that was his problem. She would not cry, not over his ass.

She cranked the engine. Who needed him, anyway? And who needed a belligerent daughter or an immature son? Sid at The

Mystic Affairs Community Bank had been coming on to her for years. She'd give him a tumble, and he'd be hers, especially with her new youthful appearance. Calvin was always flirting with her. Wouldn't Simon die if she went out with him!

That might be a good idea. Every man on earth would be interested in her now. She glanced in her rearview mirror. She looked dazzling, simply dazzling, and wasn't that all that really mattered?

As she drove home, she contemplated her predicament. Simon would beg her to forgive him, but she wouldn't, at least not until he'd declared his undying love for her and vowed to agree to all of her decisions, and fire that deceitful secretary.

As she pulled into her neighborhood, she noticed balloons on Claire O'Donnell's mailbox. There was also a large sign in the yard that read: "Happy 55th!" Several cars were parked in the driveway, and she saw Sister Mary Jean Stevenson welcoming people into the house.

Lucinda pulled her car over, practically parking on Claire's grass. She raced to the front door just in time to catch her.

"Sister? Sister. How nice to see you." She said, stalling before she mentioned the cream.

"Oh, hello. I'm very busy. It's Claire's birthday."

Lucinda's chin dropped. "She's fifty-five? I thought both of you were in your thirties."

Sister Mary Jean laughed richly. "Well, you knew Claire was a grandmother, right?"

Lucinda hadn't given it much thought.

"Lucinda, you are a hoot. But I really have to go now. We're throwing Claire a birthday dinner. We have a houseful."

"Wait," Lucinda said, placing her hand on Sister Mary Jean's elbow. "I must have more Skin Deep. That stuff is miraculous."

Sister Mary Jean giggled. "I know, right? But I'm sorry, Lucinda." She touched Lucinda's hand. "We're all sold out."

"What? You can't be."

"I'm afraid we are. The neighbors pitched in and bought our entire inventory. Muriel got her patent and sold the rights for big bucks. Everything has worked out for them. Isn't that splendid?"

"I need that cream, damn it. I have to have it. Did she leave details on how to make it?"

"Oh, yes. I know how to make my own. Everyone who contributed was given the top-secret ingredients."

"Thank God," Lucinda breathed. "Tell me, please. I have to know. I'll pay you anything."

Sister Mary Jean's gaze turned downward. "I'm afraid I can't do that. It's only for the generous at heart, for those who helped Muriel in her time of need. It's for those with compassion beneath the surface and love in their hearts, folks who care about others."

"What the hell are you talking about?" Lucinda shouted.

Sister Mary Jean crossed her arms calmly. "You really don't understand. Physical beauty is skin-deep. Real beauty comes from the inside of a person." She touched her heart. "I'm sorry for you. I wish you'd gotten to Mystic Ridge sooner."

A man appeared in the doorway. "Hurry up, Claire is about to open her gifts. Her granddaughter is chomping at the bit." He glanced at Lucinda and then back at Sister Mary Jean. "Tell the hater we're busy."

Sister Mary Jean took a step backward. "Beauty is on the inside. Think about it, Lucinda. Be beautiful to others, and you are beautiful on the outside as well."

Lucinda uttered the F-word.

Sister Mary Jean closed the door.

Lucinda couldn't move. The world seemed to spin around her. Sweat covered her brow, and a hot flash glided hotly through her. She took a step backward and stumbled to her car. She drove home in a daze and realized with horror that she was drooling.

When she entered her house, she checked her reflection in the mirror, ready to bask in her youthful appearance, but it had faded. Her momentary beauty was gone. The circles under her eyes were deeper than before. The chickenpox scar on her forehead had returned. Her blue eyes looked pale and washed out. The dry patches on her nose were back, and the brown spots on her jawline looked darker than ever.

As she turned away from the mirror, a tear crept from her eye. The house around her grew dark in the late afternoon, and she felt alone. She made her way to Simon's obnoxious recliner and sat down. It felt rather comfy, although it smelled like barbecue potato chips. She noticed the dog outside, asleep, fat and happy.

Suddenly, she spied a white cat that had wandered into their yard. It sat stoically, staring right at her. For a second, she wanted to run outside and pick it up, to hold it to her chest and feel its soft fur. It was stunning. It was so still it almost looked like a statue. But she couldn't move. She felt frozen.

Shaking her head, she closed her eyes. Tears seeped from the corners. What the hell was wrong with her? Why was this happening? She rubbed her eyes, willing the moisture away. Maybe petting the damn cat would make her feel better.

But when she looked back in the yard, it was gone. The moment had passed.

She did want people to think she was beautiful, although as she grew older it seemed more and more impossible. Was it possible that she wanted to be respected? *No, that's not it.* She bit her lip. *I need more of that cream. There must be a way.* She ground her teeth. Women like her didn't have to prove anything to anyone.

She did good things. She did. She laid her head back and stared at the ceiling. Well, she used to do good things. She drove her kids to school when they missed the bus. She picked up balanced meals on her way home from work. She took Loraine to doctors for years—psychiatrists, at that. She was always so damn busy. That wasn't her fault. Women were always jealous of her, so how was she supposed to make friends? Maybe she could have put stock in a few other things. But right now, she just couldn't think of anything.

She rose and stretched her arms over her head. Simon probably wasn't coming home, or if he did, it would just be to pack. Their marriage was over. It had been for years. And she really didn't care. She hadn't had feelings for him in years. It was possible she had never loved him at all. She wasn't sure. Maybe she had never loved anyone.

It was of no consequence. The floor needed vacuuming, and she had to iron her dress for work tomorrow. A load of towels rested in the dryer in need of folding, and there were some vegetables in the refrigerator that needed to be thrown out.

She tucked her hair behind her ears. There was no time for self-pity. She'd never been one to wallow, and she would not start now. She strutted to the kitchen, pleased to have a purpose. The day's mail caught her attention, and she riffled through it.

Simon would want to rekindle. And Loraine would need her mother soon enough. Babies were difficult. Felix would be home for Thanksgiving. They'd all be back, begging for her acceptance, apologizing for treating her badly, and needing her words of wisdom. She didn't doubt it for a minute. It was all about learning valuable lessons. That was life, and they'd learn soon enough. She was always right. They needed her. They did.

Suddenly, she noticed the empty baggie that had contained the face cream lying on the counter. She bolted to it. She tried to squeeze out one more drop out, but sadly, she couldn't. Her lips quivered. She felt ugly, hideous. Beauty was not skin deep! That was crap.

Her hands began to tremble. She noticed a small square envelope and opened it.

It was an invitation to a baby shower for Emma Parsons. Who? There was also a picture introducing a new family that had moved onto the street. A stupid photo showed them smiling on a stone staircase, The Gilberts—Stuart, Mariah and Daisy.

"Who freakin' cares?" Lucinda screamed at the top of her lungs, filling the empty house with anger. A lump formed in her throat, and for a second it was difficult to swallow. Her chest ached as she struggled to breathe. Inhaling was difficult. She clutched her throat. If she died right now—would anyone care? Would anyone find her?

She succumbed to sobs, and her chest relaxed. A tear cascaded down her cheek and landed on the photo of the family. Behind it, she noticed a donation envelope from a homeless shelter. She bolted to her purse, took out the checkbook, and stared at it. Would being generous really make her more beautiful? Was that possible? She decided to try it. And maybe the next time those silly peahens came to her door, she'd stop and listen.

# FAMILY EMERGENCY

JOSEPHINE WAVED AS THE SCHOOL BUS CARRIED HER DAUGH-ters out of sight. She blinked away the moisture from her eyes. Why on earth was she choked up?

She headed back to the house. It really was a relief. Both girls had been so bored this summer and had been thrilled the last few weeks getting prepared for school. They had meticulously picked out all their folders, scissors, glue, and crayons. School-clothes shopping had been another adventure. Lexie was ready to conquer kindergarten, and Elizabeth was now a confident second-grader. Everyone was talking about the new teacher who had come to town. The gossip was that she was kind and very patient.

A soft wind blew through Josephine's hair, and she exhaled. For the first time in what seemed like ages, she had more than an hour all to herself.

She chuckled as she stepped inside. Their kitty Elsa was drinking from a cereal bowl. The peanut butter and bread had been left open. Rupert had forgotten his travel mug, which he did practically every other day. Creamer and jelly were near the refrigerator but not in it. Pajamas were strewn in all directions. It was a complete disaster.

She tapped her tablet, and a dance beat filled the kitchen. She sang loudly as she straightened up, cleaned the dishes, made the beds, and dusted the blinds and tables. She found a few candy wrappers beneath the couch and emptied the cat's litterbox. Within an hour, the house was clean—and still.

With all the chaos lately, she hadn't even thought about what she would do now the girls were in school all day.

As she passed the sliding glass door, she noticed sticky fingerprints. She sprayed cleaner and wiped the window swiftly. She gazed at the wrought iron bench in the backyard and the huge iron wheel that leaned against the oak tree. She'd never forget Rupert's excitement when he had found the artifact in a junkyard just south of Mystic Ridge.

They'd been assisting a feral cat trap-and-neuter group when he happened upon it. The elderly gentleman who owned the junkyard said it had been on a cannon used during the battle of Fort Sanders on November 29, 1863. He insisted it had been right in the middle of the fight. He didn't have any proof, and everyone Rupert had contacted said it was quite doubtful; but he just had to have it anyway.

Their little volunteering weekend had cost her two hundred dollars and the price of transporting the heavy thing. Thank goodness his friends had helped him unload it and set it up in their back yard.

Her hand moved to her hip. It looked awkward leaning against the tree. It was so large—it was almost like a person loitering there, day after day. She wasn't sure she liked it. But Rupert was so proud of it, and had placed an ornate white Victorian bench beside it. They'd planted marigolds and tulips and azalea bushes all around it, and the area did have a uniquely vintage feel. It was Elsa's favorite spot to nap.

A small creek also flowed through their back yard. Shimmering rocks and lush grass lined the sides of the clear water. It was her favorite thing about the property. The large yard was a big part of the reason she and Rupert had been drawn to the home in the first place. It was enchanting.

As she finished wiping the glass door, she noticed tiny sparkles of light coming from the shallow water. Elsa rubbed against her leg and let out a soft meow. She patted the small furry head.

The bench and the heavenly area around it mysteriously summoned her, and Josephine longed to sit down.

She grabbed her tablet and a cup of coffee. Today she would relax just a bit, and tomorrow she would think about the best way to use her new spare time.

She walked to the bench, sat down, and ran her toes through the chilly grass. Fall would be here soon. Where had the time gone? The trees swayed. It was odd, but sometimes when she was here, it felt like she was waiting for something.

She'd spent so many years being a wife and mother that she couldn't really remember anymore what her other personal goals had been. She was good with details and a tad obsessive. When she started a project, she had to finish it to the very best of her ability. She stretched her arms up to the sky and closed her eyes. Yes, she would have to do some soul-searching to find out exactly what she was meant to do.

The trickling sound of water was refreshing. She rose and went to the tiny creek, sat on the bank, and put her toes in the water. A pedicure was overdue.

But the wheel distracted her again. She giggled, remembering the battle reenactment they had attended a few years back near Knoxville. It had been the one hundred-and-fiftieth anniversary of the battle at Fort Sanders. Rupert had been in his element, loving the period costumes, the artillery-firing demonstrations, and the storytellers who provided details of the battle in which Confederate troops sustained 813 casualties. They suffered 129 killed, 458 wounded, and 266 missing. The Union losses inside and around the fort had been minimal. It had been a poorly executed attack, and a lopsided victory for the Union.

Rupert had taken great pride in relaying the details of the battle.

Since acquiring the wheel, they had visited several Civil War battle sites in Tennessee—the Battle of Franklin, the Carter House, Carnton Plantation, the Hermitage, and Two Rivers Mansion. Truthfully, she knew quite a bit now.

But Lexie and Elizabeth hated the scary stories and were not that fond of the wheel. They begged for a swing set. She knew that next summer a cedar swing set with a slide was in order.

But she had a few more months to enjoy the uncluttered space and the lush expanse of green grass.

Josephine and Rupert had both been born in Mystic Ridge. After they were married, they'd had a quaint apartment near the downtown square. She'd loved walking to all the shops. One afternoon, as they took a drive, they'd noticed the new construction of this particular house. When they walked the lot and spied the marvelous back yard and magnificent creek, they both wanted the home. Although it had been difficult financially, they'd muddled through. Somehow, she knew she would live here for the rest of her life. It was truly home.

An hour or so passed, and Josephine's relaxation turned to worry. What if she couldn't find a job that coordinated with the girls' schedule? She had been out of the workplace for several years. What if her qualifications were out-of-date? There had to be something constructive she could do. Maybe she should volunteer at the hospital. She couldn't stand the sight of blood, but the thought of helping someone really appealed to her. She did need to be home by three o'clock. That could present a problem.

Of course, she was rather good with Excel and Word, but that was so mundane. Everyone was a computer geek these days. She wanted to do something meaningful.

She rolled over onto her stomach, keeping her toes in the water. Yawning, she placed her hands under her chin and closed her eyes.

The cool water suddenly felt warm—freakishly warm. She rolled over quickly and gasped as she realized the clear water had turned cloudy and red.

"Excuse me, ma'am."

She looked up to see a large man standing in the creek several feet away. His worn brown boots were soaked. Her body froze. He was bleeding profusely from a gash in his head. He wore a muddy, tattered gray Confederate soldier's uniform. She tensed, then relaxed.

"You must be from a reenactment group. I must say, you look extremely convincing. You scared me for a second." She sat up, chuckling.

He hung his head. "I apologize. No, I ain't with that there group you was talkin' about. I'm with the Seventh Infantry out of Macon, Georgia."

She noticed tattered yellow stripes dangling from his upper sleeves. His uniform was shredded in spots, his elbows and knees completely exposed. His hair was shoulder-length and full of leaves and twigs. A brown bandage was wrapped around his head and a small gray hat was perched on top. A homeless soldier wannabe? What the heck? What was Mystic Ridge coming to?

His jade eyes met hers, but he quickly looked back at the ground.

She studied him. His breathing was erratic, his head badly injured.

"You need medical attention!" she stated, then noticed he was carrying a gigantic brown rifle with a bayonet on it. She tensed.

"No, ma'am" he muttered. "I been lookin' fer you."

"Me? What can I do for you?" she asked. She watched as he rubbed his eyes with dirty fingers and tried to stand a bit straighter. She realized he was crying. Oh, no, even worse—a sad, injured, delusional lunatic with a gun. She stared at him.

But something about him was just so pitiful that her heart slowed its pace. She looked back at her house. She was a pretty fast runner.

He began to speak. "My...My...My boy—well, I mean my great-great-great-grandson Cade is in trouble. I...I need some help. I need *your* help."

He swayed, and for a moment and Josephine thought he would collapse into the water.

"You need a doctor. Can I take you to the hospital?" she asked sincerely.

"Naw, no, it's too late fer me. I been in the hospital a time or two. A nurse named Crystal said you was the one to speak with. She told me to come here. She said you could help me."

Now Josephine felt really confused, and utterly sad. A nurse named Crystal...

"Why don't you sit down?" she suggested. "Over there." She pointed to a grassy clearing on the other side of the creek, several yards away from her. He nodded and slowly moved to the open spot. As the breeze carried his bloody scent to her, she covered her nose.

He groaned heavily as he sat down and laid the enormous gun beside him.

"What, exactly, are you talking about?" she asked. "Which hospital were you in? Why did you leave? Who's your grandson?"

"If ya please, ma'am. You *are* Josephine Evans, ain't ya?"

She flinched. "Yes, but how on earth do you know that?"

"She said there might be a chance that you could…well, that you could help me. Help me and my kin." He took off his hat, his eyes red-rimmed and troubled. "Please, excuse my manners. I know us come from different worlds, but my family is jest about gone."

She squeezed her knees to her chest. This was creeping her out. If Rupert knew she was conversing with an armed homeless guy, he would have a fit. Maybe she was dreaming. She bit her lip. Nope, it hurt.

"I'm listening, sir, but I have no idea how I could possibly help you." *Except for getting you to a hospital*, she thought.

He cleared his throat. "Cade Watson is my name. A lotta time has gone by, and so, so many o' my kin have come and gone. Not everyone has young-uns like they used ta. Now I only got one livin' relative left. His name is Cade Watson, after me." He paused and looked up at the sky and then back at her. "He's a smart boy, he is. He goes to college. A real Watson college boy. I's proud.

"His Mama died just a year ago, and he's on his own. What he don't know is that he has the cancer." He looked up at the sky again, a worried expression creasing his brow. "I gotta get. Can you help me, please?" His dark, swollen eyes bored into hers. "Can you help save him?"

"What could I possibly do, Mr. Watson?" She watched him rise, obviously in terrible pain. "What are you asking? I don't understand?"

"Find him. Tell him he's sick. There's still time to treat it. He can live. He can carry on our good name."

"Can't *you* find him?" she suggested. "Maybe he could help you."

"I'm afraid that's not possible." He put his hat back on and picked up the heavy weapon. "I'm only able to be *here*."

She watched as he glanced at the cannon wheel.

"He belongs in Mystic Ridge. I know you can fetch him."

"I...I wouldn't even know where to look. Is he still in Georgia?" She rose, her head swirling.

He stepped back into the water and faced her. "He's at a college in Georgia, to the south. He's ailin', and he needs someone. I'd feel bad if my family perished from this here earth altogether. My thanks to ya, ma'am. I gotta get." He began walking in the creek upstream, away from her.

"No, wait! Can I get you some food? Please, come inside. I'll call my husband. I need more information."

He shook his head and looked back at her once more. "Crystal said we should keep this our secret for now. She said folks wouldn't understand. She said you was special."

"Your boots..." she began, then threw her hands up in the air. "I...I'll try to find him," she called. "I promise, I'll try."

He turned away and slowly trudged through the water. Suddenly, she could see through him. He was becoming transparent, and as he continued to walk, he disappeared completely.

Her knees gave out, and she slumped back onto the grass. Her whole body trembled. She was losing her mind. It was official. This was some sort of wacky motherly meltdown.

The water turned from crimson back to clear. Her heart ached for the man. But had he even been there? She had napped a bit. Maybe it was just a dream. She needed proof.

The rumbling sound of the school bus engine caught her attention.

"Oh, my," she muttered, shocked that so much time had passed. On shaky knees, she raced through the front yard and down to the bus stop to greet her children.

≈≈

Josephine spent the afternoon looking at the girls' schoolwork and preparing dinner. She couldn't get the vision of the soldier out of her mind, or his concerns. By six o'clock, she'd decided she had dreamt the whole silly thing. It was preposterous.

As she stirred a chicken-and-rice concoction, she decided the encounter had been just an unusual dream brought on by her thinking about the old cannon wheel. She decided to forget about it.

Rupert got home early, and they all sat down for a family dinner. He noticed the unusual crinkle in Josephine's brow as they ate.

"Is something wrong, honey?"

"No, no, everything's fine. How are things at the office? Will you be traveling a lot this month?"

"Maybe. Everyone's being conservative, but I got an unexpected call from an investor in Jacksonville, Florida. He wants to meet with me immediately about a possible merger. Can you pass the rolls, please?"

She stood, handed him the basket, turned, and raced up to Lexie's room. She gazed at the extensive map of the United States tacked on the wall. Yep, Jacksonville was only a few miles from south Georgia. She raced back downstairs and grabbed a flashlight. Her family had stopped eating and was watching her.

"Oh, sorry, guys, just checking something."

She exited through the sliding glass door and ran to the creek. Her heart pounded in her chest. The sun had almost set, and a peaceful red glow lit up the yard. She checked up and down the creek. She shone the flashlight on the spot where Cade had sat. There was a rust-colored spot there about two feet wide. She covered her mouth with her hand as chills crept up her legs and down her arms. Cade had sat in that exact spot. Bleeding.

There was her solid proof. He had been there. Now the future of his family rested on her shoulders.

As her mind raced, she turned off the flashlight. "I'll do what I can," she whispered.

She hurried back to the house and into the kitchen.

"Something wrong with your precious creek?" Rupert chuckled.

"Oh, no, of course not."

"We know how you love that creek," he commented.

The girls laughed.

She couldn't think straight. "Listen, I've got to check a few things on the computer. I can't eat another bite. Y'all enjoy your meal, okay?"

The three of them exchanged glances, then nodded.

"Rupert, when are you going to Jacksonville?"

"Well, if you had let me finish," he began, showing his irritation, "I was going to say I'd normally fly down on Friday and come right back. But the companion ticket is super-cheap. I was thinking you could come along, and we could have a weekend getaway instead. I spoke with Bea, and she can take the girls while we're away. We could fly home Sunday afternoon."

Josephine's mouth dropped open. "Absolutely."

Rupert nodded.

❦

She spent the entire evening on the internet searching for colleges in the southern region of Georgia. She found several, but Georgia Southern, a small college in Statesboro, piqued her curiosity. At this point in her life, she was going to listen to her intuition. Something inside her knew this would be her starting point.

She printed detailed directions and phone numbers and contacted a rental car agency. Two vehicles would be waiting at the Jacksonville Airport, one for her and one for Rupert. Finding Cade wouldn't be an easy task, especially on the weekend. So many students went home on weekends. So, it was imperative she get there as early as possible on Friday before the admissions office closed. Once again, she wondered if this whole scenario was real.

She looked up Civil War statistics and browsed through screen after screen of facts on the battle of Fort Sanders. Finally, she found a list of soldiers killed in the battle. Many of the names were not complete. As she scrolled down the enormous list, she held her breath as she reached the W's. Her heart seemed to freeze as she saw *C. Watson.* Was it him?

A rustling behind her startled her, and she turned to see Rupert scrutinizing her.

"I'm just looking up a few things," she blurted.

He looked at the screen. "You're Googling Confederate families?" he asked.

"Well, I was thinking about writing a biography about a Southern family, the Watsons." She just blurted it out, unsure of where that idea had come from.

"Oh, now, that sounds interesting."

"I may drive around a bit while you're in meetings."

"Allright. I'm going to read in bed. Take your time, honey."

Josephine pondered for a moment. Where had that book idea come from? It was genius. Maybe she should jot down a few notes as she began this crazy quest. It was going to be a challenge, and a life was at stake, and a family name. It wasn't just fun and games—this Cade Watson VI could die if she didn't find him. A tinge of anxiety filled her.

She spent the rest of the week investigating every detail about the battle of Fort Sanders, the Watson family, Georgia Southern College, and, most important, cancer hospitals in Georgia. By Friday, when she boarded the airplane to Jacksonville, she had an entire folder of pertinent information.

As she soared over the clouds, she began wondering why she had been chosen for this mission. Maybe she was just gullible enough to believe everything. Maybe someone was videotaping this nonsense. Maybe she was going to be part of a television prank. But she clearly recalled the soldier disappearing as he walked away. That had not been her imagination. And she did value the importance of family, and she had always been totally dedicated to it. Family was everything.

She thought of the young man she was searching for. How would she approach him? What would she say? How could she make him listen and believe her—a total stranger? She knew she had to convince him to seek medical attention. It was critical.

She closed her eyes and tried to take a nap. Sleep would not come. There was a mystery ahead of her, a life-or-death dilemma, and she was chosen to assist in the preservation of a family. And again, it plagued her. Why her? That was an even bigger mystery.

Whatever the reason, she had to succeed.

～≫～

Josephine propped her cell phone in the car's cup holder, making sure the GPS app was functioning. She took a deep breath and peered over the unfamiliar steering wheel. She was amazed at how easily she'd gotten away from Rupert. Just one mention of Civil War research, and he was totally agreeable. He did insist that she stay in touch with him throughout the day while he attended his meetings.

A couple of hours later, as she entered the campus of Georgia Southern University, she felt overwhelmingly emotional as she surveyed the area. Beautiful weeping willows decorated the narrow streets. Young adults walked, sat, and held hands in almost every direction. It would not be easy to find Cade.

Following her computer-printed map, she located the Administration Office. She straightened her skirt, took a deep breath, and entered with high hopes.

Forty-five minutes later, Josephine exited feeling defeated. The student administrative manager took her job very seriously. She was very protective of her students' privacy. At first, she wouldn't even look up Cade. But Josephine concocted a story about a family emergency, saying his great-uncle was very ill, and they needed to find Cade and see if he had the same blood type. After several frustrating arguments, the stern woman at the desk looked up Cade on her computer and was pleased to inform Josephine that he did not attend this college.

She strolled through the crowded campus streets. Deep in her soul, she felt he was here, somewhere. She walked into the student center and found a picture of the football team. She prayed and prayed as she searched the names, but...nothing.

She found a candy-bar machine and indulged in a chocolate treat. Several students were also buying snacks, so she decided to ask a few if they knew of a Cade Watson. She stopped several and asked if they had heard of him. Again, nothing. What if she was at the wrong college altogether? Anxiety consumed her, and the sugar didn't help. Her stomach churned. She located a bench and sat down to think.

First of all, the ghost or whatever he was had only said it was a college in Georgia, in the south. What if it was a junior college or a college in Atlanta or some other college altogether?

If she was going to another school, she needed to get there quickly. She took out her tablet, went to a Georgia Southern social media site and searched for "Cade Watson". Nothing came up. She searched a social media site for a school in Milledgeville.

A female student sat beside her and began digging through a floral backpack. She flashed a brief smile, and Josephine decided to try one more tactic.

"Excuse me, I'm looking for my nephew, Cade Watson. By any chance, do you know him, or have you ever heard of him?"

"Um..." The girl concentrated. "I've heard of a guy named *Charlie* Watson. I don't know if he's Cade. Charlie's a Kappa Sigma Chi brother."

Josephine's mouth dropped open. Charlie? Maybe. "Do you know where I can find him?"

"Oh, the Kappas are having an epic party tonight. It's gonna be sick. They have a house near downtown, just a couple of miles past McDonald's, on the left."

Josephine felt elated. "Thank you so much. You, my dear, are a lifesaver." She grabbed her purse and hurried to the car.

"I know," Crystal muttered, smoothing her blond hair as a gradual smile spread across her young face. "Booya."

❦

After a phone call to Rupert, Josephine found a restaurant and ordered a soup and salad. She assumed the fraternity party wouldn't be starting until later. She had a few hours to kill. Clicking through her phone, she checked her email and called the girls.

❦

As Josephine entered the fraternity house, she felt very old. Uninhibited students were dancing everywhere. They kissed and groped each other openly. The music was horribly loud and pulsating. She looked around and pondered how she was going to find Charlie. And what if he wasn't even Cade? And if he was, how would she bring up cancer in a place like this?

She looked for someone sober enough to talk to. It was difficult. So, she began looking for someone who seemed to know everyone. Finally, she saw a young man singing karaoke in the corner with a girl on each arm. He would have to do.

She waited until he finished an awful rendition of "I Love Rock 'n' Roll".

"Excuse me." She held up her hand. "Can I talk to you for a minute? I'm looking for someone."

He acted smooth and cocky. "That was badass, right?"

Josephine felt her lip rise. "Yeah, super badass," she managed.

He straightened up a bit. "Okay." He motioned for the girls to go away, as if they were suddenly annoying. "What can I do you for?"

"I'm looking for Charlie Watson. Do you, by any chance, know where I can find him?"

"Dude, he's already puking. Such a lightweight." He pointed down a hallway. "He cannot hold his liquor."

"Thanks." She pushed and shoved her way through the crowd. Several girls gave her dirty looks as she inspected the line. "I'm just looking for someone. I promise. Have you seen Charlie Watson?"

A girl with an irritated scowl spoke up. "Yes, he's in there, hogging the bathroom, like no one else matters. Rude. I'm dying here."

Interesting choice of words. Josephine leaned against the wall. He was just a few feet away. Her heartbeat sped up. She'd finally found him, she hoped.

Suddenly, the door opened, and a tall, pale, thin young man stumbled out. He had long but clean brown hair. When he gazed at her, he had the same jade eyes she'd seen in her backyard. Could it really be him?

She wasted no time. "Are you Charlie Watson?" she shouted above the thumping hip-hop beat.

He nodded.

"Have you ever heard of Cade Watson?" she yelled.

His brows crinkled. He examined her from her head to her toes. "Yeah, that's me."

Relief flooded Josephine's entire body. Yes! She closed her eyes then opened them again. The loud noise and the smoke all seemed to disappear. She could only see Cade. And he looked feeble and frail.

"I have got to talk to you. It's very, very important."

He shrugged and motioned for her to follow him. He wove through the crowd. She prayed he was sober enough to digest all the information she was about to lay on him.

Finally, they reached the back door, and he guided her to a bench several yards away from the house. He waited for her to sit first, and then he sat down.

She knew she had to try and explain this delicately. "Have you always been called Charlie?" she asked him sincerely.

"Actually, no. My mother always called me Cade. In high school, a few friends called me Charlie, and it just stuck. She never liked it. After she passed away, I just stayed with Charlie. She was all I had, so being called Cade reminded me of her. It was just easier to be Charlie. I miss her. Did you know Verina Watson?"

"No, I didn't. But I'm sure she named you Cade for a reason." Suddenly, she realized he was not intoxicated at all.

"Actually, I'm Cade the Sixth."

She couldn't help but grin. "Yes, your great-great-great grandfather fought in the Civil War."

He leaned back and squinted at her. "How in the heck did you know that?"

"I...well, someone told me, someone who loves you very much. Don't you think you should be proud of your name and of your heritage?"

"You sound like my mother," he said as he grinned. "I guess you're right." He slumped a tad and wiped the sweat from his brow. "So, why were you looking for me?"

Josephine crossed her arms and prayed for the words to come. "It's a little hard to explain. My name is Josephine Evans, and someone who cares a great deal about your family sent me here." She took his large hands in hers and gazed into his eyes. "It's an emergency. I was told you are very ill."

He straightened his posture, then squeezed her hands. "How do you know that?"

"I just do, that's all that matters. I know you're busy with school, but you have to see a physician immediately." She took out all the internet listings of cancer hospitals in south Georgia.

He glanced at them. "Cancer?" He rose, putting his hands on his hips. "Shit. I *have* been throwing up a lot for a while now. I assumed it was just nerves. I'm graduating soon." He ran a hand through his hair, sat back down, and stared at her. "For real?"

She could feel his breath on her face. She nodded. "I'm so sorry."

"I went to the Army recruitment office last week and threw up all over the lobby. I didn't even have the strength to enlist. It was freaking awful." He rubbed his forehead with his hand. "I guess I won't be a soldier any time soon."

"No," Josephine told him.

"Am I gonna die?" he asked her in a shaky voice.

She swiftly gathered him in her arms and hugged him tightly. He was trembling.

"I don't think so. That's why I'm here. To make sure that doesn't happen." She moved him to arm's length and gazed at him. "You must see a doctor, pronto. If you've been vomiting, be sure he does an x-ray of your stomach. Do you have medical insurance?"

"Yeah, before my mom died, she hooked me up with full coverage legit." He slowly released her. "If you don't mind me asking, what are you, an angel?"

"I'm just an ordinary wife and mother from Mystic Ridge, Tennessee, honest."

Three drunken fraternity brothers fell out the door and onto the grass. Cade looked embarrassed.

She glanced at her watch. It was after eleven. She quickly took out a pen and paper and wrote down all her phone numbers and her email address.

"Here's my information. I have to know how everything goes for you. Get to the doctor immediately—tomorrow. Let me know what he says and start treatment as soon as possible. Please text me or email me and give me an update on your condition."

"I will," he said softly. He keyed her number into his contacts. "I didn't expect to get any digits tonight."

She touched his hand once more. "I want to see you again. I have a feeling we will be friends—forever. Do you have plans for Thanksgiving?"

He shook his head.

"No one should be alone on Thanksgiving. I'll set a place for you and have a room ready. Mystic Ridge isn't too far. Rupert and my girls will adore you. I'll prepare some foods you can keep down." She took a deep breath. "And I'll show you something a bit spooky in my backyard."

His brows rose. "That sounds good. I'm going to the hospital first thing tomorrow. I'll email you as soon as I know something." He looked down at his feet. "Of course, when I wake up tomorrow morning, I'm going to wonder if this was all my imagination."

She stood. "I know exactly how that feels, believe me. But it wasn't easy to find you, Cade Watson."

He rose. "I still have a lot of questions."

"Come for Thanksgiving and we'll talk, in depth." She pulled him into another embrace. "No matter what conclusion you come to about me, you have to get help. You are the last of the Watsons. Your ancestors are depending on you to carry on the family name."

He smiled awkwardly.

"Good luck." She kissed him on the cheek, went back into the house, and scooted through the crowded corridors and out the front door. Hallelujah.

✎✎

Josephine spent the rest of the weekend with her husband, pondering the importance of family. She got a text from Cade late Saturday that he had gone to the emergency room and gotten x-rays and nausea meds. They'd assigned him a local doctor, and he had a meeting Monday to discuss the findings. She felt a wave of relief.

The flight home was uneventful, and that was just the way she wanted it. When they returned to Mystic Ridge, they picked up the girls from Bea's house and hurried home to get ready for the following week.

After dinner, Elsa began meowing as she gazed out the sliding glass window. Rupert went over and looked out.

"Josephine, you have to come see this. Come here, hurry!"

She rushed over. The sun was just beginning to set, but nothing looked out-of-place. "What?"

"Look," he shouted. "There are red and white azaleas growing near the creek. They're huge. That's freakin' impossible. We were only gone a few days. I didn't even plant them. I've never seen such a thing."

She smiled.

He regarded her. "Do you know if someone came over and planted them?"

She shrugged and shook her head. The spectacular azalea bushes were in the exact spot where Cade Watson the Elder had sat. They were a gift, a heartfelt thank you—for her. Somehow, he knew she had spoken to Charlie/Cade.

Tears streamed down her cheeks, and she turned away while her family marveled at the sight. She found a dish towel and wiped her face and then joined them back at the window.

Josephine's eyes were attracted by the faint outline of two men walking in the creek. Crap. Her heart seemed to stop beating. She could barely see them, but gradually they became more and more visible.

They were dressed in tattered blue uniforms, carrying a cot with a wounded soldier on it. She looked at her family, but they were still laughing and chatting about the weekend as they walked away from the window. She was the only one who could see the soldiers.

She stared. These were Union soldiers. She pressed her face closer to the window. The wounded man lying on the cot waved to her and motioned for her to come out. *He needs me.*

Elsa meowed.

She grabbed a pad and a pencil as quickly as her feet would move. "Rupert, I'll be right back. I'm just going to the creek for a second."

"Those azaleas are pretty incredible. Get a photo with your phone, and I'll post it. I'm getting in the shower."

She chuckled, enjoying the fact he was oblivious to the soldiers waiting for her. She felt a bit honored. Apparently, they were for her eyes only.

She slid the door open and squared her shoulders. Apparently, there was another family emergency!

# BUBBA'S HONKY-TONK

CHARLENE EASED INTO A CONTENTED SMILE. "HOW WAS YOUR catfish, honey?"

"It was just fine, and your salmon?"

"It was very good, a little drier than usual, but still the best in the South."

Emmett rubbed his full stomach. Charlene looked around The Cavern Cafe. It was beginning to get crowded.

"We finished just in the nick of time. Let's get home—I want to read Poovie's newest article in the *Gazette.*"

Emmett's mouth spread into a thin-lipped smile. "I'll bet there's a nice sunset out there." He pointed towards the window.

Charlene looked where he pointed and then back at him. Her back ached. She didn't answer.

"It's Saturday night," he pointed out.

"So?" she remarked.

"I think we're getting into a rut."

Charlene spoke sternly. "I've given birth to two children, changed their diapers, taught them to drive, argued over curfews, help put them through college, and married them off." Her voice escalated. "Wyatt and Tammy are happy. I have three grandchildren, and babysit all too regularly." She crossed her arms tightly. "I welcome the rut. The studio is running smoothly. It's my turn to relax, dang it."

"Well, I'm all for relaxin', but we need a change of pace. The Senior Smiles Retirement Home isn't too far off."

"Baloney," she muttered.

Emmett began rubbing his left shoulder.

"Change of pace?" Charlene repeated. "You've lost your mind. Our pace is perfect. And don't start that 'my shoulder is tryin' to tell me something' routine. It conveniently hurts when you want it to. It doesn't mean something strange is going on. And I take pies to The Senior Smiles all the time. It's a nice place." The waitress handed them their check. "Now, pay Dolly. I'm tired."

"And grouchy," he said under his breath as he handed Dolly a wad of cash.

"Everything okay?" she asked, clearly sensing tension.

"Delicious. Thank you," he said.

Dolly's eyes lit up at the large tip.

Charlene smiled. "Tell your mama I said hello."

"Will do. She's feelin' a bit better—that hip surgery really kept her down for a while, but you know Joanne. Nothing can keep her down for long."

"I'm so glad to hear it. Did she like the apple pie I brought by?"

"She loved it, and Daddy also thought it was mighty tasty. You two have a great evening. Stay out of trouble, ya hear? Bye, now." Dolly disappeared into the kitchen.

Charlene glared at Emmett. "You are too old to be lookin' at that girl's behind, so stop it! Eli would not appreciate it."

"Don't walk a thing like her mama," he said with a laugh.

"And isn't that a good thing!" Charlene insisted as she rolled her eyes. "I'll bet Johnny ate every bit of that pie. Joanne probably didn't even get a taste. Oh, well, come on, let's get."

They slid out of the booth and held hands as they walked through the restaurant. Charlene spotted one of her friends waiting in the lobby.

"Howdy, Matilda."

"Hey, there, sugar. How are you?"

"Fit as a fiddle, and you?"

"Busy, busy, busy, just trying to keep up," Matilda said. A small girl clung to her leg. "Did you know our granddaughter Vera has moved in with Earl and me?"

Charlene patted the child's cheek. "No, I didn't. She's growing like a weed, bless her heart."

Matilda put her hand on her hip and leaned in close. "Me and Earl just love this child to death. Unfortunately, Loretta's run off again. I just don't know where she gets that wild streak."

Charlene almost laughed, but instead just said, "Loretta's a smart girl. I'm sure she'll be back real soon. It was nice to see you, Matilda. Call me if you need anything. You take care, now."

"See you at church," Matilda called after her.

Charlene and Emmett left the restaurant. As they neared the car, he stopped.

"Just look at that sunset." Crimson clouds stretched across the vast horizon. "It's unusual."

Charlene halted and stared. "It is nice."

He wrapped his arm around her shoulders.

"What are you thinking, old man?"

He rubbed his own shoulder again, and then placed both of his arms around her and looked down at her.

"I was thinking about making a wish."

Charlene leaned back. "A wish? What could you possibly wish for? We've been blessed time and time again. Maybe you ought not push your luck. Something bad might happen."

"I don't want to win the lottery or anything. I'd just like a night of excitement, like we used to have."

"Oh, you are an old fool. The grandkids are coming over tomorrow after church. That's as much excitement as you can stand, and sometimes you can't stand that much. What's gotten into you?"

A shooting star darted across the sky, leaving a trail of tiny, glistening lights in its path. Their eyes met, and he whispered, "Someone was listening."

Charlene tried not to smile, but gave up. "He's always listening, Emmett. Maybe you should come to church more often. Now, let's get home." She kissed him lightly on the cheek.

Emmett opened the door of the vintage Ford truck, and she climbed inside. As they rode home, she began planning her Sunday dinner menu. The only thing the kids would eat was macaroni and cheese. Still, she would broil some chicken, and dessert was a must.

Suddenly, she noticed they weren't on the road home. They were driving away from Mystic Ridge on a small two-lane road.

"Where on earth are we going?"

"I felt like driving, that's all."

"Driving where?"

"I don't know." He let out a deep breath. "Cruising, like we used to."

"Have you seen gas prices? Cruising? Oh, Lord." She looked out the window. The sky was black, except for the thousands of shimmering stars. "You're gonna get lost."

They passed an old abandoned Texaco station. She thought for a moment.

"I remember this road. This is the way we used to go to Bubba's."

"Yep."

"Didn't that old dive burn down years ago?"

"Yep."

"Well, then, why are we driving in that direction."

"Don't know. Just felt like it."

She glared at him. "I hope my cellphone has a full charge. The kids are gonna think we have Alzheimer's if we have to call them and say we're lost. Do we have a full tank?"

"We do."

She crossed her arms, her annoyance obvious. She checked the clock. It was getting late. She was just about to complain again when she was distracted by a strange magenta-colored fog ahead of them.

"Goodness, what is that?"

Emmett leaned over the steering wheel. "Maybe it's a fair or something." He pushed down on the accelerator, and the car swiftly approached the phenomenon.

Charlene blinked several times as the familiar neon sign with the giant cowboy boot towering into the dark Tennessee sky appeared.

Emmett slowed down.

"Bubba's Honky-Tonk!" She faced him. "Are we going crazy? It's exactly the same. It hasn't changed a bit."

He pulled into the empty gravel parking lot. Shadows of people dancing drifted past the windows. He rolled his window down. They could both hear music, shouting, and singing.

He looked at Charlene. "What do ya think?"

"I think we've just driven off a cliff, and we don't know it."

"We're dead?" He pinched his arm. "No, that hurt. This is incredible. Maybe it was rebuilt, and we didn't hear about it."

"There aren't any other cars or trucks," she pointed out. "Just us."

He smirked. "But it's a perfect replica of its former self, that's for sure."

"I'll say. I never heard one thing about it being resurrected. I think we've just entered the Twilight Zone." She looked around. "Maybe Dolly drugged us at the cafe."

He cut the engine. Charlene's mouth dropped open. "Good God almighty, you don't think we're going in there?"

He grinned. "Oh, yeah. We're goin' in." He got out of the truck, walked around to her side, and pulled her out.

Charlene was speechless. The Tammy Wynette song "Stand By Your Man" began inside the saloon. Her heart pounded, but she could not speak as he pulled her toward the door. The sound of people shouting and singing, and glass breaking, got louder and louder. When they reached the door, he kissed her.

"Don't fret. Everything will be all right."

She squeezed his hand. "Remember what I said about not pushing your luck? What if I lose you? I'm scared. What if we lose each other—forever?"

"Don't go overreacting, Grandma. Let's just have some fun." He pointed toward the mounted steer horns above the door.

"Impossible," she muttered, even though nostalgia was flooding through her.

"Come on. Let's go."

He opened the door, and a thick cloud of lilac fog drifted out and engulfed them as they weightlessly drifted inside.

Charlene let go of his hand and covered her ears. The music was loud, but it was classic country music. Tammy Wynette had always been her favorite singer, and she smiled for a brief second until she realized she could no longer feel Emmet's hand. Her body tensed. He was gone!

Before she could properly panic, she looked down at her attire. She was wearing a red denim skirt and white fringed cowboy boots.

"Oh, my." She touched her stomach. She had on a plain white T-shirt, but the blacklights gave it a purple glow. There was a red bandana around her neck.

She giggled, remembering how many times she'd worn this exact outfit. It always made her feel like a genuine *Hee-Haw* celebrity. She touched her hair and recognized the feel of her long, silky curls. She was young again!

Confusion overtook her mind. The unruly atmosphere was intoxicating. She looked toward the bar. There were hundreds of people crammed into the rocking saloon—yelling, swearing, ordering drinks.

Blacklights decorated the ceiling, and everything was lit up in a neon hue. There were glowing paintings of rodeo riders, cactus, illuminated sunsets, and starry skies. There were long tables containing buckets of peanuts, half-empty pitchers of beer and red plastic cups. She noticed the familiar jukebox, altered with extra four-foot speakers.

Looking towards the bar, she saw men and women filling every seat, flirting and laughing with each other. Men in huge cowboy hats waved money at the overwhelmed bartenders.

She giggled again, and covered her mouth with her hands. The aroma of her mama's famous meatloaf tickled her nose. She stared at her hands. Had she helped make meatloaf for dinner? She concentrated. Yes, yes, she had.

She remembered it all so clearly. Her mama had shucked the corn while she mixed the ingredients. Her sister had spent the entire evening complaining as she kneaded dough for biscuits. The kitchen had been boisterous, but she'd enjoyed it. She pictured her mama's face so clearly, her proud, simple expression as she tended to some important household duty. No one on earth could cook like her mama.

A loud shriek startled her as someone grabbed her arm. "Charleeeeeeene!"

❧❧

Emmett rubbed his shoulder as pain shot down his sides. His toes ached. He looked down to see worn black snakeskin cowboy boots. These had been his favorite. He lifted a gray Stetson off of his head and admired it.

"Perfection," he said as he placed it back on his head.

He felt his face melt into a smile as he gazed around the chaotic room. Now, this was cool. Men and women cavorted and danced in every corner of the bar. How on earth did he get here?

He reached into his pocket and pulled out the keys to a Chevy truck. He studied the rabbit's-foot keychain. Oh, yeah, he suddenly remembered. He had stolen his brother's truck. There would be a ruckus in the morning. Coming to Bubba's was always an adventure. It was worth any repercussions that might arise the next day.

He tucked the keys into his tight Wrangler jeans. The twang of a slide guitar filled the room, and he felt like dancing.

❧ ❧

"Charlene, you're late." Matilda held up her wristwatch. "Sugar, *everyone's* here. I've been looking all over for you." She surveyed Charlene's outfit. "Oh, you look darling, good enough for television." She entwined their arms. "Let's have a look around." She guided her through the crowd to the bar. "Look." She pointed. "There's Johnny. He thinks he's as cool as Johnny Cash, but he's about as sexy as Buck Owens."

The two women laughed heartily.

"Let's get us a drink. You ready?"

"Sure. I'll have a beer," Charlene answered.

They squeezed through the crowd at the bar, and Matilda somehow managed to get two beers. Charlene squeezed her friend's elbow.

"Oh, dear, there's Earl. He took me to the picture show a few weeks ago, and now he calls me constantly. I just can't stand him; you've got to hide me."

Matilda stood on tiptoes and checked him out as Charlene hid behind her. After he passed, she turned to Charlene. "Actually, he's not too bad. Those sideburns remind me of Elvis. Did you kiss him? Is he a good kisser?"

"Ugggh, no. You've got to be kidding. Let's go to the ladies' room." Charlene led the way as Matilda followed. When they entered, they found their friend Joanne sitting on a small stool near the sink. She had a bottle of tequila and a large needle. Ladies were lined up in front of her.

Charlene put her hands on her hips. "Joanne, what in the world are you up to?"

"Piercing ears. Wanna go next?"

"Absolutely not. Do you even know what you're doing?"

"Of course, but I'm about to take a dancing break. This stool ain't doin' nothing for the shape of my tush." She held her hands up high and stood up. She wiggled her large hips as she adjusted her bra. "Just a short intermission, girls. I'll be back in one hour." All the girls moaned and quickly dispersed.

Matilda rolled her eyes and whispered to Charlene, "I've seen her cross-stitch, and it's a sloppy mess. I can't imagine letting her stick a needle through my ear."

Charlene adjusted her curls, applied a thick layer of red lipstick, and strolled out confidently. They found a spot to lean against the bar. After a few minutes, Matilda elbowed her in the stomach.

"Oh, my, look who's back from Vietnam."

Charlene looked to the left and didn't see anyone new. She looked to the right, and saw Emmett Huff, her first love—her only love.

Her heart began pounding in her chest. He looked better than cold lemonade on a hot summer day. She couldn't take her eyes off him. He was rubbing his shoulder.

She turned toward Matilda.

"I heard he was hit by a stray bullet."

"Yep. He was taking pictures of his squadron when they got ambushed by the Viet Cong. His entire shoulder was shattered. How painful."

Charlene watched him. "Poor thing. He...He gives me goosebumps."

Matilda laughed. "I'll bet he'd give you more than that if you'd let him. He's always fancied you."

They watched as Joanne walked straight toward him.

"Look, Charlene, the hussy's moving in. You've got to do something."

Charlene couldn't move. She watched as the couple sauntered onto the dance floor and began the two-step to the Loretta Lynn song "Coal Miner's Daughter." In dismay, she chugged
her beer.

Matilda shook her head in disappointment. "You are a chick-
en, my friend." She returned her attention to the dance floor
and began singing loudly. Then she stopped and said, "If I ever
have a little girl, I'm going to name her Loretta."

Charlene wasn't listening. Her heart was aching watching
Joanne and Emmett. He had written her one letter from Vietnam, and she had read it a hundred times. She'd written him
back, but it had been returned to her marked insufficient address; and then no more letters came. Emmett Huff had broken
her heart.

She looked away, unable to watch them another second.

"Excuse me, Charlene, would you like another beer?"

She looked up to see Johnny Lee. He had taken off his hat
and had his long hair tucked behind his large ears. She glanced
at the dance floor, and Joanne still had Emmett in her arms.

"No. Dance with me, right now."

His eyes lit up. "Okay."

She took his hand and strolled out onto the crowded dance
floor. They swiftly began the Texas two-step. The country beat
was rhythmic and bold; it felt good to float around the room.
She could almost close her eyes and pretend it was a dream.

Johnny squeezed her hands as the beat of the music guided
them in every direction of the neon-lit room, but abruptly, he
stopped. She was startled. She peered behind him and saw Emmett. He had apparently tapped Johnny on the shoulder. His face
possessed a no-nonsense expression as he held his large silver belt
buckle and sneered at Johnny.

"John, Joanne wants to take a spin with you," Emmett said
sternly as he pointed towards Joanne in the corner of the dance
floor, adjusting her blouse. Johnny frowned but walked away.

Charlene's heart leapt with joy. She felt her knees shaking
as Emmett wrapped his arm around the small of her back. He
had a serious expression as he pulled her close to him. "Love Me
Tender" began on the jukebox. They started to sway with the music in perfect unison.

He seemed so much taller than she remembered. He felt powerful, his chest broad and muscular. He'd grown into a man.

She touched his shoulder. "Are you okay?"

He moved her hand to his waist. "I'm gonna live, I'm just a little sore."

"I'm sorry you got hurt," she said. He grinned down at her and pulled her even closer.

Charlene felt her whole body come alive. It felt so natural being close to him. She had never wanted any other man. She laid her head on the right side of his chest.

"I'm so grateful that you're all right."

"I'm glad you're here." He stroked her soft blond hair as they danced. "I've wished for this moment for two long years. Now I never want it to end."

She leaned back and gazed up at him. "How come you only wrote to me once?"

"I wrote you hundreds of letters. They were the words of an immature boy in a terrifying situation. It gave me hope, writing them, but I just couldn't mail them. I couldn't."

She caressed his neck as he spoke. He sounded much different from the cocky boy who had bravely departed for the other side of the world. She was in awe of this new Emmett.

She buried her face against his throat. Blood coursed through her veins like a newly awakened river. It was unfathomable, but he was even more handsome and desirable than when he'd left. She remembered the tiny peck on the cheek she had given him before he departed. It seemed so insufficient now.

"I would have welcomed your letters. I missed you so," she confided as tears began forming in her eyes. Their bodies continued to sway. "I just thank God that you're here with me now."

He placed his hands behind her neck and pulled her face towards his. Charlene closed her eyes. Their lips met with a need that had grown and matured in the past two years. His lips were gentle yet searching. Shivers of a new desire raced through her body. She responded eagerly. Time stood still as they kissed unabashedly.

Suddenly, they were startled by the sound of glass shattering, and the romantic moment ended.

"What the hell was that?" Emmett said.

Matilda and Earl were arguing fiercely, a pitcher of beer broken at their feet. They watched as she slapped him across the face.

"Oh, no!" Charlene shouted, and ran to her friend. She grabbed Matilda by the arm. "Great balls of fire, what is going on?"

"That no-good redneck was dancing with me and pinched another girl on the fanny. Can you believe that?"

Charlene squinted at Earl, who stood with a shocked expression on his face and his hands out by his sides. Matilda was on the verge of tears.

Charlene turned to Emmett, who had followed her. "I'm going to take her to the ladies room to calm down. I'll be right back."

He nodded. Charlene noticed the red lipstick smeared on his face and giggled. "Maybe you should check out your kisser. My color is a little dark for your complexion."

His eyes grew wide, and he rushed toward the men's room.

Charlene pulled Matilda by the elbow. "Come on."

"Men! I hate them all." Matilda ranted. "That no-good liar was just telling me how glamorous I am. And I was actually falling for it. His ugly sideburns were starting to look sexy. We were slow-dancing so close my mama would have had a stroke. I stepped on something and looked down, and I saw him pinch this skinny girl right on the rump. The nerve of that guy. I am done with hanky-panky Earl." She noticed Joanne was back to calmly piercing ears. "Good grief, Joanne. Why are you still doin' that?"

"All the girls in California have their ears pierced, sometimes more than once. Even guys are doin' it. Flower power, baby. We are way behind the times here in Mystic Ridge. I feel it is my personal duty to get us ready for the seventies."

Matilda thought for a moment. "Do me next, then you can do Charlene."

"What?" Charlene bellowed. "Oh, no, not me."

"Suck it up, buttercup," Matilda drawled. "I hate to tell you, but we are not sixteen anymore." She sat down in front of Joanne. "I'm ready." She closed her eyes and didn't flinch as Joanne pierced each ear, placing tiny gold hoops in them.

Charlene was amazed.

"All done." Joanne pointed proudly towards the mirror.

Matilda walked to it, leaned close, and smiled at her reflection. "I am one cool babe." She turned her head from side to side, stood up straight, and faced Charlene. "You're next."

Charlene shifted from one foot to the other. Smoke billowed overhead, beer bottles littered the counter and women came and went, washing their hands and lighting cigarettes. Her friends seemed to know what was best, and it obviously hadn't hurt. She walked over to the small stool and sat down. She wasn't a child anymore. It was time she behaved like a real woman.

Joanne washed the needle in the sink and poured tequila over it. Charlene cringed, and her stomach tightened. She nodded, closed her eyes, and held her breath. The needle stung badly as it pierced her earlobe. She sobbed as Joanne quickly put the gold hoop through her ear and wiped the blood away.

"Good grief, that hurt," Charlene cried. "Matilda, you big faker. You know it hurt like the dickens." The sound of chairs crashing distracted her. "What was that?"

Matilda peeked out the door. "Holy shit-fire, Johnny and Earl are fighting." She brought her hands to her hips. "Joanne, I'll get Earl, you get Johnny. We gotta stop this before the sheriff gets here."

The two brave women dashed from the bathroom into the crowd, toward the chaos.

Charlene exited and scanned the crowd for Emmett. Suddenly, a hand took hold of her arm, and she turned to face him.

"Hey." But her excitement quickly turned to concern as she saw the worried expression etched on his brow.

"Charlene, my brother's here. He's looking for the keys to his truck, and he's hotter than fire. I guess I should have asked. I've got to skedaddle."

"But..." she began, and then broke off.

"Come with me." He held a hand out. "We got all night. I don't want to leave you again, not ever." His eyes pleaded with her.

She had no reservations. She took his hand. "From now on, I will go where you go."

He quickly kissed her on the cheek. "We belong together."

"We do," she agreed.

Emmett charged through the crowd, ducking around people, pulling Charlene every step of the way. Everyone seemed to be engrossed in the fight and the two women clawing at the rowdy men. She hoped Matilda and Joanne would be okay. They were pretty darn fearless. Earl and Johnny probably didn't stand a chance when those two intervened.

They reached the front door, and Emmett took off his hat. "You still with me?" he shouted, squeezing her hand.

"Forever," Charlene answered him. He opened the door and smoke billowed out. Holding hands tightly, they darted outside.

The next step seemed to last several minutes as the fog enveloped them. They drifted through space and time surrounded by astral beauty. In a simultaneous instant, their feet touched down in the gravel parking lot. Still hand-in-hand they faced each other...

The vintage years had returned.

Charlene busted out laughing. "That was some kiss, Grandpa."

"And you, kissing like that in a public place. I'm glad your grandkids didn't see that." He put his arms around her and hugged her. They could still hear the commotion coming from inside Bubba's. "I dodged my brother for a week and then ended up doing his chores for a month. Mama wouldn't let him kill me, since I'd come so close once before." They began walking toward the car. "Do you remember how that night ended?"

Charlene shrugged, pretending to be confused. "Nope."

Emmett laughed. "Oh, yes, you do. How about if I remind you?" He opened the door for her. "Sweetheart."

Charlene giggled, unable to contain her embarrassment. Emmett hurried around the car and jumped inside.

"You are an old fool, you know that?" she declared.

"Yep, a lucky old fool—at least, I'm hoping."

He started the truck and headed toward Crystal Caverns Park.

Charlene studied his ageless profile. Timeless love coursed through her. His rugged smile and handsome face still caused her heartbeat to quicken. Things hadn't changed one bit!

≈≈

"Pass the potatoes, please," Emmet asked politely.

Tammy handed them to him. "Why did Mom make meatloaf? I'm not sure the kids will eat it," she whispered.

"Hogwash, this is her mama's famous recipe. They'll love it."

"It's amazing!" Wyatt wolfed it down. "I'm so tired of college cafeteria food."

Charlene watched with anticipation and glee as the entire group sampled the meatloaf. She knew it was delicious. And she hadn't made it in years. Corn fritters made the perfect side dish.

It was a proud feeling to have remembered her mother's secret recipe after all these years. She was thankful memories of her mother had returned.

Tammy turned towards her. "Mom, this is really terrific. I must get the recipe, and you have to teach me how to make it."

"I was planning to." Charlene felt so blessed as she watched her daughter, her son-in-law, and their three kids enjoying the meal. Wyatt hadn't even taken a breath since she served it. It was a pleasure having everyone around the dinner table again.

The night before was still fresh in her mind. Had it really happened? Was it a dream? Whatever magic those tiny stars contained had brought back precious, forgotten memories, and some much-needed excitement for Emmett. She had to admit, it had been thrilling.

"Mom, I was wondering if you and Dad could babysit next Saturday night?"

Emmett answered. "No. No, we have plans." He winked at Charlene.

Tammy stopped eating and stared at him. "Okay, Dad. That's fine."

Wyatt chuckled.

Tammy resumed eating, a suspicious gleam in her eye. After a few moments, she leaned close to Charlene. "Mom, you and Dad are acting like frisky teenagers. What is up?"

Charlene giggled but didn't reply.

"And seriously, Mom, why are you wearing one gold hoop earring?"

# IMAGINE THAT

A HUGE CRASH OF THUNDER SHOOK THE HOUSE. MILLIE BOLTed to a sitting position in her bed as rain hammered loudly on the roof. Flashes of lightning lit up the dark room.

"Surely that woke you," she barked at her husband Abe. "Surely that woke you," she barked at her husband Abe. "This storm is a doozy."

"Yes," he answered. "But I'm not going to get up and debate it." He rolled over and resituated himself comfortably.

"I closed the shop early today because they were calling for bad weather."

"Yeah, and you closed it last week because you saw one random snowflake. I don't know how Enchanted Treasures is ever going to stay in business if you keep giving away everything and closing for no reason. Now go to sleep."

Still sitting up, Millie heard a faint meow from underneath the bed.

"Did you hear that?" She shook Abe's shoulder. "I heard a cat."

He groaned loudly. "You're just imagining things. Snowbell has been dead for over a year. Wendy is at the shop, curled up on her heated bed. Now, go back to sleep." He adjusted the covers tightly around his body.

She poked him in the back. "You know how Snowbell always used to wake me up when one of the girls wasn't feeling well."

"Yes, she was a gem, but I have to get up in four hours. Leave me be."

Millie ground her teeth. He was so irritating. How in the world could anyone sleep with the possibility of tornadoes, and with ghosts of dead cats gallivanting through their home?

She had grown up in the Midwest, and had experienced several devastating storms. They'd frightened her then, and they frightened her now.

She glanced at the clock; it was two a.m. Her shoulders slumped. If only the girls weren't so far away. Betsy was in Chicago attending a culinary school, and Susie was a freshman at University of Tennessee in Knoxville. If they were here, they would play cards with her until the storm passed. They understood her fears.

Oh, how she missed their card games. Susie and Betsy got extremely competitive in the late-night hours. It was so enjoyable for her to referee. It always took her mind off bad weather. She wanted to call the girls at this very moment, but it was the middle of the night. She must resist the urge.

Another clap of thunder shook the house. Chills raced up her arms, and her stomach churned. Sleep was not going to happen, so she got up. She put on her heavy robe, her warmest slippers, and went downstairs and fixed a glass of iced tea. She needed to distract herself. She went into the family room, selected a photo album, sat, and spread it on her lap.

A smile crept across her face as she saw a photograph of Betsy on her first birthday. Abe was holding her hands as she took her first steps. An expression of sheer joy lit up the baby's face. She spotted a picture of herself, a year later, holding Betsy perched across her ample stomach. Not long after that photograph, Susie was born.

What a joyous yet exasperating time in her life! Betsy had been into everything. Every light socket, trashcan, lamp cord, and drawer seemed to beckon her. And Susie wanted to eat constantly. It was quite challenging to keep up with the busy girls.

She looked at pictures of the girls taking baths, making messes, modeling dresses, and playing with special toys. Each page rekindled a memory. She knew her family had been blessed with so many happy times.

When she turned the last page, Betsy was in the third grade and Susie was in the first. She sipped her tea. Why didn't she look at her albums more often? They were so delightful.

She carefully placed it back on the shelf. There were at least seven more to relish.

Millie's eyes began to glaze over. Oh, how she missed the girls. She hadn't expected it to be so difficult, but it was. She missed them each and every day. They had grown up so fast, and now they were gone.

The thunder continued to blast overhead, and uneasiness still lurked in her stomach. Maybe she would watch a little television.

She switched through several channels, and found music videos, cartoons, talk shows, old golf tournaments, and infomercials. She took a deep breath and continued to search. She stopped on *The Dick Van Dyke Show*. She could remember when it was on during prime time. She used to fix popcorn and watch it every week. The predicaments Mr. Van Dyke got into were always very amusing, and Mary Tyler Moore was so cute and gullible. In this episode, they ventured into a men's prison to do a vaudeville show.

She put down the remote and relaxed. It wasn't so bad being awake in the middle of the night.

She did miss having a cat. There was nothing like a purring feline to calm her nerves. The funny thing was, she had pictured herself with Snowbell for many years to come. In one daydream she had seen herself caring for a grandchild as Snowbell played with the baby's tiny toys. It was so unexpected when the cat died of kidney failure. Now, with the girls *and* Snowbell gone, she felt lonely, and emotional.

Lightning lit up the room. Life went on, things changed, and there was nothing she could do about it. She turned her attention back to the television.

After the show ended, Millie turned off the television and decided to go back to bed. As she climbed the stairs, she heard faint voices. She immediately sat in the dark stairwell and strained to make out the words. Was someone in her home? She held her breath and listened.

The voices seemed far away. They sounded like women, happy women, giggling. She closed her eyes and concentrated as she sat in the darkness. The thunder made it difficult to hear. She could still see the flashes of lightning through her eyelids. Oh, why wouldn't the thunder stop? She had to hear the voices again. They were trying to tell her something.

Owning the largest and most unique antique shop in the South had taught her to listen to her inner voice, and everyone else's. Enchanted Treasures contained some truly ghostly items. She had learned to be open to unexplainable coincidences, too. In Mystic Ridge, unusual events happened all the time. It was their claim to fame, and she was proud to be a part of it all.

She waited for several minutes, then began to picture her daughters. Her imagination ran wild. She was pretty sure it had been their voices. At least, it sounded like them. They were laughing. What could possibly be funny?

She opened her eyes, and a bolt of lightning struck nearby. Once again, the house rumbled. Chills started on her calves and slowly crept up her entire body. Her hair stood on end. She was scared, scared for the girls. What was happening?

Her body began to tremble. She closed her eyes again, trying to compose herself, but the voices reappeared. They were screaming this time, and it was much louder. The stairwell seemed to fill with their screams, mingling with the loud claps of thunder.

Millie raced up the rest of the stairs and looked in Susie's room. Nothing seemed amiss. She hurried to Betsy's room. Everything was in its place. She dashed back down the stairs and looked out the dining room window. Her breath caused the window to fog, so she wiped it off with the sleeve of her robe.

The streetlights swayed in the strong wind. She looked for a person, anyone. *Somebody* had screamed. Who had it been? Sweat dripped down her sides as she scanned all the neighboring houses. There were no lights anywhere.

She trudged back to the stairwell and sat down again. Her body shook in a bizarre fashion she had never experienced before. She wrapped her arms around her waist and rocked back and forth. The voices were gone, and it was hauntingly quiet, the thunder now just a soft, defeated grumble in the distance.

She felt confused. *I heard it. I know I did. Abe! Maybe he heard them, too.* She raced to the bedroom and shook his shoulder.

"What...what is it?" he asked as he sluggishly sat up.

"Did you hear it, the screams? I heard Susie and Betsy. First, they were laughing, and then they were screaming." As she spoke, she realized how insane it sounded. She slowly sat on the bed.

Abe shut his eyes and opened them again and made a heavy sigh. "Millie, come to bed. Your overactive imagination is really getting the best of you. I talked to Betsy the other day. And you talked to Susie about her meal plan. They are both fine. Everyone is fine. Let's get some sleep."

Millie wanted to cry. "I heard them. I did."

He took her hands in his. "I believe you. I know it's been hard for you adjusting to the empty nest. And it was a beast of a storm. But everybody is okay. Their holiday breaks will be here before you know it. You've got to be tired. Lay down. We both need our sleep."

Millie stood. "No, you go ahead." Her nerves felt shot. She needed to stay busy. "I'm going to get a bowl of cereal."

"Are you sure, darling?"

"Yeah." She kissed him on the cheek and left the room.

The whole thing was ridiculous; she knew that. Thunder sounded in the distance. Maybe it had been the storm. Rain continued to fall.

She went to the kitchen and fixed a pot of decaffeinated coffee. She knew it wouldn't help her jittery nerves; but hot coffee had always been comforting to her, and she desperately needed something hot. Sleep was not an option. She looked at the sofa. She couldn't sit, either. She had to occupy her time.

Opening the cupboard, she spied a box of cake mix. Chocolate supreme was always Betsy's favorite. She decided to prepare it. She also noticed the enormous box of oatmeal. It would go stale if she didn't use it soon. Susie loved her cinnamon oatmeal raisin cookies. She decided to make those, too. Hopefully, the rain would move on through, and she would just forget about it. She took off her fuzzy robe and got busy.

❧❧

At exactly 7:20 a.m. Abe entered the kitchen. "Wow, something smells great."

"The cake is cooling. I'll have it frosted when you get home from work." She handed him a cup of coffee. "I had to do something all night. You hungry?"

"Starved, what's for breakfast? I have a busy day."

"Cornflakes and oatmeal cookies," Millie answered.

Abe's eyebrows rose. "Seriously?"

"Yep, have a seat." She pointed at the table.

He sat down. "Are you feeling better?"

She poured him some cornflakes and put the milk on the table. "I guess. But it was such a long night. Claire is going to fill in for me today at Enchanted Treasures. I really thought I heard the girls."

Abe stood and wrapped his arms around her. "I'm sorry I couldn't help. I was just pooped. You must have been up all night. Relax." He helped her put her robe on.

Millie exhaled and put a plate of cookies in the middle of the table. She sat with a thud. "I'm going to call the girls today, just to make sure they're okay."

Abe added more coffee to his cup and sat back down. "I won't stop you. It's a good idea."

Millie ate a cookie. "I'll wait a while."

He poured the milk onto his cornflakes and dipped a cookie into the bowl.

"De-licious." He took out his tablet and began reading the morning news. Usually, Millie did the same, but this morning she couldn't concentrate on anything—not until she spoke to the girls.

After Abe left, she began calling them. Neither answered. So, she texted them both and waited. No replies. Frustrating! Sadly, she had no alternate numbers.

The tears flowed, and this time she didn't even try to stop them. She just sat in the messy kitchen and sobbed openly. What the hell was going on? She felt alone, but she also felt that something was not right. She wiped her face. *Damn it, what can I fix now?*

❧❧

Millie found sausage and ground beef in the freezer. She browned it and added tomato sauce and spices. As it simmered, she boiled noodles. She layered the mixture with the noodles, cottage cheese and mozzarella. Her sausage-and-cheese lasagna was quite famous in town. Neighbors regularly got a pan during hard times or holidays.

As she covered it with foil, she realized she and Abe could never, ever eat the enormous pan of food. Maybe she would take half to Pearl Hathaway and her kids. She placed it in the refrigerator. Her arms felt heavy and her knees weak as she shut the large door. Leaning against it, she frowned. Neither girl had replied to her texts. A wave of helplessness engulfed her. *What should I do now?*

Dragging her heavy feet, she went to the couch. She lay down and positioned the pillow underneath her head. She situated her robe over her ankles. She was too tired to comb her hair or even brush her teeth. She laid the phone near her breast and checked the clock. It was nearly three in the afternoon. She needed a shower, but weariness demanded that she rest her head for a moment. Then, she would call again. As a light drizzle tapped against the windows, she finally found sleep.

❧☙

"Mom? Mom."

Millie opened her eyes and was startled to see Susie standing over her. She quickly sat up.

"Suse, dear, what...what...?" she stuttered, her mind fatigued. "Give me a hug. Are you really here? Are you all right?"

Susie sat on the edge of the couch and leaned toward her. "I'm fine. What's up with you? Are you sick? You're still in your pajamas, and it's five-thirty in the afternoon."

Millie moved her to arm's-length and studied her. "I had a bad night, and I've been calling you for hours." A door shut, and Betsy came in from the garage. Millie's chin dropped. "Both of you? What are you girls doing here? Why didn't you tell me you were coming?"

Betsy slowly crossed the room and kissed her mother on the cheek. "We wanted to surprise you. It's fall break for both of us. I flew into Knoxville yesterday, and Susie picked me up." She winked at her sister.

Millie straightened her messy hair as her bottom lip began to quiver. "I...I've been losing my mind. I was imagining such awful things." She stood up and went to the mirror in the foyer. "Oh, Lord, I look atrocious." She wiped the dampness from underneath her eyes. "You girls look perfect. I'm so relieved you're here."

"Something smells amazing," Susie remarked and went into the kitchen. Betsy and Millie followed her. She inspected the dishes in the sink. "It's good to be home." She moved a few bowls around. "It smells like your sausage lasagna. What a mess. Did you know we were coming?"

"Absolutely not," Millie grumbled, as she leaned against the refrigerator. "I've been worried sick, and neither of you were answering my calls or texts. I'm still upset about that."

"We wanted to surprise you." Betsy was snooping in the cupboard and found the oatmeal cookies and chocolate cake. "Jackpot, chocolate supreme cake." She turned to her mother. "Are you sure you didn't know we were on our way?"

"No, no, I just couldn't sleep. I was scared. I had to do something. There was this tremendous storm, a doozy. I thought I heard..." She paused. "Forget it. I was just being a worrywart. Mothers are allowed." She hugged each of them again.

The sound of the garage door opening distracted the conversation. Abe walked in carrying a box with handles.

"Hey, hey," he shouted. Both girls went to him and squeezed him tightly. "I didn't know you gals were coming."

"We wanted to surprise you, too," Susie explained. "What do you have there?"

"It's a present for your mother. She's been a little depressed without you two. I think she reached the breaking point last night. So, I wanted to get her something special." He pointed toward a chair. "Millie, have a seat."

Millie crossed her arms and sat down.

Abe was all smiles. "Okay, I got you something to keep you company through any bad storms in the future." He lifted out a white kitten. "This little girl was at The Pet Palooza. This kid named Jason insisted she was the girl for you."

Millie shrieked loudly. "Oh, she's precious. Snowbell Two."

"Sweetness," Susie agreed.

"Holy cow, Dad. Best gift ever!" Betsy added.

Abe beamed proudly.

Millie hugged the kitten to her chest as it licked her chin. She held her up and gazed into her tiny jade eyes.

"Are you going to warn me about things, too? I was sure there'd been some kind of disaster last night. Did I hear you meow?"

Abe, Susie, and Betsy exchanged glances and rolled their eyes.

Millie cuddled the kitten to her chest. "I knew there was another kitty in my future. I can't explain it." She gazed lovingly at her husband. "Abe, it's a wonderful, thoughtful gift. Thank you. I needed a new buddy."

She inhaled deeply and exhaled slowly. Everyone was okay. *I let that silly storm get the best of me. They are all here and everyone is simply perfect.* Her eyes weighed a million pounds.

"I have been so panicked. I am spent, simply spent. Now that I know everyone is safe and sound, me and Snowbell Two are going to bed."

"Bed?" Abe repeated.

Millie stood. "Yes, bed. There is definitely plenty of food. Girls, you know how to bake the lasagna. Make yourselves at home. I have got to get some shut-eye."

The girls hugged her again.

Millie dragged her feet as she left the room, trudged up the stairs, and closed the bedroom door.

∽∾

Abe crossed his arms and pointed toward the couch. Susie and Betsy went in and sat.

"Now that your mama's all snug in her bed, do you two want to explain how you got here? There isn't a car in the driveway. Did you Uber?"

The girls exchanged a long glance. Betsy groaned as she rolled up her sleeve and showed her father several stitches going up her left forearm, and a huge purple bruise running down the length of it. "I have two broken ribs, too."

He gasped and then turned to Susie.

She lifted her long skirt and displayed stitches across each of her thighs surrounded by amethyst bruises.

"We tried to come home last night. It happened just outside of Nashville," Susie explained. "We hydroplaned. My car is totaled."

Abe's mouth dropped open.

"It was so late," Betsy interjected. "We didn't want to call and alarm you guys in the middle of the night, and we were okay. Really."

Abe swallowed hard, making a loud gulping noise. He opened his mouth, but no words would come out. He shook his head, stopped, and then shook his head again. He began to rub his chin and looked at their wounds once more.

"I'm just so grateful you're both all right." He looked toward the stairs that led to the bedroom. "She...she..." he began. "I didn't be—" After a moment, he looked back at the girls and sighed. "Imagine that."

# SATURDAY WITH POOVIE LAMAY

DOLLY POURED PEARL HATHAWAY ANOTHER CUP OF COFFEE and handed each of her children another individual-size carton of chocolate milk. She placed the altered check on the table.

"Y'all have a good day now." It made her feel good to give Pearl a bit of a discount. Pearl's ex-husband hadn't been seen in Mystic Ridge in quite a while; rumor was he had left them all high and dry to pursue his career in Music City. She'd had it rough, and the $6.20 bill was still probably barely in her budget.

Dolly untied her yellow apron, went to the beverage station, and poured herself a cup of coffee. She carefully placed the steaming carafe back on the warmer.

"Aggh!" she shrieked as someone pinched her backside. She turned around to see her best friend and fellow waitress Eve Davis smiling devilishly, a large glass of lemonade in her hand. "Girl, I almost threw this coffee sky high. Are you cray-cray?"

Eve fluttered her eyelashes and raised her drink. She lightly touched Dolly's cup with her glass. "That's what people say."

"You, my friend, are a nut. My customers are finishing up. You ready to relax and read the paper with me, and tell me all about this week's rescue kitten escapades?"

"Lordy, am I ready. These new blueberry pancakes are so popular. Everyone in town's coming in. It's gonna be the death of me," Eve said.

Dolly grabbed the *Mystic Gazette*. "Honey, you are preachin' to the choir. I have got to get off these sore feet. My dogs are pounding. I'll be in orthotics before I'm forty."

Eve followed her to a booth in the back corner of the diner. They slid in and began to unwind.

The Cavern Café's new manager, Tyrone Rogers, stopped at their table. Dolly inspected him. He was an eager African American fresh out of graduate school. He'd taken over management of the café from his grandfather Arno. He'd own the café soon enough. She liked him. He did a top-notch job, but he never knew how to handle them, outspoken as they were. And that was a good thing.

"Great job, gals." He paused. "You wonderful ladies were crushing it today!" He glanced at the paper. "Oh, heck, no. Y'all are the only two people in the whole world still reading a real newspaper. You know all that crap is online. Easy peasy! It's simple to see what's trending. I could teach y'all."

"Shut your mouth, Tyrone," Eve said. "Computers are only for Facebook and online shopping. We like to do some things the old-fashioned way."

"Yeah, we're vintage gals," Dolly agreed, snapping her fingers and motioning him to go. "Now, get."

He rolled his eyes and walked away.

Dolly let out a sigh of relief. It was a treasured Saturday morning ritual the girls had shared for years. Everyone else knew not to disturb them after they had finished their five-to-ten a.m. shift. Tyrone was just learning. The weekends were always extremely busy, and the two women worked hard. When it was over, they yearned for their corner-booth sanctuary, and a few moments of peace before heading home.

Some Saturday mornings they sat in silence just reading and catching up on all the events taking place in Mystic Ridge and the rest of the world. They discussed Eve's cat rescuing efforts, and any new babies she was fostering. Dolly got to complain about her husband Eli and his long hours as a park ranger. Still, she was always quick to point out his thoughtfulness.

She also liked to talk about her kids, and the struggles she encountered.

Other Saturdays they talked about politics, and the nutty fake news that Mystic Ridge residents were known for ignoring. They read and rotated each section of the paper approximately every fifteen minutes. To onlookers it was like clockwork—planned, anticipated, and relished. To the two women it was as important as their weekly paycheck. Maybe it was catching up on the news. Maybe it was the cherished friendship. Neither cared; they just knew it was a treasured time.

Dolly added more sugar to her coffee and lowered the paper. "Any new adoptions?"

"Yep, my last litter is all gone. I'm gonna miss those sweet little biscuits."

"Ah, the life of a cat lady."

Eve crossed her arms. "Cat ladies get a bad rap, but we are hot, affectionate women who know that felines can see right into our past lives, and comfort us accordingly. It's a big responsibility. We have to rescue as many as possible."

"Sexy," Dolly drawled.

"Exactly." Eve's chin rose.

"Here it is," Dolly proclaimed, lifting the newspaper. "Our favorite little section." She folded the paper in half and waved it toward Eve. "'Saturday With Poovie Lamay'."

"She's the best," Eve opined.

"The queen," Dolly agreed. She squinted at the small black print. "I sure would love to meet her. I mean, just to be in the same room with her would be an honor. No one tells it like it is like Poovie. And the coolest thing of all is that she's a regular gal, like us."

"Regular—but so skilled at writing the exact things I'm thinking. She has a way of making me feel like a server of gourmet cuisine to English royalty." Eve leaned over the table close to Dolly. "Poovie's made it clear to me that the regular gals, like us, actually run the entire world." She cackled loudly and then whispered softly, "it's just our little secret."

"Booya." Dolly nodded in agreement and held up her hand for a fist bump, Eve obliged. "That bit last week, 'Sack Lunches for the Senate', was a total crack-up. It wouldn't hurt them to save their ketchup packets, like we do."

"Damn straight." Eve agreed. "I'd like to see a television show about two broke politicians serving corn dogs."

Dolly tapped her long nails on the table. "I've seen her a few times at Mystic High, during student shows and presentations. No one bothers her. The rumors about her having agoraphobia must be true."

"So, she's afraid of crowds and public places?"

"Yep, almost never leaves her home."

A busboy approached the table. "Mrs. Dolly, your daughter is on the phone. She says Nicolas and Henry are fighting."

Dolly crossed her arms. "Is anybody bleeding?"

The bus boy bellowed toward the kitchen, "Is anybody bleeding?"

They waited. Dolly tapped her foot loudly as Eve chuckled.

"No," came from the kitchen.

Dolly pointed her finger at him. "You get on that there phone and tell my daughter to send their butts to their rooms, and I'll be home in one hour. No more crap." The bus boy quickly scurried away. Dolly shouted towards him. "And don't bother me again, unless it's the hospital calling."

She took a deep breath and sipped her coffee; thankful it was still warm. "Jesus, Joseph, and Mary. Eli was supposed to be off today, but some nut job spotted Bigfoot at the Crystal Cavern Park, so he had to throw on his dirty park ranger uniform and hightail it over there. All I ask for is one hour of peace with my friend, a cup of java, and a good laugh from Poovie. You'd think we were starring in an episode of *Mission Impossible*."

"Tell it," Eve agreed.

"Anyhoo, sometimes I envy you being single and free and cat-infested."

"I'll know the right man when I see him," Eve said. "Until then, I'm not kissing a bunch of frogs. Here, give me the paper, and I'll read it out loud. You read it last week."

"Go, girl." Dolly handed it to her.

Eve took a swig of lemonade and adjusted her apron. "Okay, the title is 'Reality Check'. 'You know you've come to grips when...'" She glanced up. "Oh, this sounds good. Here we go."

"'You've started to come to grips when your husband gawks at other women and you couldn't care less.'"

"Care," Dolly interrupted. "I've started critiquing."

Eve continued. "'You finish two things on your to-do list of ten, and you're happy.'"

"I'm happy with one," Dolly giggled.

"'Your child wants Oreos and Coke for breakfast, and you give in.'"

Dolly scratched her chin. "Been there, did that. My kids are so pushy. What's the point?"

"'You ignore the roll.'"

Dolly held both of her hands up over her head. "Have mercy, I won't even go there, girlfriend."

"'You cheer for Bs and Cs.'" Eve peeked over the paper. "Do Ds count in that scenario? My poor mama saw Ds." She continued. "'It's dinner. If they don't like it, then they shouldn't eat it.'"

"Oh, absolutely," Dolly interjected.

"'You'll pay for and sit through a cartoon, alien, wizard or superhero movie just for the popcorn.'"

Dolly pointed a finger towards Eve. "You cannot beat movie theater popcorn, and that's a fact."

"Amen," Eve agreed, and then continued. "'You have accepted that housework is not a perfect science.'" She shuffled the paper. "Not in my dang house, that's for sure."

"My kids can't even get their dirty clothes into the laundry basket—beside it, yes. But in it, no," Dolly stated flatly.

Eve sat up a spec straighter. "'You finally realize that nobody can give you self-esteem.'"

"Yep," Dolly agreed. "You gotta grab it by the balls, all by yourself."

"And the last one—Oh, Dolly, this is you. "'The evil glare is starting to work.'"

Dolly scooted out of the booth, stood beside the table, and took a bow in every direction. Eve cackled loudly, and several customers turned around to see what the commotion was all about. She bounced back into her seat, smiling proudly.

"I do declare, I am the goddess of the evil glare. When I squint my eyes just right, my husband, kids, and even my dog will stop dead in their tracks."

"Your dog?"

"Yep, even Buster."

Eve exhaled. "Poovie seems to think it's working for her, too. You've got to teach me, please, please."

"Well, if you insist. If me and Poovie got it goin' on, it's definitely your turn." Dolly snapped her fingers.

"Oh, and her famous last words: 'Be safe and stay sweet.' I just adore Poovie," Eve cooed as she folded up the paper. "I feel like she's my friend."

Dolly placed her elbows on the table and relaxed her chin in her hands. "Me, too. She's a real visionary."

The women spent the rest of the morning practicing the perfect squint and the proper eyebrow position, the pressing of the lips, and the all-important hands on the hips. By lunchtime, Eve had it down to an art and hurried home, eager to try it out on her cat.

Dolly reveled in her unique power of the evil glare, and as she tossed the paper in the trash can, she marveled at how Poovie Lamay had pointed out pride in calculated eyebrow positioning. Yes, Poovie had a talent for bringing attention to the small, unappreciated, unnoticed, splendid aspects of being female and fabulous.

≈≈≈

School had gotten out early today because of teacher meetings. The weekend was starting early, but Archie exhaled in exasperation as he slumped in his chair. He crossed his arms on the antique wooden farm table. This would be embarrassing. Well, maybe not embarrassing, but awkward.

He watched his famous mother, Poovie Lamay, rushing through the kitchen like a woman on a mission. Their cat Moon sat on the counter watching Poovie perform her frenzied tasks. Archie surmised it seemed unusual, even to a cat.

It was all his fault. He had made the mistake of telling her he was taking Hannah on a picnic. Now, she was filling a basket with plastic plates, chicken sandwiches, tiny packets of ketchup, macaroni and cheese, juice boxes, and cupcakes.

His shoulders felt heavy. Dang it, he was in the eleventh grade. Showing up with this kind of picnic basket, or a picnic basket at all, was not cool. He'd planned to drive through a fast-food restaurant. But he'd opened his big mouth, and she'd gone to work so fast he'd been unable to protest. He cringed as she added red-checked napkins. But her face lit up at their addition, so he kept quiet. Hopefully, she wouldn't add candles. *Please— no ambiance.*

He straightened his posture as she regarded him, trying to read his mind, knowing she always succeeded.

Hannah would understand, hopefully. She respected his mother a ton, maybe more than he did. Everyone knew who she was. Her column, "Saturday With Poovie Lamay," was always trending. Hashtag Poovie was a big deal. Everyone loved her and her special down-home wit.

Archie continued watching her. He'd have to text his sister Vivian at the UT. She would get a good laugh out of this.

Their mother was something else—truly different from other mothers. She was more than just a stay-at-home mom. She never left the house, or only if she absolutely had to. His dad said she had agoraphobia, but honestly, she wasn't afraid of crowds or gatherings. Entertaining was one of her greatest joys, but it had to be in her own home.

What she had was an issue with leaving. That was her real fear. She loved people. She adored seeing old friends and neighbors, or welcoming new folks to Mystic Ridge. She invited people over regularly. He didn't see a social anxiety problem. He had Googled it. Something unusual plagued her. He was sure of it. She was mind-boggling, but everyone respected her fears and the boundaries she had put on herself.

They lived on the outskirts of Mystic Ridge at the base of a row of majestic smoky mountains, near the famous caverns. Archie knew his parents had met in the fourth grade, and that it had been love at first sight. Although they attended different colleges in different parts of Tennessee, they reunited after graduation and settled in Mystic Ridge.

The home they'd picked had a big yard with a splendid view. His dad, Donald, had even built a pond in the back yard and stocked it with goldfish. Poovie took a job writing for the *Mystic Gazette*, reporting on high school events, local elections, minor law infractions, and bake sales. It wasn't until her pregnancy with Vivian that her phobia began.

While at a high school football game, she'd fallen on the bleachers. Thankfully, Sister Crystal Grace had caught her. But Poovie had passed out cold. The ambulance took her directly to Smoky Valley Hospital.

She was unconscious for more than thirty minutes, and then awoke without remembering even going to the football game. The paramedics had been stumped. She only suffered a sprained ankle, and the baby was fine; but something in that experience had changed her forever. She built her life around her home and never leaving it. His dad had tried to understand it, and explain it, but he struggled.

They all tried to ease her fears and help her, but she would just smile and shrug it off. Poovie was the master of changing the topic of conversation, especially if it involved questions about her feelings. She gave no clues and refused professional help.

Everyone knew she hated to drive and hardly ever did. Only in times of complete necessity did she get behind the wheel of a car, and then she drove perfectly but cautiously. When Archie and Vivian had been younger, she'd always organized rides for them.

She repaid kindnesses with homemade desserts and homegrown flowers. Occasionally, she would accept rides with others to school plays or important functions, but she always looked uneasy and didn't seem to enjoy her outings. She wanted to stay in the comfort of her own home, and that was all right.

Poovie was unique in many ways. She never lost her temper. She professed her undying love for everyone in the family daily. She used her trademark words "be safe and stay sweet" all the time. She tried to make each day unique and exciting.

Sometimes, when they were kids, Archie and Vivian had to rise early and hunt for their school lunches. Instead of cartoons in the morning, they watched Elvis movies while she lectured them on the fascinating aspects of his personal life. She insisted being different was okay. And she marveled at Elvis's love for his mama.

Occasionally, she blew bubbles during breakfast. He'd never forget her allowing them to eat Oreos and milk. She insisted it was their little secret. Her playfulness was infectious. Those wondrous mornings would stay with him forever.

When the weather was nice, and her websites were updated, she would walk to the school and help out in the library or the nurse's office. Archie tried not to be annoyed when she would come by his classroom and blow him kisses. But it was impossible not to be irritated when she rode the school bus home with him. She definitely didn't have a fear of crowds. There was no tougher crowd than a bus full of hormonal teenagers.

As he got older, he noticed that she lived each day like it would be her last. He yearned to know what demons made her so afraid of the outside world.

One Christmas Poovie had spent the whole day crying. She just could not stop sobbing. Everyone tried to be cheerful, but it was impossible. She was inconsolable. By one o'clock in the afternoon, she had taken to her bed, overwhelmed with grief.

As he, his dad, and Vivian sat down to eat the meal Poovie had prepared, his dad soberly crossed his arms. He confided that, all those years ago when Poovie had passed out at the football game, she'd had a premonition—a vision of her future. She never shared what it was, but it had shaken her to the core. He said he'd told her over and over that it was nothing but anxiety, brought on by pregnancy and the fall. But she wasn't consoled, and whatever it was she'd seen had broken her heart. He said all they could do was love her.

Archie tried to understand. He actually yearned to be like his mother. Words could not express the admiration he had for her. He was editor of the school newspaper, and had to approve each article, Instagram and Facebook post, and Tweet. Poovie was immensely proud.

She wrote all the time. He thought about all the journals in the garage. When Vivian was born, Poovie began to write to her —notes and advice about life and love. She wrote about pride, trust, self-respect, love, relationships, war, drugs, Patsy Cline, the Beatles, Ronald Reagan, Princess Diana, Fleetwood Mac, and many other topics. She handed over the journals to her daughter two years ago when she'd graduated from high school. Vivian shared some of it with him. It would take his sister years to read them all. She had taken an entire box to college with her. Archie knew he had a huge stack coming his way on graduation day. He looked forward to his mother's wisdom.

As his father had read over the notes in the journals to Vivian, he'd marveled at Poovie's gift for humorous writing and pride in everyday life. He insisted she show her boss at the *Mystic Gazette* and "Saturday With Poovie Lamay" was born. No more interviews with spelling bee winners or details of Little League home runs.

The column was instantly popular, and eventually went into syndication; the list of its publication outlets grew and grew. Women everywhere could relate to Poovie's simple views; and for her, the greatest thing was that she never had to leave the house. The articles were emailed weekly.

She also read each one on her personal podcast. She thrived on social media. The public embraced her, and a star was born. She was successful, and Archie couldn't have been prouder.

Someday, he would get her the psychological help she needed. He longed to take her to the ocean and the towering metropolitan cities, and the desert. But mostly, he just wanted to protect her from whatever it was that made her so sad.

"That should do it, honey." She brought over the enormous wicker basket, two crimson roses poking out decoratively.

"You really didn't have to go to all that trouble."

"I know, I know," she said and waved a hand dismissively. "Hannah will enjoy it."

He took the heavy basket out of her hands. "I'm not gonna lie, Mom. I can't wait to eat it. Would you like to come along?"

"Oh, no, you two kids go enjoy the day. I have a lot to do around here. And I don't want to interfere."

"You wouldn't be interfering. You need some fresh air."

"I have fresh air right here in my own back yard." She brought her hands to her hips.

"Ooo-kay. I'll send you a pic when we get it all out."

She clapped her hands. "Oh, good, spread it out in a nice circle. I'll Tweet that." She lifted the cat and scratched her chin. "Picnic lunch photos are always popular."

He studied her. "What are you gonna do?"

"I need to rake a few leaves from the front porch, and I'm going to weed the garden a little bit. I need to tend to the pumpkins. They're looking solid and stout. Plus, I haven't spoken with your sister in four days. I've texted her a few times, and she hasn't replied. She hasn't updated her Facebook or Twitter accounts, either.

"I'm going to call her. I need to hear her voice. I know Fridays are busy. So, if I don't reach her today, I'm going to call nonstop in the morning." She pondered for a moment, snuggling Moon. "Also, your dad is going out of town tomorrow, so I want to spend the day around here readying his suit and packing for him. Even though it's a Saturday, he's gotta go."

Archie shrugged. "Okay, tell Vivian I said hello. That sorority keeps her pretty busy. I'll be home later, and thanks again for the chow." He stood up. "Oh, Hannah's family is going to Chattanooga tomorrow to visit the aquarium. Is it okay if I go along? They're leaving super early."

"Of course—such unique marine life. I looked at it online. Superb."

"You can come."

"Oh, no. After your father leaves, I was thinking about starting an article titled 'The Popcorn and Fudge Existence.' I think I'll churn it out. It's been bouncing around in my brain for a few days now." She put the cat down, crossed the room and hugged him. "Don't keep Hannah waiting."

He embraced her. "I love you, Mom."

Her shoulders began to quiver. "Archie, I love you so much, so very much. You never forget that." She leaned back and began to straighten his collar. "You look very handsome, mister newspaper editor. Now get. Drive careful. I'll see you tonight. Be safe and stay sweet."

"I will, Mom." He kissed her cheek and left.

❧❧

Eve grabbed Dolly's arm. "Oh, my God, come here right now."

Dolly put the plate of biscuits back underneath the warmer. "Sweet Jesus, what is your problem, girl?"

Eve dragged her to the back of the diner, tears cascading down her cheeks.

Dolly was beginning to panic. "What happened?"

Eve pointed to a booth. "Sit down."

"It's Sunday morning. I missed church, and I've got sinners to serve."

Eve shot her the well-practiced evil glare, then wiped her face with the back of her palm.

Dolly sat.

Eve inhaled then exhaled slowly. "Listen to this. It's on the front page. *Beloved Poovie Lamay Dies in Devastating Car Accident.*"

Dolly gasped and placed her palms on her chest. "No."

Eve cried openly, and they sat in silence for several seconds. She situated the paper in front of her, obviously trying to steady her trembling hands. She wiped her eyes again and read in a broken voice:

"Beloved writer Poovie Lamay was pronounced dead upon arrival at the Knoxville General Hospital late last night. While driving from Mystic Ridge to Knoxville she lost control of her vehicle and plummeted into a ravine. She was killed instantly. Poovie Lamay was a well-loved member of the *Mystic Gazette* staff. Her weekly column has delighted women of all ages, all over the world. She will be greatly missed!'"

Eve picked up a napkin and dabbed her wet cheeks. Dolly's eyes were closed, her elbows firmly planted on the table, her head resting limply in her hands.

Eve put the napkin down and read the rest to herself.

"Tell me," Dolly pleaded.

"Apparently, she had been on her way to see her daughter, a student at University of Tennessee. who was holed up in the school infirmary for dehydration. She'd had a terrible case of the flu. Poor child couldn't keep anything down. She was afraid to tell her mama, because she didn't want to upset her. But Poovie kept calling and found out she was feeling poorly. Well, Poovie jumped in her car and headed to Knoxville."

"I thought she didn't go out," Dolly cried.

"I know," Eve agreed, and then continued. "'The accident occurred just ten minutes away from the school infirmary.' Oh, that sweet mama never made it to see her baby."

"What about Vivian?"

"Oh, she's feeling physically fine today. But she lost her mama, so she's emotionally devastated." Eve sobbed openly. "That poor family."

Dolly grabbed the paper and began meticulously reading. "'Mrs. Lamay is survived by her loving husband Donald, her daughter Vivian and me, her son Archie.'" She gazed up. "Oh, sweet Jesus, her son wrote this article."

Eve wailed even louder, and several of the diner's customers turned to see what was happening. Dolly squared her shoulders and continued.

"Listen to this. 'My mother taught me about Oreos, blessings, kisses, bubbles, picnics, gardens, writing and so many other paths to happiness. But most of all, she taught me how to express love and to relish every moment of my life. She will be forever in my heart. As my mom always said, 'Be sweet and stay safe'. A candlelight vigil will be held at Crystal Caverns Park today at one p.m. Archie Lamay."

Dolly scrambled out of the booth and slid in beside Eve. The women embraced. Eve dropped the paper on the table as Dolly hugged her, their bodies slumped in despair, and squeezed her tightly as her tears soaked Dolly's shoulder. Dolly's tears streamed down the front of Eve's yellow apron.

"I can't believe it. I just can't," Dolly sobbed.

Eve squared Dolly's shoulders. "Do you think Poovie knew she was going to die? Do you think maybe that was the reason she never went out?"

Dolly wiped her face with a napkin. "I doubt it. How would anyone know that?"

"This *is* Mystic Ridge," Eve whispered.

They heard footsteps, and looked up to see Tyrone staring at them. With tear-filled eyes and wet cheeks, still holding each other, they mustered their best evil glares. Silence loomed. He took in the emotional scene but didn't speak. The commotion in the diner seemed to cease. He took a step back, exhaled, and quickly scampered away.

"We've mastered it. We have," Dolly gulped as tears glistened on her face. "Thanks to Poovie."

Eve faced her. "Let's go to the vigil. It's only eleven. We can still make it."

"What? Look at us? We can't go like this." Dolly motioned to her jelly-covered sleeve.

"You said you always wanted to hang out with her. Well, she'll be there in spirit, soaring above everyone. She's a real angel now. She wouldn't miss this. It's our last chance. And I do declare, she'll appreciate two hardworking women like us being there, even if we're forced to come as we are. Why, I'll bet the place will be flooded with women like us. She'd love that."

Dolly stood up. "When you're right, you're right. We've got to go. Think of how many times she made us laugh, even when we were exhausted. She made me feel...worthy and proud. She was one of a kind. People like Poovie don't come along every day. We owe it to her."

"Yes, we do," Eve agreed. "She was a rock star."

The two women rushed through the diner, handing their unfinished meal checks to other waitresses and gathering their jackets. When Tyrone approached them, a questioning frown etched on his face, they pressed their lips together tightly.

Dolly spoke up. "Don't even start with us, mister. We've got an emergency. We have to pay our respects, even if we do look like haggard waitresses. We're outta here."

"But..." he stammered.

Eve placed her arm through Dolly's as they headed toward the door. "Be safe and stay sweet."

# PSYCHIC SECRETS

D AISY HELD HER TINY MIRROR FIRMLY AND INSPECTED HER purple lip gloss. "Does this color look okay on me, or is it too trendy?"

Tilly squinted for close inspection. "Girlfriend, that color is radical. I saw it on TikTok. It was trending, fo' sho'." She stroked the dozens of tiny braids that hung loosely in her long hair. "This isn't too many, is it?"

"No way, girl. Adore," Daisy drawled, and then leaned toward the front seat. "Mom, are we almost to Nashville?"

"Yep, the Tennessee State Fairgrounds are just ahead."

The teenagers shrieked in unison. Mariah jolted in her seat yet kept the car steadily between the yellow lines. She'd enjoyed listening to the enthusiastic girls for the past hour. They spoke pretty candidly about boys and Smoky Valley Middle School and their girl squad. They were a total riot. She couldn't help but grin. Oh, to be young again.

She was so glad Daisy had adjusted so quickly; they'd only moved to Mystic Ridge a couple of months ago. Their transfer from Brown Mountain, North Carolina, had been rather sudden. One week her husband Stuart was plotting locations for new strip retail stores, the next he was in charge of finding a location and renting out the spaces in Tennessee, near Mystic Ridge Mall.

Their home in Brown Mountain sold in days. It was all a whirlwind of changes in a minute of time. Thankfully, Daisy had settled right in. But a pang of sadness filled Mariah. She missed her friends, neighbors, and her job. Her new neighbors had been quite welcoming, showering her with banana bread, chicken casseroles, and some incredible wrinkle cream, but it wasn't home.

Claire O'Donnell seemed super-thoughtful, and had told her all about the fair. Claire had insisted she come and try some of the state's best pies and meet some of the residents of Mystic Ridge. Although she was eager, Mariah was also nervous. Making new friends as a grown woman wasn't that easy.

She had lifelong pals and close confidants, but she'd always kept her personal life private. She'd adored Brown Mountain. It had an otherworldly ambiance, with those unexplainable dancing lights in the night sky. True, Mystic Ridge had a real paranormal reputation to go with its rolling smoky mountains and low opaque clouds.

She felt like she was caught up in a tornado, like a force was directing her path—a force she could not decipher, a force more powerful than herself. The universe was changing her path. Someone or something had tampered with her calm, stable existence.

Uncertainty was not something she liked. Truthfully, she feared change. She knew she had special skills she wasn't using. That she was capable of more. But she'd always been leery of taking chances. What if people found out she was different? She hid in the safeness of everyday life.

She admired Daisy. Her daughter embraced newness with gleeful anticipation. At fourteen years old, she was fearless. She wanted to experience everything life had to offer. To her, each day was a new adventure. She said she had FOMO—fear of missing out. Mariah chuckled to herself. They needed an in-depth mother-daughter discussion very soon.

"Let's do a selfie," Tilly gushed. "Come close."

"Okay, cheeeeese," the girls said in unison.

"Oh, we look lit," Tilly said a moment later.

"I know, right? I'm gonna pull up my Facebook and check us in at the fair." Daisy giggled.

Mariah was pleased but conflicted. Daisy and Tilly were BFFs already. She was glad for Daisy, but a tad lonely. Daisy was sharing all her hopes and dreams with someone else. They didn't talk like they'd used to. Now, Tilly got the lowdown.

Daisy texted her new friend constantly and was obsessed with social media. Her voice even had a new Southern twang. It was humorous. But Mariah knew these years had been pivotal in her own life. She desperately wanted to be there for Daisy and remain close. A BFF could never replace the years of knowledge a mother possessed, although friendship, too, was a natural thing.

Her brows creased, and the butterflies in her stomach churned. Her mother's intuition was on high alert. Something was going on with Daisy, something even Tilly didn't know.

"Last year all the boys from Mystic High were here," Tilly gushed.

"Really? Daisy cooed. "High school boys?"

"Yeah, so keep that lip gloss handy."

High school boys? Mariah suddenly questioned this trip. Maybe it was a bad idea. Her hands began sweating on the steering wheel.

Just ahead, an enormous magenta glow lit up the dark sky, and the girls squealed. She exited the highway cautiously. As they neared, she could see the towering Ferris wheel and several monstrous roller coasters. It was a wild spectacle.

"We have to do the Mega Drop and the Tilt-a-Whirl," Tilly insisted. "Have you met Jason Barnes? He's a junior. He works at The Pet Palooza in Mystic Mall. He lives on a big farm. His parents bring pigs every year. I hope he's here. He's straight fire."

"I don't think I know him. Oh, look, a funhouse. We must do that," Daisy yelped.

Mariah pulled into the gravel parking lot, paid the fee, and inched carefully to a parking spot. The trio slid out of the car and took in the sight before them. The aromas of popcorn, French fries, and barnyard animals enveloped them. Mariah felt nervous. The sun was almost set, and the expansive carnival gave off a glow of intense hues. Hundreds of people moved in all directions.

A woman's voice pierced the air. "Wait! Stop! Wait!" she screamed.

A small blond preschool-aged girl wearing a red-checked dress and pink cowboy boots appeared. She threw her arms around Mariah's waist, hugging her tightly.

"I'm Ruby," she squeaked. Then, she urgently moved to Daisy and embraced her as well. "I'm Ruby. I'm soooooooo happy to finally see you."

A woman gasping for breath was close behind. "Holy crap, kiddo. That is bad, very bad. You cannot just run off, and you cannot attack perfect strangers."

Daisy knelt. "It's okay. She's so cute."

"Whatever," Tilly muttered.

The woman held her hand out to Mariah. "Please, excuse my rambunctious daughter. I'm Virginia. This crazy cowgirl is Ruby. We were just leaving, and I think the cotton candy and corn dogs have gotten to her."

Mariah laughed out loud. "It's so nice to meet you. I'm Mariah, and this is my daughter Daisy and her friend Tilly. We're new here. Well, me and Daisy are new to the Mystic Ridge area."

Virginia cocked her head sideways. "We're from Mystic Ridge, too. My little carnival clown must have seen you two somewhere."

"Maybe," Daisy said, obviously still enjoying the girl attached to her leg.

Virginia pried her off. "We've got to get you home and into a tub."

Ruby released Daisy with a pout, and then her expression turned hopeful. "Can you babysit me?"

"Yeah, that'd be cool," Daisy agreed.

Virginia took out her phone and got Daisy's number. Mariah studied the small girl as she fidgeted with her arm full of pink bracelets and licked the sugar stuck on her lips. She had a slight ivory glow around her entire body, like an angel. It was beautiful. Was she the only one who saw it?

Ruby hugged her again, and she felt deeply connected to the child, like they somehow had something in common. She watched as Ruby hugged Daisy again, completely ignoring Tilly. Interesting.

Their new acquaintances said goodby and disappeared into the crowded parking lot, Virginia still struggling to hold on to her exuberant child.

"I like her," Daisy said.

"Let's get a groove on," Tilly insisted.

Mariah met Daisy's eyes, and questions lingered between them. Daisy's expression was astonished and confused all at the same time. Had she seen the glow, too?

Daisy chewed her lower lip for a second, then turned to Tilly. "Yeah, let's hit it."

Mariah rolled her eyes and followed the girls. They paid admission and went through the congested entrance.

"Wait. Don't run off yet," Mariah said. "Whatever y'all do, stay together. If you get separated, meet at the baking tent. I'll be there the whole evening. I'll keep my phone handy. Make sure your purses are zipped up and across your bodies. Don't talk to strangers."

They both nodded grudgingly.

"We will meet here at nine o'clock. Not one second later."

They nodded again.

Mariah held her hands up, and they bolted away. Abruptly, she felt worried about Daisy. A part of her wanted to follow them, but teenagers needed a degree of privacy and a show of trust. She just couldn't get a read on Daisy. It was like she had plans she was not sharing. It felt like she was keeping secrets, big secrets. How was she going to mother this new, fearless, unpredictable daughter of hers? *I am a hot mess.* She caressed her belly. Maybe some pie would help.

❧❧

Daisy gasped for air and encouraged Tilly to slow her pace through the crowds. The rollercoasters had been awesome.

She took a deep breath, reveling in the multitude of unusual scents that surrounded her. As people bumped into her and brushed against her elbows and swept against her shoulders and arms, she felt their joy, their excitement, and their pain. It consumed her, and left her dizzy and overwhelmed and exhilarated all at the same time. Daisy knew something unusual was happening to her, a new intuition or maybe a superpower. She wasn't sure.

"Let's do the Tornado again," Tilly shrieked.

"Maybe the Mega Drop one more time," Daisy suggested.

Tilly laughed. "Oh, hell, yeah."

Daisy grabbed a pinch of Tilly's cotton candy. "That was wicked funny that Jason's pig won first prize. It was a hefty thing. It was great seeing so many kids from school."

"Everyone was checking out the new girl. You are badass."

"I wouldn't say that."

Tilly tilted her head sideways. "You might as well enjoy it. They won't be curious forever. I'm not gonna lie, your fascination with quilts and embroidery does concern me."

"That shit is hard to do," Daisy insisted. "I can appreciate the time and expertise it takes to make those things."

"It would ruin your reputation if the world knew you were obsessed with that crap. Let's get back to some bitchin' stuff, maybe the Fireball coaster."

"Ugg," Daisy groaned. "My stomach is still in the clouds."

Tilly wound her arm through Daisy's, and they walked for a few minutes. Daisy adored the dizzying music and flashing lights. A jubilant feeling coursed through her. Since moving to Mystic Ridge, she had felt weirdly at home, like she belonged there.

"We could get a psychic reading," Tilly said.

Daisy was pleased her suggestive power had worked so perfectly. "Yeah, let's do that. I'd like for that funnel cake to actually stay in my stomach."

"There's one." Tilly pointed to a brown tent with a flashing yellow sign that read "Your Future From Fiona."

Daisy studied it. "No. It looks lame." As Tilly groaned, they walked a little further. Finally, she spotted the one she'd been seeking. "Look at that."

She pointed. A black-and-purple tent with a burgundy awning and red scrollwork lattice loomed before them. She read the sign in front of it out loud. "'Simza, Psychic Readings, Fascinating Fortunes. Ten dollars.'"

"Ten bucks!" Tilly spouted. "Oh, hell, no."

Daisy faced her. "Listen, I'm just getting my bearings here in Tennessee. I need a reading. Who knows what my future holds? Honestly, you need to untangle that hair mess before anyone from school sees you—hashtag crazy do."

"What?" Tilly pulled out her phone, reversed the camera and gazed at her reflection. "Oh, my God. It's a shit show."

"Yeah, it's wrecked." She pointed to an ice cream-covered picnic table. "Sit down, work on that disaster, and I'll be done in a few."

Tilly was panicked. "Holy crap, I hope no one saw me."

Daisy guided her over to the table. "Sit, calm the threads. I'll be quick. I promise."

As Tilly slowly sat and began tugging at her braids, Daisy took a deep breath and walked toward the ominous entrance. The scent of cherries and tobacco reached out to her as she neared. It looked spooky. For the first time in her fourteen years, she felt independent and brave.

When she reached the silky red sheet that sufficed as a door, a towering, dark-skinned wall of a man came out. He gazed down at her and crossed his muscled arms. He wore indigo satin pants and a crimson-and-gold vest. He was no stranger to working out.

"Ten dollars," he grumbled.

"The others are way cheaper," she said, reaching in her purse.

He didn't answer.

She handed him the bill. "Is she legit?"

He placed a fist on his chest. "Simza sees all, knows all. Wait here."

Daisy felt her heart thundering in her chest. If he was meant to be intimidating, he was rockin' it. He made all of her thoughts run together. Rubbing her forehead, she contemplated leaving. No, she had to put on her big-girl panties. She couldn't deny the things she knew the way her mother did. What a coward.

Suddenly, the silky sheet moved to the side. She slowly stepped into a dark room. The bold cherry scent was a bit nauseating. The floor was a combination of dirt and sawdust. A black cat sat unmoving in the corner, its unblinking purple eyes fixed on her. Was it even real?

The sides of the tent were lit by a soothing aquamarine lamp. It almost seemed like they were moving, like waves on the ocean. It was dizzying. There were twinkling stars on the ceiling and illuminated crystals hanging everywhere. It was pretty in a gaudy, trashy way. She was impressed. Kudos for the digs. Maybe she would tell fortunes one day.

She spotted a crystal ball on a small table. There were two wooden chairs, so she sat down.

All the lights went out. WTF. She listened as something rustled. Suddenly, the lights came back on, and a woman was sitting across from her. Daisy gasped. The woman smiled, enjoying her surprise. Her teeth were covered by a gold grill, gleaming in the soft glow of the lamp. Her eyes were the exact same violet as the cat's. She wore long robes in colors that matched the ones of the giant dude at the door. Blond hair with black roots peaked out from beneath her ornate headscarf. Hoop earrings dangled from her ears, and rings decorated every one of her fingers.

Her right eyebrow rose a fraction "What may Simza do for you?"

Daisy shrugged. "Just my future, I guess. Will I ever graduate from middle school?"

Simza waved her hands over the crystal ball, and an emerald hue lit up the tiny sphere. She hummed and swayed from side to side. "Simza sees that you are very smart, and that you do well in schooling." She mumbled unfamiliar words. "Simza sees that you have a special boy in your life. You and he will marry and have five children. You will travel great distances and explore endless continents."

"Stop right there, Gypsy Rose Lee." Daisy stood. "Five children? I don't think so. I have no stomach for diapers. And you obviously didn't see my last report card. I'm totally unfocused. I don't have a boyfriend. I puke like a frat boy when I fly in airplanes. You are nothing but a big fat fake." She brought her hands to her hips. "And, full disclosure, you charge way too much, more than nachos."

Simza rolled her eyes. "The great Simza has spoken. No refunds."

"What about your son, vagabond woman.? Do you see him, too?" Daisy spat.

"I have no son," Simza growled, grinding her ornate teeth together.

Daisy placed her palms on the table and leaned forward. "Oh, yes, you do. You left Rahul with your sister in Sarasota over ten years ago. He's been calling me telepathically. He needs help."

Simza gasped and grabbed her throat.

Daisy crossed her arms and smirked. "Own it, old woman."

≋≋

Mariah had tasted samples of pumpkin pies, banana cream pies, chocolate pies, peach pies, and apple pies. She'd never, ever been so full. Claire O'Donnell had introduced her to so many residents of Mystic Ridge she couldn't possibly remember one name. As the pie judging began, she found a wicker chair and sat down. Unexpectedly, she was having a lot of fun.

She noticed a couple of nuns across the room; a tall nun pushed an elderly one in a wheelchair. They greeted everyone they passed. They looked a little out-of-place in their long black robes, white scapulars and black veils, especially amidst all the red flannel and floral prints. But they seemed to be quite popular—everyone went out of their way to speak to them.

They neared her and when they stopped right in front of her, Mariah grinned nervously.

"Hello."

"Good evening," the tall nun said. "I am Sister Mary Jean Stevenson, and this is Sister Crystal Grace."

"Nice to meet you," Mariah replied and started to stand.

Sister Crystal Grace motioned for her to stay seated. "Please, relax."

Suddenly, Sister Mary Jean's phone began to ring. She reached into her pocket. "I'm so sorry. It's Father Harrison. Do forgive me. I'll just be a second." She walked several yards away.

Sister Crystal Grace flashed a tired smile. "Thank you for coming."

"I love me some pie," Mariah joked.

"No. I want to thank you for coming to Mystic Ridge; you are an answer to my prayers. Honestly. Bless you." She spoke urgently, worriedly. Her eyes were compassionate and sincere and somehow familiar. It was as if Mariah had seen those eyes her uneasy.

Sister Crystal Grace reached out and took her hand. The world seemed to spin around her until she finally focused on the face before her. She gazed into those emerald eyes as a queer feeling consumed her. It seemed like she was lifting off her seat, hovering weightlessly.

She felt her mind pour into Sister Crystal Grace's. It was as if she became a liquid and drained into the nun. She floated into another dimension altogether, and her chin slowly lowered as her eyes fluttered and closed.

She saw Sister Crystal Grace—really *saw* her. At first, she was a baby being cuddled by her mother in an old rustic farmhouse, warm and content. Then, she was a toddler, running through fields of wheat, laughing with each step. Suddenly, she was a bold young girl with tousled golden hair, climbing up a steep mountainside and entering a black fissure into a deep cavern. She saw her face distorted in terror as she fell into a dark, endless hole. She gasped.

But then the sun was illuminating her young face, and she appeared thriving and jubilant.

There were flashes of her in different times, once wearing a poodle skirt with her hair in a ponytail, and then in Egyptian robes with sashes of gold and silver. She saw her in a long dress with a huge hat and a cameo at the base of her neck as she sang and played the piano. She saw her waving her hands in the air, her long hair adorned by flowers as she danced amongst thousands of young people. The places and times flashed so quickly it was impossible for Mariah to keep up.

As the visions slowed, Sister Crystal Grace appeared lying motionless in a bed as several nuns applied compresses to her head. Finally, Mariah saw her as a contented young woman embracing others and holding her hands up to the heavens.

The scenes played over and over in her mind, faster and faster. The chronological order became jumbled and out of sync. The world spun around her.

None of it made any sense. It was always the same face, and always the same sympathetic smile, but the lines on the face clearly morphed from old to young and back again.

After what seemed like an eternity, Mariah felt her body jolt. As her eyes opened, the visions ceased. Sister Crystal Grace touched her cheek.

Mariah lifted her head and felt she would vomit. Sister Crystal Grace caressed Mariah's hand urgently, her expression hopeful.

Mariah's stomach slowly settled.

"You understand, don't you?" Sister Crystal Grace asked.

Mariah was mortified, mostly because she *did* understand. She understood the incomprehensible. Sister Crystal Grace was a time traveler. There were circumstances in the world she had never dared to admit, even though she had the gift of seeing them. She'd never acknowledged the things she had suspected.

"I don't know what to say."

"Say we can be friends," Sister Crystal Grace countered. "I need a confidant and a real friend. And you, my love, have sight. You were born with it, but I stumbled upon it." She squeezed her eyes tightly shut. "I was so brave and adventurous. I wanted to be a queen and a politician, an actress, and a free spirit. I wanted to do it all, and I have. But I've learned that it's not all about me. It's about helping others. I can give back. I've done my best, but there are limits."

Her eyes opened with an urgent seriousness. "I can't always change things. Only small things are possible—big world changes are out of my realm, and probably yours as well." She exhaled. "Now I am old, so old, and much more fearful. Mystic Ridge needs you. *I* need you. I have much to teach you, sweet darling."

Mariah stared at the nun. Although she was slumped in the wheelchair, she didn't really look a day over forty. Her skin was smooth, and her eyes bright.

Mariah was perplexed by so many of the things she'd said. She'd come to realize the world wasn't always as it seemed, but this was more than she had ever expected. Words were difficult.

"I only see things, crazy things sometimes. I have a little power of suggestion. But I don't leave my present circumstances. I can't travel through time." Her shoulders rose. "And I'm not Catholic," she confessed, chewing her lower lip. "I'm agnostic at present."

A slow smile spread across Sister Crystal Grace's face. "Then I shall have to love you all the more." She paused as the winner of the pie contest was announced, and the room erupted in applause. "I must confess something as well. I need a monumental favor from you and your daughter. Your girl Daisy, she's special, too. Right?"

Mariah's whole body trembled at the thought of involving her daughter. She wanted to protect her from the unexplainable and the supernatural.

Sister Crystal Grace seemed to read her mind. She touched her cheek softly. "She's already been testing her limits, significantly more than you have."

"Oh, no!" Mariah's eyes filled with panic. "We've never discussed things such as this."

"You must. Don't let her be confused. I just want to help you —both of you." A lone tear drifted down her cheek. "I never meant to frighten you. Forgive me. I see you are more tender-hearted than I'd expected. Please trust me. I know it's difficult."

All Mariah could do was nod. Sister Crystal Grace leaned forward and hugged her, and a joyful cocoon of euphoria enveloped her. She exhaled, calmly.

"Come see me at the convent as soon as you can. It's so very urgent. I need you desperately. I have a..." She paused. "...situation. You must bring Daisy."

Sister Mary Jean rushed to them. "Y'all, I am so sorry. Father Harrison went on and on about getting the carpets cleaned in the foyer before Sunday." She wiped her brow. "He went on and on. I don't know anything about carpet cleaning."

Mariah exhaled and slumped in her chair, feeling as if she had just stepped off a rollercoaster.

Sister Crystal Grace's green eyes became hooded as a troubled look overtook her features. The upward tilt of her lips suddenly turned downward. She released Mariah's hands.

"We have much more to discuss, but you should go, quickly. The future of your family is at stake. Daisy is playing with fire, you must hurry. Find her."

❧ ❧

Daisy paced around the tent, continuing her assault on a bewildered Simza. "You never loved Rahul. He was just an inconvenience, standing in your way, blocking your selfish path. You treated him like garbage. You told your sister you'd be back to get him. Big fat liar," she shouted.

"No. No," Simza cried. "I wanted to keep him. But I was a dancer, and I had auditions. I was traveling from city to city."

Daisy pressed her lips tightly. "It's all about you, right? Who cares about a small boy forced to tend to an old woman riddled with cancer? That's not okay."

"Cancer?"

"You knew something wasn't right with your sister, but did you keep in touch? No! Lame! She's been ill for years, and poor Rahul has been caring for her day and night. He's a terrific kid who's been living in a horror show."

Simza trembled.

"Well, spoiler alert, she's dead. He's twelve and homeless now. Way to go, psychic extraordinaire." She waved her arms wildly, enjoying the revelation.

Suddenly, Simza pulled a gun out from beneath the table and pointed it at her; her hands shook wildly. "You are a sorceress. The devil has sent you. You taunt me with lies."

Daisy didn't respond. Crap. Maybe she had gotten a little carried away. She slowly began to inch toward the doorway.

The gun hung unsteadily in the woman's hands. "Go away, Judas. Leave me be. Take your evil visions and disappear. I curse you and your family."

Now Daisy was angry. "Blah, blah, blah, big fat fakers can't curse anyone."

Simza lifted the gun higher. The perspiration on her hands glistened in the odd neon lighting.

"Oh, but I can," she growled, and began chanting in an ancient language as her eyelids fluttered wildly.

The air in the room began to move in a circular motion. Daisy's hair blew upward as did Simza's. The black cat let out a pained shriek. Simza moaned yet appeared distracted. Daisy knew it was her chance. Even if the hag couldn't tell fortunes, she might be able to affix a curse.

Abruptly, she felt a large hand on her shoulder. She turned to see the tall, muscled man. He pulled her swiftly through the red silky doorway and put himself between her and the curtain. She drew in a sharp breath and was startled to find his onyx eyes glazed over with moisture. He steadied her on her feet and released her.

"Thank you." He bowed in her direction. "I will find my son. I will leave Simza this night. She told me her sister stole him and disappeared with him. I have been searching for many years."

Daisy straightened her purse and smoothed her hair. "That woman is bat-shit crazy." She regained her composure.

"Don't underestimate her. She is dangerous."

"Well, I'm not afraid. Listen, Rahul is a great dude, but if you don't find him soon, he'll have to start stealing to survive. He's gifted, like me. He's living near the ocean in an alley between a pizza place and an arcade. There's also a bicycle shop." She concentrated for a few quiet seconds. "Google 'Palm Street Wheels'. I think that will get you the closest."

His lips trembled. "You are not a demon. You are a prophet sent to me by the heavens above. I am Ramir, and I am forever in your debt." He bowed his head.

She chuckled. "I dunno about all that. He's a good kid, though."

He handed her ten dollars back, and then an extra ten. "You gave me my future."

"Cool. Thanks, dude. Good luck." She turned, delighted with what had transpired, a new feeling of pride within her.

*He's coming, Rahul, hold on a little longer.*

Feeling very pleased with herself, Daisy began walking toward Tilly, who was still at the picnic table wrestling with her messy hair. Just as she started to laugh, she noticed her mother across the sawdust path, leaning against a livestock sign, her arms crossed, a thin smile etched across her face. Shit.

Warily, Daisy approached. "What's up? Is it nine o'clock?"

"Almost." Mariah exhaled and uncrossed her arms. "That went pretty well, but I hope you realize that interfering in other people's problems can be quite risky."

Daisy felt her body break out in a sweat.

"Did you like my vertical windstorm?" Mariah chuckled and pulled her into an embrace. "Oh, Daisy. I'm proud that you chose to listen to Rahul and to help him. But we must be very, very cautious. That woman is vicious."

Leaning back, Daisy inspected her curiously. "Whaaaaaaaat?"

Mariah giggled softly. "Like I said—much respect, but a mother-daughter talk is long overdue."

Daisy chewed on her lower lip. "A windstorm. Truly cool, kudos. I'm so impressed." The side of her lip rose a fraction. "Is that curse crap anything to worry about?"

Mariah shrugged. "I don't think so," but as she said the words, she had a vision of a young boy cuddled up on her couch as she wept nearby, a purple-eyed black cat peering in the window. Her heart seemed to skip a beat. A loud bell clanged, and the vision was gone.

"Mom?" Daisy said worriedly. "Did you see something?"

Mariah hugged her again. "We need to be careful. It's all so complicated. The good news is that I met someone tonight, someone unique, who's going to help us. She also said she wants us to help *her*."

"Do what?" Daisy asked.

"No idea, but she was genuine. She was simply astounding—and a nun."

"A what?"

"Yep, a time-traveling nun." She nodded.

Daisy's mouth opened wide. "Legit."

Mariah chuckled. "Daisy. I have a lot to tell you. We have a lot to tell each other. It's imperative. I don't want any more secrets between us. None! Lives and futures could be at stake. No more secrets?"

Daisy's eyes lit up. "Okay, Mom. No more secrets!"

# FINDING JOY

**L**ORAINE SAT DOWN HEAVILY IN THE UNCOMFORTABLE WOOD-en kitchen chair as its legs wobbled beneath her. The table needed sanding or painting or something. It looked awful. She stared into her mug. As she lifted the full cup of coffee to her lips, she knew what the results would be, and it was just as she had expected—freezing. She couldn't even enjoy a cup of coffee anymore. And she hadn't had a hazelnut latte in more than a year! Absurd!

Suddenly, the baby in her lap began fussing. She moved him to her shoulder and patted him gently on the back.

"Shhhhhhhh, sweet Brooks. Daddy's still asleep." He made a few more gurgling sounds then nestled his head beneath her chin and settled down. She closed her eyes, relishing the feel of him and loving him more than she'd ever thought possible.

Her pregnancy had been a surprise, but such a welcome blessing. In truth, she'd never even imagined being a mother, playing pat-a-cake and washing bibs. When she'd completed law school, she assumed she would work at her father's firm, obsessed with her career. But she wasn't obsessed with it at all. She dreaded practicing law, and picturing that scenario now was even more difficult.

Years of listening to her mother Lucinda telling her exactly how to live, what to do, and how to feel had taken its toll—she'd been diagnosed as clinically depressed when she graduated from high school. But truthfully, Loraine knew she had been depressed long before that. Simple decisions were difficult. Lucinda's constant insults and the complete manipulation of everything she did left Loraine emotionally stunted and incapable of trusting her instincts. The judging and critiquing had left her defeated and afraid to think for herself. She'd been broken.

Her father Simon had tried to be loving and understanding, but he'd failed as well. He was depressed himself. She didn't blame him. Years of therapy should have convinced her it was not her fault, and that she was a victim. But she still heard her mother's voice beating down her every idea and thought. No amount of medication or affirmation could make it go away.

She exhaled and kissed Brooks's soft cheek. After years of struggling with the depression, she'd thought breaking away from her mother and starting a family of her own was the answer. She'd assumed this baby would set her free from her feelings of hopelessness. But little Brooks was here, and the depression continued. Why? Why couldn't she silence her mother's awful voice? Why couldn't she just be happy? Why did she feel joyless? The doctors said it was postpartum depression. She knew better.

Cradling the baby in her arms, she opened the refrigerator. There was nothing but eggs, cheese, coffee creamer, condiments, and baby formula. Good wives and mothers kept a full refrigerator, with cookie dough, vegetables, and ice cream. She sat back down with a thud.

Looking out the kitchen window, she noticed the glow of the sun rising. A part of her wanted to go outside and take it in, but she felt so tired. The huge stack of bar exam study notes loomed before her. It had been two years since she had graduated from Harvard Law School, and she still hadn't taken the bar exam. What was her problem?

Philo had passed it right after graduation, but she couldn't bring herself to even attempt it. She'd studied and studied, and had even googled times and places to take it; but so far, she hadn't made an appointment. It terrified her. What if she failed? What if she passed?

She closed her eyes, remembering all the effort she'd put into that damn degree. When she had been accepted at Harvard, she'd expected her mother to be thrilled and proud, and she was—for five minutes. But then a whole new set of rants began, mostly about the cost of tuition, boarding, books, meal plans. Loraine pasted on a happy expression for the world to see when inside she was melting like the Wicked Witch in Oz.

Faking happiness while melting inside weighed on her. When she got to college, she'd reveled in her solitude and freedom, thankful there was no one she had to impress day after day. But as soon as quietness surrounded her, negative thoughts crept into her mind. She started finding fault with everything. She questioned her own decisions to an unhealthy level and obsessed over tiny failures. She threw herself into a world of lectures, notes, debates, trials, exams, and papers.

Loraine opened her eyes and took a deep breath. She'd contemplated suicide, or disappearing into the famous caverns, or jumping on a flight to Morocco or Bolivia. Instead, she found counselors at the student services department and began weekly sessions. It saved her life and gave her strength. Some weeks she went three or four times. If felt good, voicing her darkest thoughts and troubled upbringing.

She wanted to walk away from law school, but her mother had bitched and moaned so much about the cost and the burden of the tuition that she persevered and graduated with a superb grade-point average. The warm summer day she walked across the stage and received her diploma, she knew something was not right. Her path was all wrong.

Brooks made a small snorting sound, and she knew he was asleep. She rose and took him to the nursery. It was still unpainted and undecorated. The crib bedding was splendid, with baby animals and Noah's ark caricatures. Her father had picked it out. He tried to be kind now, but a part of her wondered if it was just too little, too late. It was hard to take him seriously.

She exhaled loudly. She'd meant to add animals and vines to the walls, but all she had done for the past nine months was study for the bar exam. The room was still painted an ugly off-white.

She laid Brooks down carefully and covered him with a blue cotton blanket. He deserved a lovely room. He deserved a mommy who took the time to embellish his surroundings, not a woman who stared at lecture notes and studied books all day. He deserved more. She was failing as a mother.

As a tear cascaded down her cheek, she returned to the kitchen and stood frozen for several seconds. The enormous pile of books and notes loomed before her like a bomb—ready to blow her mind and her complete existence.

She dumped her coffee out and started a fresh pot for Philo. How on earth had she found such a wonderful man? She'd seen him often in the campus library, and then one afternoon he invited her for coffee. It had been love at first sight for both of them. Just after graduation, he presented her with a tiny engagement ring. For the first time in a long time, she felt hopeful. They traveled to Mystic Ridge for family introductions. He marveled at the gorgeous mountain views.

Loraine knew Lucinda would be difficult. When she introduced them, Lucinda didn't hold back her disdain. She riddled them with comments about the differences in their families and backgrounds and their aspirations. None of which made any sense. She'd pointed out Loraine's shortcomings, completely humiliating her. She forbade them from even dating, ignoring the engagement ring. Simon had been a silent bystander. Philo was floored by their rudeness.

After the terrible meeting, they drove directly to Florida for Loraine to meet Philo's family. They welcomed her with open arms and threw together a whimsical beach wedding in no time. She and Philo were married the next week. She was eternally grateful to his family for pulling it off so brilliantly. They were lovely people, and she felt blessed to be part of their family now.

Right after the wedding, Loraine felt bold, carefree, and proud; but within weeks she was again plagued by self-doubt and unworthiness. Philo understood fully and insisted she get back into therapy, which she did. But therapy hadn't helped. It explained her pain, but it did not heal her. She longed for healing.

They moved to Mystic Ridge after Philo passed the bar. He prayed she would find some kind of belonging there. He commuted to his new job in Chattanooga.

She felt disheveled and remiss. She couldn't complete anything. Every task she started sat unfinished. Her heart wasn't in anything. She floundered for a year at different jobs in the local courthouse.

When she became pregnant it was a relief. They were both ecstatic. Yet fear had swiftly followed. What kind of mother would she be? Would she be like Lucinda?

Now Brooks was here, and she adored everything about him. When he grew up, he could be whatever he chose. She'd never insult or badger him. She was happy and blessed but remained stagnant. What was her problem?

"Hey, honey," Philo said, entering the kitchen as he toweled off his dark straight hair. "It's gonna be a nice fall day out."

She poured him a cup of coffee. "There's a slight chill in the air. You'll need a jacket. You'd better hurry, or you're going to be late."

He hugged her. "It's Saturday." He kissed her thoughtfully, deeply.

She relished his tender touch, then moved her face to the crook of his neck. "Shit, I'm so out of it."

"That's pretty standard for new mothers, especially new mothers studying for the bar exam. That messy hairdo thing is really working for you. Sexy." He caressed her back. "I love you, Loraine."

"I love you, too." She sat down.

"Hey," he said, "why don't you get out for a while? Me and Brooks can watch a little football. I got this bottle thing down. I am a pro. Go do some shopping. Get your nails done up or buy yourself something—lingerie, maybe."

Loraine crossed her arms. He looked so handsome with his dark skin and prestigious Roman nose. What on earth did he see in her? "We do need groceries."

"Oh, now, that sounds thrilling," he joked.

"I could go back to bed," she commented. "A nap sounds good."

"Only if you're gonna be naked. It's naked nap or no nap, just sayin'." He rubbed her shoulders, and his lips curved into a devilish smile.

"I'll go to the grocery store." She stood. "I'm just too tired to get busy with you right now."

"I get it. No judgment. It's sunny outside. Why not lay off the meds today? All that vitamin D would be good for you."

"I can only pray," she joked.

Within minutes she was in the car, teeth brushed, hair combed, light makeup in place. As she drove, she noticed the colorful leaves and the pumpkin-filled harvest decor the neighbors were putting out. It was homey and sweet. Lucinda would say those folks clearly had nothing important to do, or that they were desperate for entertainment. What a bitch. *When will I stop hearing her voice, her negativity? She haunts me like an incurable disease.*

Thanksgiving was coming. It was a time to reflect and be thankful. And she wanted to get Brooks's picture taken amongst some big fat orange pumpkins. The corners of her mouth tipped. *So, I'm silly and sentimental. Sue me.*

The sun was warm and possibly a tad uplifting. Today she would allow herself to smile.

A daze seemed to overtake her as she drove. The radio was off, and it was quiet except for the hum of the car engine. She cracked the window, and the cool breeze seemed to surround her and give her an exhilarating hug.

She was approaching the Enchanting Treasures Antique Store. The last time she had gone in, she'd become nauseous. Little angel figurines and dainty porcelain teacups had seemed to glow, and look freakishly familiar. She'd thought she spied a hat she'd worn. But she couldn't have. A stunning white cat had followed at her heels. It was a bewildering, haunted little store. She couldn't leave fast enough. They needed to call a ghostbuster in the worst way. She sped up.

The road called to her. She turned on the radio and sang along. Music had always lifted her spirits, and she could carry a tune.

Suddenly, she realized she had traveled to the far edge of town. A high-end market stood on the corner. She wasn't familiar with it, but she pulled in anyway. The sign boasted of a café. That might be a good thing. Caffeine was a necessity.

Loraine picked out a grocery cart and began exploring the store. She checked several prices and noticed they were higher than at her regular store. Since she didn't have a job, she was cautious of spending unnecessary money. She didn't put anything in her cart, but she continued to stroll up and down each aisle. For some insane reason, it felt relaxing.

Questioning her sanity was not a new thing. She listened to the soft music playing from unseen speakers and smiled at the people she passed; most were elderly. They seemed kind, and content with their lives. What was their secret?

When she got to the pharmacy and personal care section, she stopped. She was definitely in need of medication. Nothing worked.

Abruptly, there was the sound of breaking glass. She turned and saw juice seeping all over the floor among large slivers of a broken bottle. A man in a wheelchair was looking up at her—his basket had emptied in the middle of the floor. A tiny white dog sat in his lap.

The woman pushing him was frantically trying to gather the rolling cans of food and the bags of cheese and a head of lettuce. Loraine began helping as the juice spread out in all directions.

"I got this," the woman said.

"No, I want to help," Loraine insisted, fishing a lip balm from beneath a shelf and grabbing a melon as it rolled down the aisle. A store worker appeared with a mop and began cleaning up the wet mess and glass pieces.

The woman rose with the basket and the items. "Thank you so much."

Loraine placed the lip balm and melon in the basket. "No problem."

"I...I knew it was you," the old man stuttered. "Your eyes are exactly the same. I'd know you anywhere." He paused. "But you're very troubled. I can see that by the arch of your brows."

"Excuse me?" Loraine replied.

"Can we talk for a moment, just a few minutes? I'd like to buy you a coffee."

Loraine locked eyes with the woman who held the handles of the wheelchair.

"He's harmless." She petted the dog in his lap. "And she's a joy." She pointed toward the café at the front of the store. "I could get our shopping done while you two catch up." Her eyebrows rose a fraction. When Loraine hesitated, she spoke again. "You'd be helping me out." She held up a list.

"Of course," Loraine heard herself say.

The woman pushed him up to a table in the café area then took his basket. "I'll be back in a few minutes. Y'all enjoy a short chat." She winked at Loraine and hurried toward the bakery.

Loraine parked her empty cart near an ice machine and sat down across from the man, feeling confused and a little uncomfortable.

"I'm Loraine," she managed.

His old weathered face melted into a smile as a lone tear drifted from his eye. "I'm—"

The barista appeared at their table. "I only wait tables for you, Mr. Edgar. Would you like the usual?"

"Yes," he replied. "And coffee for my friend, too. Add a touch of hazelnut for my Jewel."

"Got it." He scampered away.

The old man patted the tiny white ball of fur in his lap. "They call me Edgar. Tell me about your life. Is it a good one?"

"I...guess. I have a baby boy."

"Oh, I'm so pleased to hear it. Children are a blessing, and we were never able to have any. We did have a houseful of critters—dogs, cats, chickens, rabbits. You doted on them day and night."

Loraine shifted in her seat. This man was delusional. The barista returned with their drinks. She took a large gulp. It was delicious, and hazelnut, her favorite. The warmth coursed through her, and she felt her body relax. So, she would humor the old man a little longer.

"I'm married to a man named Philo," she told him. "My baby is Brooks."

He rubbed his chin. "Is he a football fan?"

Loraine smiled. "Yes."

"Good." He sipped his coffee. "You're twenty-seven, right?"

Her eyes grew wide, and she nodded.

"Jewel passed away on a cold, snowy night in February twenty-seven years ago. Were you born in March?"

She nodded again. Coincidence.

"What brings you to me? It must be important. Are you searching for something? Are you content?" He stared at her with a deep, brown-eyed gaze that seemed eerily familiar. Chills ran down her spine.

"I'm good. Totally fine." She glanced toward the grocery aisles. *Where is his caretaker?*

He laughed heartily. "Are you singing and painting and moving everything around? Ah, you have the voice of an angel. Even the songbirds in our back yard hushed to listen to you serenade them."

She cocked her head sideways. "I can sing a little. But no one has ever heard me sing—not Philo, Lucinda, or Simon. Only Brooks, my baby." She chewed her lower lip. "I'm too embarrassed."

He pointed a thin finger at her. "Be proud, fine lady. You join your church choir today, or the local glee club. You have pipes straight out of the Vatican in Rome. They'll be blessed to have you. Singing brings you alive. It lifts you up. It's your gift. You must share it with the world."

She felt abruptly emotional, and her eyes filled with moisture.

He continued. "Are you painting?" He waved his hand from left to right. "You painted every single day of your life—critters, fruit, candles, sunsets, everything and anything. You had a little studio in the back of the house. It brought your soul so much pleasure. You also painted the rooms in our house and the cupboards and the baseboards, and anything that wasn't covered in fabric. Our home was an ever-changing sea of vivid hues.

"It's not good to deny your God-given gifts, it's stifling what's inside you. You have many talents. You must let that wonderment out." He lowered his hand to the tiny animal in his lap. "No one can tell you how to live your life, not even your folks. You must do what you were created to do, not what others want you to do." His voice lowered. "It's the only way to live a truly happy life."

Using the napkin on the outside of her coffee cup, Loraine wiped the wetness from her cheeks and finished her drink. She held it out toward him.

"This is the first time in a year I have finished a cup of coffee while it was still warm."

Edgar chuckled.

She stared at him as he stared at her. Was he for real? Were these the answers to her years of depression? Her mind swirled with ideas. The house could use a good painting. And wouldn't it be lovely to capture Brooks's tiny face on canvas? She didn't attend church every Sunday. Would the church even accept her in the choir? She somehow knew they would.

Edgar scratched his head. "You're a strong spirit, Jewel. Listen to what's in here." He placed his hand on his chest. "But be who you are now."

They sat in silence for a few more minutes, and it was oddly comforting.

Finally, she spoke with deep sincerity. "I thank you, Mr. Edgar. You've been more helpful than a thousand hours of therapy. I've been trying to find some joy in my life for such a long, long time."

He lifted the small dog in his lap and handed it to her. "Joy will love living with you."

"Oh, no," Loraine began. "I didn't mean that. I couldn't take your dog."

He crossed his arms. "You need Joy more than I do. She's smart and trained and very loyal. She'll keep you company while you sort everything out."

The dog licked her hand, then settled into her lap. She'd never had a pet—not ever—not even a fish.

"I...feel horrible taking her."

"She'll remind you of me and to stay on the path of real happiness."

The caregiver returned with a handful of bags. She placed them in a basket behind Edgar's wheelchair.

Loraine met her eyes. "I can't take his dog."

She nodded. "Oh, yes, you can. We're expecting puppies any day now at The Senior Smiles Retirement Home, and we have a pregnant cat, too. Little Joy is actually a lot of Joy. She'll be a good addition to your family. Your husband will enjoy her, and she'll be gentle with your baby. They can grow up together."

Loraine was flabbergasted. She hadn't told the woman she had a husband or a son. What was going on?

She gazed downward at the white ball of fur. Its large dark eyes were tender and simply adorable. Her heart felt full of love—instantly.

"We'd better get going," the lady said. "I'm Mariah Gilbert. I'm rather new in town. I'm trying to help out here and there, as much as I can. It's so nice to meet you."

Baffled, Loraine rose. "I'm Loraine, Loraine Priscus."

"I know," Mariah smiled.

Edgar patted the dog's head once more and then lightly touched Loraine's elbow. "Please take care of yourself. Live your life the way you want to. Follow your heart."

Mariah reached into a grocery bag and handed her a bag of dog food.

"She likes the little kibbles the best, but she'll eat practically anything. Have a lovely afternoon." She paid the barista and pushed Edgar through the grocery store and waved as they exited through the double doors.

Loraine's mouth fell open.

≈≈

Loraine rushed into the house. "Philo, I'm home."

He raced into the kitchen cradling Brooks in his arms.

"Oh, my God, Loraine. It's been hours. I've been worried sick, and your cell phone is going straight to voicemail."

She bit her lip. "I'm sorry. I don't think I turned it on all day." Her eyes lit up. "Guess what? You'll never guess. I stopped by the church, and I joined the choir, just like that. I sang a short hymn with another lady, and we were *amazing.* They were so glad to have me." She bounced on her toes. "I felt welcomed. Then, I went to the hardware store and got paint for every room of the house. I was thinking cranberry for the bedroom, hunter green for the family room and a pale blue for Brooks's room."

A furry head peeked out of her purse. "Oh, and this is Joy." She lifted the dog out. "Isn't she precious? And she even fits in my purse. A convenient companion, am I right? I am taking her everywhere I go from now on. She's going to be my service dog, for a lifetime of depression and anxiety disorder." She chuckled. "If that's even a thing. But I think it's a thing. Anyway, it's going to be my thing."

Philo shifted from side to side, soothing Brooks, struggling to process her giddy behavior. "Did you take something?"

"Nope." She kissed the puppy on the head. "Not one thing. I did finish an entire cup of coffee, though, with hazelnut—quite miraculous, if I do say so myself."

"This might be a manic outburst. It could be."

"Nope, I'm listening to my heart and doing the things I've only dreamt of doing." She kissed Brooks and held Joy close to him. He cooed excitedly. "Oh, I also bought crates for toys; I'm going to paint them bright red and blue. And I also got a cozy little doggie bed for Joy. I picked up a pizza for dinner, and I got some marshmallows."

"Marshmallows?"

"For the bonfire we're going to have."

Philo tilted his head sideways.

"Burning all those." She pointed to the stack of legal materials. "It's going to be so freeing. I can hardly wait." She cuddled Joy. "I did spend a little bit of money, though. I'm sorry about that."

"I'd give every penny I have to see you happy." He pulled her into an embrace with Brooks and Joy wiggling between them. "I'm making plenty now. Relax, and enjoy Brooks for a while."

"I'll find a way to generate some income. But it will be something that I have a passion for. First, I'm going to turn our house into a home."

Joy licked the side of Brooks's face, and they all laughed.

Philo kissed each of her cheeks and the tip of her nose. She kissed him deeply, and then pulled back and winked at him.

"About that naked nap..."

He howled with laughter. "Now, that's what I'm talkin' about."

# SHE GOT SOCKS

A GUITAR-SHAPED NIGHTLIGHT PROVIDED JUST ENOUGH ILLU-mination as Pearl picked up George's building blocks, underwear, cheese wrappers, and crayons. She straightened a pile of stuffed animals and tossed several pairs of sneakers and boots into the closet. Glancing at him as he slept, she worried. He was only four years old. Would he remember his dad at all?

He'd only been two when Quinn left. They hadn't made any real memories together. She caressed his soft hair. He was very well-behaved at daycare and was already learning his ABCs. He was a happy boy, and that was really all that mattered. She placed a soft kiss on his cheek and adjusted the covers around his small body.

She took in John's side of the room. There were neon stars and planets stuck to the walls and ceiling. His first-place trophy for his intergalactic science project was on his nightstand, near the head of his bed. A planet Earth nightlight helped her see to gather the tiny toys that littered his side of the floor. She pulled off his socks and tossed them into a full laundry hamper. She put the array of schoolbooks into his backpack and tucked the covers around him as he snored loudly.

For an eight-year-old, John was very mature. He was the peacekeeper in the family, and the first to tell her what was really going on. She kissed him on the forehead. Sugar, their old white cat, rested on the bottom of the bed. Pearl rubbed her chin softly, and Sugar stretched out in response.

Exhaling, she tiptoed into the next room, where there was a glow of the computer. She picked up candy wrappers and four shirts. She hung them on the back of a chair, reminding herself to inquire as to which ones were clean. There were bowls of half-eaten cereal and empty sports drink bottles. She added a blanket to Paul's messy array of untucked sheets and moved his baseball glove from the bed to the nightstand. He was such a good athlete. Watching him compete was thrilling. But with her work hours, it was getting more and more difficult.

She went to the computer, saved a few school documents, wrote down the details, and shut it down. At eleven, Paul was pretty much on track, but she worried about him as well. He missed his father, and he clearly remembered Quinn coming and going and bragging about his gigs and connections. All, obviously, more important than his own children.

She knew Paul was on every form of social media just waiting for his father to reach out. She expected he wouldn't. Quinn had run out of plausible reasons as to why he wasn't interested in his family.

Entering Penny's room, she found her lying in bed texting. "Hi, Pumpkin. Who ya talkin' to?"

"Daisy."

Pearl sat on the edge of the bed. "She seems very nice."

Penny sat up. "Oh, she is. She came over tonight and taught me how to cook Hamburger Helper. She said her mother taught her. We made a feast. The boys loved it, and there's even some left over for you."

"That's terrific. Where did you get the hamburger meat?"

"Daisy brought it over. Her mom had some extra, and she didn't want it to go bad."

"I like Mariah. Those granola snacks she brought over were delicious. She seems so sincere and eager to be my friend." Pearl rubbed her chin. "That doesn't happen very often at my age. I'm glad they moved here."

"Me, too."

"How did you do on that algebra test?" Pearl inquired.

"All right, I think, but probably not an A." The phone let out a ping, and she glanced at a text. "It's Tilly. She says that Caitlyn's little sister Isabella doesn't need her wheelchair anymore. Some kind of wack-a-doodle miracle."

Pearl nodded. Surely, there was more to that story. "Sophie is my hero for adopting a special needs child with three children of her own."

"And they got her from the circus—epic!" Penny glanced at her phone as it pinged again. "Daisy says Isabella just had asthma and never needed the wheelchair in the first place."

"That makes more sense." Pearl stood. "Darling, it's almost eleven. Tell your friends goodnight and get some sleep."

While Penny texted, Pearl picked up several scarves and a furry hat. "Thank you for looking after your brothers. I don't know what I would do without you. I'm sorry to burden you."

Penny put her phone on her bedside table. "I'm sorry Daddy is an asshole." She scooted under the covers.

"Language," Pearl groaned. She wanted to cry, but she just sighed instead. "I love you. Get a good night's sleep." She closed the door and leaned against it. She was all cried out.

All those years ago, a messy-haired, blue-eyed musician had seemed like a good idea. Not! Quinn spent most of their marriage in Nashville, singing on the streets and dropping recordings at studio doors. There was always another gig or a group in need of a baritone. It was all he focused on. As the children arrived, he was temporarily ecstatic, then off again to the next gig or promising opportunity. She'd been the breadwinner and a single parent as well.

He had drained their account several times for studio time and amplifiers and demo discs. His needs came before anyone else's, even the children's. It was ludicrous. When he'd announced, he was going to Colorado to entertain at a lodge, she filed for divorce. He returned the papers quickly with an announcement introducing his new band and their performance dates. Were they supposed to be impressed? She'd tossed it in the trash without a second glance. She was on her own.

Two years had passed, and she'd even received more flyers, but not one inquiry about his children. Didn't he want to know about their lives? He probably feared paying any kind of child support, so he just stayed away. Quinn was a selfish child himself, and she was so glad to be done raising him.

As she made her way to the kitchen, she was thankful that she and the kids were still together under the same roof. There had been times when she'd doubted she could make ends meet. She stopped by the dining room, which was officially her room. They'd never had dining room furniture anyway, and the boys needed space, and Penny deserved her own room. So, she'd moved her bed to the dining room and created a master suite.

She pulled her heels off, and her toes throbbed. She worked at the law firm about fifty hours a week, but Paul, George, John, and Penny were worth it. She hated being gone so much, but she had utility bills, insurance bills, grocery bills, and the mortgage. When her bosses, Simon and Calvin, had begun talking about hiring another secretary to concentrate on research, she'd insisted that she could do the job in the evenings. She promised she would continue to excel at her current responsibilities.

Simon had a big heart, however broken he was, and he couldn't refuse her. So, she had two jobs at the firm, and that was okay! The pay and benefits were excellent. They were flexible on game days and school events. It kept a roof over everyone's head. She was thankful.

She took off her clothes and pulled on a fleece robe. Exhaustion consumed her. She sat on the edge of the bed, gathering her strength to tackle more cleaning.

Having an affair with Simon had not been her best moment, but she'd needed affection; and he was even more needy than she was. His wife Lucinda was truly a despicable woman who had absolutely no feelings whatsoever. He'd insisted she wouldn't even care.

But after six months, she'd realized *she* cared. He was still married, and she couldn't get past that. She was ashamed. What would the community think? What would her children think? She broke it off.

Thankfully, they were still friends, and there was minimal weirdness at work. He knew how much she needed that job. He was respectful, and she knew he still cared about her. He was a good person, and deserved more than living in Hell with Lucinda.

She adored his daughter Loraine. Loraine had redecorated the law office, and they had become quite close. They spent many evenings together chatting as Loraine painted and Pearl researched cases. On the rare Sundays they made it to church, Loraine was always waving and insisting Pearl's whole brood sit with her and her family.

Loraine called her constantly with questions about baby care. Admittedly, she did have a lot of knowledge when it came to children. It made her proud to answer the inquiries. And when Loraine brought little Brooks to the office, she loved doting on him. Simon adored being a grandfather, too. It was cute. Maybe someday, when Simon was divorced, they would give it another try. Presently, all she could really concentrate on was paying the bills, feeding the family, and staying close to all of her kids. Her priorities were firmly in order.

Sliding into her furry white kitty slippers, she trudged to the kitchen. The dishes were cleared, but the table was covered with crumbs and milk puddles. The sink was full of character glasses and superhero silverware. Burnt cheese was baked onto the stove burners. Water was spilled all around the cat's bowl, and lunchboxes full of the day's leftovers were stacked near the refrigerator. As much as she wanted to abandon the mess, she wanted a nice tidy space for them to enjoy breakfast. It was the only meal she was able to eat with them, and it had to be special. Tomorrow she would make waffles and sausage—their favorite. And maybe she would blow some bubbles, like Poovie Lamay had suggested in one of her articles.

She opened a diet soda, grabbed a cookie, and began the daunting tasks.

～～

The house was quiet and peaceful as Pearl finished loading the dishwasher. She wanted to hum, but it just took too much effort. She was careful not to make any loud noise. She didn't want to wake anyone. She wiped the counters, swept the floor, and took the garbage into the garage. She laid out items for tomorrow's lunch boxes. She gave Sugar some fresh water and a scoop of cat food. Finally, she surveyed the area, and it was—decent, which was going to have to do!

As she returned to the makeshift master suite, she noticed her fingernail polish was cracked and chipped. She plopped down on the bed. It was late. Penny had all the polish upstairs, and that was so far away. The staircase might as well have been a mile long. She was too tired. Her legs felt like lead weights. So, she would have chipped nail color tomorrow. Who cared?

As she pulled on a large teeshirt, the familiar anxiety began. How would she handle all the challenges that were coming her way? She had four children with four distinct personalities. Each had their own problems and worries. They were the challenge of her lifetime. Was she qualified? Would she be able to keep them all content? How would she teach them all to drive? How would she afford a second car? How would she put them through college?

As she crawled into bed, she felt very alone. A chill crept up her spine. She drew her legs up close to her body. Her first priority was making the house payments. This was her home. She'd spent an entire summer stenciling around the fireplace. She had each drawer lined perfectly. The laundry room had extra shelving and hooks for the kid's jackets. It was perfect, and she had worked years to make it that way.

She pulled the covers tightly around her. Her feet were cold. Her feet were *freezing*. As she wiggled her toes, she could barely feel them. She sat up and looked at her dresser. Even though it was only a few feet away, it seemed like miles. She scooted back down under the blankets. She would just have to be cold.

She buried her face into her pillow and squeezed her eyes shut. Her lips began to quiver. Tears seeped over her nose from one eye to the other. She could feel a wet spot forming on her pillow, and she heard herself groan softly. As she began to sob, she remembered how early she had to get up. She did not have time to feel sad and stressed. She had to get control of her emotions. There was absolutely no time for this panic.

She rolled onto her back. The ceiling was uncaring, unfeeling. She rolled onto her side. The mattress felt hard. She was so utterly tired and chilled. And if she didn't get to sleep soon, she was going to wake the entire neighborhood with her screams of frustration.

Her body began trembling. *Why? Why is it so cold? I am so cold.* As she wiggled around, she felt something at the bottom of her bed, pressed between the sheets. She reached down and pulled out a thick boot sock. What in the world? She reached down again and found the other one. As she looked at them, astonished.

"Yes," she said out loud. What were these doing down there? She'd not worn them in months, and she made her bed every day. They were huge. She couldn't have overlooked them.

She stroked the soft, fuzzy cotton. *Oh, what does it matter?* She quickly put them on her icy toes. They felt wonderful and cozy, like a warm hug. Her tense body warmed and relaxed. Her anxiety lifted. She had made it this far on her own. She'd take it one day at a time, and she'd keep her family together, no matter what.

The corners of her mouth tipped as a feeling of thankfulness and gratitude enveloped her. Finally, she would sleep. The socks were a sign. She could feel it, and sank into the old mattress.

Someone was watching. Someone cared about her and her family.

"Thank you," she whispered.

At that moment, she knew they would be okay. She was not really all alone, because when her feet were so very cold, she got socks.

# THE EMERALD NECKLACE

**E**MMA STOOD IN FRONT OF THE MIRROR ADMIRING HER HUGE belly. She was so happy—beyond happy. She adored teaching at Smoky Valley Elementary, and Caleb's job was secure. She felt a peacefulness she had never known.

But most important, her baby was growing right on schedule, and all the medical tests were normal. The doctors had been so wrong, or maybe it was a miracle. Her miracle. She was going to be a mother, something she thought would never happen. Life was truly wonderful. *Thank you, Lord! And thank you, Mystic Ridge.*

She grinned sheepishly. If living in Mystic Ridge had taught her anything, it was that prayers really were answered, and that sometimes life was unexplainable. Fate had brought her here. Meeting Violet had been critical to her life. And although she'd never be able to explain what had happened, she wouldn't question it.

She had been given a gift—a child. She'd been somehow chosen, thanks to Violet. It gave her joy to bring a deserving soul into the world, and she vowed to do everything in her power to give this child a peaceful, happy life—like Violet would have wanted.

She knew the stress having a child would bring, but she welcomed it—all of it! Living in Mystic Ridge might even bring unexpected challenges. Whatever came her way, she would put her baby first.

She adjusted her large pink kitty teeshirt. She knew she looked a tad juvenile, but she didn't care. Her students loved it when she wore quirky attire; and it was highly possible she might run into one of her second-grade students at the grocery store. She usually did on Saturdays.

As she swirled, she caught a glimpse of her kitties lounging on Violet's pink tapestry chair. It was probably not what Violet's son had envisioned when he insisted Emma take it. The kitties were drawn to it.

They had really grown since Caleb had found them in the parking lot. And somehow, she felt that Caleb's rescuing them had played a pivotal part in Violet's approval of him.

She walked to the cats and rubbed their heads. She clearly recalled the day she had shown them to Violet. She missed her neighbor, and the friendship she had lost. As a further reminder, Violet's home directly across the street sat empty. But she still felt Violet's presence around her.

Suddenly, the sound of a truck with squeaky brakes distracted her thoughts. The cats ran under the bed. She rushed to the window. A huge moving truck and a red two-door car with a dented back fender were crammed into Violet's small driveway. Several people were milling around. Her heart sank a little. Someone was moving into Violet's house.

There hadn't been a sale sign in the yard, and Owen had cleaned it out; but she hadn't anticipated anyone else ever occupying the house.

Her eyes welled with tears. All three kitties jumped onto the windowsill and began meowing. What were they trying to say? Maybe that it was a grand, picturesque Victorian home, and that someone should enjoy it. Or maybe that Violet wouldn't want her home sitting empty, rotting, gathering dust. Violet would want celebrations and birthdays and Christmases to fill her home. Life continued!

She wiped her cheeks and hurried down the stairs. This was a good thing.

The stairs creaked, and she grinned. Caleb was not the best at home repairs. He had good intentions. He'd insisted he was going to caulk around the fireplace today; but when a colleague had called with new maps of the caverns, he had rushed out to explore. Emma chuckled; she couldn't blame him.

She glanced at the painting of *Christ Blessing Little Children* Violet had left her. It hung to the right of the fireplace, above a glass shelf of family photos. The corners of her lips curved.

She slid into a jacket and grabbed her purse and keys. As she stepped outside and locked the front door, she heard a female voice in the distance. She turned and saw a petite woman with wavy blond hair wearing a sharp burgundy blazer and stylish black knee-high boots. Emma's heart sped up. She walked carefully down the front steps and across the street.

"Hello," she called out as she crossed the street. The woman grinned and headed toward her. They met at the foot of the driveway near the back of the truck.

"Hi, I'm your neighbor," Emma said. "I'm Emma Parsons, and my husband is Caleb. He's out right now, but he'll be back soon. Welcome to the street!"

The woman shook her hand awkwardly. "Thank you. I'm Polly. It's just me and my son Murphy. He's five. He's inside playing with his action figures."

Emma nodded. "It's so nice to meet you."

Polly ran a hand through the ends of her hair. "You, too. Congratulations on your impending addition." She motioned to Emma's large belly. "They change your life, I tell ya. In a good way. I'm so nervous about meeting new people. I've never lived in a small town before. We're from Atlanta. I'm divorced." She ran her hands down her sides and inhaled deeply. "Too much information, right? I like to divulge, that's me. I'm a little tense. I just keep thinking that this...this deal is gonna fall through, somehow."

Emma narrowed her eyes.

Polly spoke fast, her breath erratic. "Violet was a distant relative. I only met her once at a big family reunion at Lake Lanier, many years ago. I can't believe she even remembered me. I'd just had Murphy, but I do recall she was enamored with him.

She held him practically the whole day. I even got to play in the family softball game.

"Most elderly women do love babies, but I never expected this. Why would she leave her home to me? It's completely paid for. I don't deserve it. Maybe she made a mistake." Her chest rose and fell swiftly. "I still can't digest that it's mine. It's like I'm dreaming."

"Violet was a wise woman. Trust me, she knew what she was doing. She took a shine to some people. She must have thought you and Murphy belonged here. I only knew her briefly, too, but we really hit it off. I miss her terribly."

Two men awkwardly descended the ramp with an old worn brown couch. Polly turned.

"Be careful, take your time. Please don't fall."

Suddenly, a small boy with messy brown hair appeared in the doorway of the house, a curious look on his face. Emma felt herself smile.

Polly waved. "We're coming in."

The boy had deep hazel eyes and a bit of a sad expression. Suddenly, the baby inside her moved. She enjoyed the feeling, but it seemed a bit more intense than usual.

"Let's go," Polly said. "I want you to meet my son." She led the way past the truck to the door and knelt beside the boy. "Honey, this is Mrs. Emma. She lives across the street."

He grinned at Emma, and then studied her neckline. "Are you wearing the green one?" he asked. "The necklace?"

Emma touched her necklace and pulled out the tiny silver cross. "No. I don't own a green one."

"Oh." he said. "I have three superheroes and two dinosaurs."

"That's wonderful," Emma said, inspecting the treasures in his hands.

He shrugged, then ran inside.

Polly laughed. "He likes you. He's not usually that friendly to strangers. Sometimes, it can be seriously awkward."

Emma stepped into the foyer and was overwhelmed by the smell of fresh flowers and sweet cinnamon. Violet's home would forever contain those glorious scents. All the stunning paintings were gone. The floors were bare and dark. The baby inside her moved again. Her pulse sped up. Being back here was difficult; she expected Violet to appear at any moment.

Polly touched her arm. "You don't look so good. Please come to the kitchen and sit down."

"That's a good idea," Emma said, hand on her stomach.

"Do you know what you're having?"

"A girl."

"Are you sure you're, okay?"

"I'm fine. I just feel emotional, and I think my baby senses it." She sat down in a red aluminum chair at a black iron table. She noticed several bottles of pills on the counter exactly where Violet used to keep hers. "Polly, are you or Murphy ill?"

"Oh, no," she breathed. "I just have terrible anxiety. Sometimes I feel like I'm crawling right out of my own skin. I just want people to like me, that's all."

Emma was perplexed. How did pills help anyone feel more liked?

Polly exhaled. "I have so much to worry about."

Emma felt her baby settling down and her own heartbeat slowing. She crossed her ankles and took deep breaths. She watched Polly pacing the kitchen, mumbling about her awful furniture and her bleached roots and her beat-up old car and her inability to keep her bank account organized. It was so tiring to behold. This woman was making herself miserable. She was frantic and getting worse by the second.

Emma reached out and took her hand gently. "Why don't you sit down as well?"

Polly looked dumbfounded. "O-kay."

"You should be enjoying this moment. Violet would want you to. She'd want you to be thrilled."

"And grateful," Polly completed her thought. "Oh, I am. Really. I just can't fathom that this is really happening."

"I understand more than you know."

"The closing was a piece of cake. It didn't cost me a dime. Isn't that bonkers?"

Emma crossed her arms. "Then it is time for you to relax and rejoice."

Polly's eyes seem to well up. "You think? That's so hard for me. I'm very high-strung."

"You don't have to be if you don't want to be. Mystic Ridge operates at a slower pace than Atlanta. And you *are* living mortgage free. That's a true blessing."

"It is. It is." Polly chewed her lower lip. "Security is new to me. I'm a nail technician. I've struggled to make ends meet all my life."

Emma nodded. "My friend Rosalie's sister Nancy Connors works at Mystic Ridge Salon and Spa. I could have her put in a good word for you."

"That'd be great, truly great."

"I'm a teacher at Smoky Valley Elementary, second grade."

"Oh, you must have patience for days. You are my hero."

Murphy entered the kitchen. "I'm thirsty. Where's my bed gonna go? Can we put the TV on the wall by the window? I want to see the people pass by. Can I get a dog or a cat or a hamster?"

Emma chuckled. "I'm so in the way. I must get going." She stood.

Polly rose and exhaled. "I'm glad you came by."

Emma hugged her. "Friends."

"Friends," Polly repeated, giving her a small squeeze.

"I've got to get to the grocery store," Emma confessed. "Caleb will be home for a late lunch, and the cupboard is literally empty." She walked toward the front door. "It was so nice to meet you both." She turned to see Polly holding Murphy's hand, looking like a deer in the headlights. She walked back to her and touched her arm. "Relax, just a little. You've been given a gift."

Polly nodded. "You're so right."

"I can't wait to meet her," Murphy said.

Emma looked down at him. "Who?"

"Your baby," he said softly.

Emma chuckled. "Oh, well, we'll both have to wait a few more weeks. But she'll be here soon." Her brows furrowed. Had she told him it was a girl? She smiled at them again and exited the front door. She walked carefully past the truck as two men lifted a chair out of the back end. "Have a nice day," she called to them.

Climbing into her car, she exhaled. The visit had been exhausting. Polly and Murphy were high-energy.

On her way to the grocery store, she decided to stop at Enchanted Treasures and get them a housewarming gift, something to help Polly with her constant worry. Millie had added some adorable vintage signs at her antique shop, and Emma was sure she could find the perfect one.

~~☙☙~~

Sunday morning, Emma returned from church and rushed through the kitchen.

"You look like a woman on a mission," Caleb said, kissing her on the neck as she opened cans.

"I am."

"I haven't seen you this frantic since you were off to meet Violet."

Emma faced him. "Really? I'm just taking some goodies across the street."

Caleb poured a cup of coffee. "I met Polly and Murphy yesterday while you were out running errands. Good people. Nothing gets by that kid. He seems really smart."

"Yeah," Emma breathed as she diced cooked chicken. "There's something unusual about him."

"I agree he's not your average five-year-old. I like him, though. I moved their couch around a bit. Murphy didn't like where the movers put it. He wanted a better view of the neighborhood."

"That was helpful." She took out a large baking dish and added the chicken, soup, vegetables and topped it off with pastry. She covered it with foil, then wrote out baking instructions and taped them to the top.

"I'm gonna get rid of some of the dead weeds in the back yard. Holler if you need me," Caleb said as he hurried out the back door.

Emma grabbed the casserole and the bag of gifts and headed out. She carefully descended her three front stairs and crossed the street.

Murphy opened the door before she even got there. "Hello," he said as he came out and took the bag from her. "Presents?"

"Yep."

Polly appeared. "Hey, let me take that." She took the casserole. "I'm so glad to see you again. You didn't have to bring food."

"And presents," Murphy added.

Emma followed them into the kitchen. "Oh, just a few welcome-gifts."

"Sister Crystal Grace and Sister Mary Jean Stevenson came by yesterday afternoon and dropped off two pies. I had a huge piece last night and a nibble this afternoon. I'm going to gain a ton of weight living here. I know it already. None of my clothes are going to fit."

"Sister Crystal Grace likes to travel. She's going on a new adventure." Murphy said as he dug in the gift bag. "I love bubbles." He pulled out the bubble shooter Emma had brought for him.

"I'm so glad." She helped him peel off the plastic wrapper. He quickly moved to the kitchen sink to pour in the bubble mixture.

Emma handed Polly the bag, and they sat down at the table. "A few things for you too."

"Girl, you are too sweet." Polly reached into the bag, pulled out the first wooden plaque and read it out loud, "'Bless this house'. Oh, I love it." She pulled out another. "'Life is too short to be anything but happy.' So sweet! I'll put this in the foyer."

"There's one more," Emma told her.

Polly pulled it out and read it. "'Breathe, be calm and make biscuits.' Oh, it's perfect for my kitchen." She rose and hugged Emma. "Thank you so much. You must let me give you a manicure. You are so thoughtful. I'm feeling more at ease already."

"The house looks great," Emma observed.

"It's a bit empty. We just had a one-bedroom apartment in Atlanta. I'm ecstatic that Murphy has a yard now. I want to get him a swing set. He's been so much more talkative since we got here. I feel like he's coming out of his shell. I feel the same. I'm more focused. Honestly, I feel like a new woman. And I've made a big decision." She paused. "I'm going to start going by my real name—Opal."

Murphy turned and blew some bubbles their way. "Mama told the nuns her name was Opal."

"Darling, it is Opal."

Emma laughed openly. "It's beautiful, and so is Mystic Ridge. You guys were meant to be here, honestly."

Murphy rejoined them, a troubled look on his face. "Are you wearing it today?" he asked Emma.

"What?"

"The green necklace." His lower lip puckered.

"Honestly, darling, I don't own a green necklace."

He pointed to her large belly. "Hers."

"Murphy," Opal interjected, "the baby isn't even here yet. She doesn't own jewelry. Now, take your bubbles out on the porch, sweetie."

He frowned as he gathered his goodies. He turned once more.

"I saw your kitties in the window. I want a white cat."

"There's a lady in town named Eve. She rescues cats and kittens. I know she can help you."

He smiled. "I'd like that. I hope you can find that necklace." He exited the back door.

Emma was perplexed. "Poor guy, I can't imagine why he thinks I have a green necklace."

"I'm so sorry. A cat—that was news to me. He's been acting so flighty." Her voice took a concerned tone. "Yesterday, Sister Mary Jean insisted on showing me Violet's prize azaleas in the back yard, even though they're dormant right now. She went on and on about how they would bloom in the springtime. Murphy and Sister Crystal Grace were in deep conversation. I couldn't imagine what they were chatting about. After they left, I asked him, and he said they talked about emeralds."

"That *is* rather odd," Emma agreed. She thought about the women. "They are truly angels. They help folks all over town. When there's trouble, they show up. I'd trust them with my life."

Opal rubbed her forehead. "Murphy must have sensed it. He usually shies away from strangers. But he hugged Sister Crystal Grace. I don't know whether to be excited or worried."

"Don't panic. People are kind here. Maybe he feels it. And honestly, everyone likes to hug a nun. Right?"

Opal giggled.

Emma stood. "I'd better get going. I've got to get ready for class tomorrow."

Opal walked her to the front door. "Thank you again for the casserole and the thoughtful gifts. Lord knows I need constant encouragement."

"You are quite welcome...Opal. I like that better. It fits you."

They hugged, and Emma made her way across the street. Allira was perched in the dining room window. Jasper and Jing were on each side of the bedroom window. It looked like a painting. She chuckled out loud. Nosey felines.

Inside, she sat down on the staircase. Her face clouded with uneasiness. She couldn't help thinking about Murphy. He seemed somehow intuitive. And his questions were unusual for a child his age. He was oddly interested in her and her baby. It bothered her.

A protective feeling engulfed her as a bead of sweat dripped down the side of her face. Something about him reminded her of Violet, and now he was buddies with Sister Crystal Grace. That woman had more secrets than the Federal Bureau of Investigation, but Emma wasn't about to tell Opal that. She'd lose her mind. *Like I'm losing mine!*

Caleb thundered through. "That yard gets bigger and bigger each day, I swear." He studied her. "What's wrong?"

"Murphy has asked me twice if I was wearing my green necklace. Caleb, I don't own a green necklace. Why would he ask me about one? Why would a little boy care about my jewelry, and something so specific? It's creepy and weird."

Caleb thought for a second. "Didn't you tell me there was one in that box of stuff under the bed?"

*Oh, my God.* Emma felt goosebumps rise up her spine and then float down her arms and legs.

"The items Violet left me." She hurried up the stairs and cautiously got down on her knees beside the bed. She reached under it and retrieved the box Owen had delivered so many months ago. She'd taken the books and the painting out, but nothing else. She hadn't looked in it since the day Violet had passed, and that day she had been so distraught.

She spied the videos but hurried past them. She carefully moved the lace handkerchief. Was there a green necklace? She lifted out the dainty embroidered gloves and spotted the black velvet-covered box. Her heart pounded. She sat down on her backside and crossed her legs. The kitties surrounded her.

Caleb appeared in the doorway and approached. "Yep," he said, standing over her. "Looks like a jewelry box to me."

Emma inhaled and exhaled and pictured Violet's face.

"You gonna open it? I need to get back to the yard."

She opened the box, and the light immediately reflected off the large pear-shaped emerald and the two smaller stones. It glistened, and the thick silver chain looked sparklingly new. It seemed to glow on the velvet backing. The earrings in the middle looked like they had never been worn, but somehow, she knew they had.

Her hands trembled. These pieces had a past; she knew that. And now she felt they had a future as well.

"Awesome," Caleb said. "Told ya it was here. It looks Middle Eastern. No idea how the kid knew about it. Owen probably told him. Well, I'm gonna finish up outside. Holler if you need me." He touched her on the shoulder and left the room.

Emma stared at the treasure. She rose awkwardly then moved to the dresser mirror and took off her tiny chain. She carefully removed the emerald necklace from the velvet box and put it on. She stared at her reflection.

It looked awkward and out-of-place on her. It was glamorous and worldly and exotic. It had an Egyptian look to it, and she wondered how old it really was.

Her mouth felt dry. It wasn't something she would wear. She had simple tastes. Maybe someday, if she attended a fancy wedding or a fancy staff event, she could wear it.

She tried to remove one of the earrings and had to lift the interior velvet cardboard out. A small yellow scrap of paper fell to the floor at her feet. Allira meowed loudly.

Emma retrieved the paper, and her heart thundered. The yellowed scrap read: "Please give this to Everly on her eighteenth birthday. It will ensure she finds her true soul mate!"

A wave of dizziness overtook her. She rushed across the room to the bed and lay down. The room spun for a second and then steadied. The kitties surrounded her, concerned and comforting.

Emma steadied her breathing and rubbed her belly. The baby moved. Her brows creased. She didn't believe a necklace could ensure anything. Or did she? There were so many unexplainable happenings in Mystic Ridge. She had not questioned any of it. She was too grateful and thankful.

But it felt like Violet was orchestrating events. And although she had passed, it still seemed like she was in control. Emma felt unhappy for the first time in many months.

*And somehow, Sister Crystal Grace is involved, I can just feel it.* She closed her eyes. This baby was hers and Caleb's. They were her parents. She chewed her lower lip. Yes, undeniable, they'd had help—somehow—someway. But the baby was hers just the same. She stroked her belly softly. Was anything in the world just random? Was everything destiny? Was there a set path for everyone? Did angels constantly intervene to set things right? Was life already written? Was fate—fate?

After thirty minutes of worrying and trying to digest what was happening in her and her baby's life, she sat up, determination etched on her brow. It was time she took charge.

She returned to the dresser, unfastened the necklace, and put it in its box. Tomorrow, she would take it to Enchanted Treasures and let Millie sell it. This whole thing was insane!

She held the sides of the dresser for support and gazed upward.

"Thank you, Violet. Thank you from the bottom of my heart. I love this baby more than I can put into words. But my daughter will be her own person and choose her soul mate. She'll make her own choices and decisions. She'll be whomever she wants to be and love whomever she wants to love. Her future is not set. She will be strong and independent. I will give her life, and I will give her freedom."

⋙⋘

Several months passed. All the homes of Mystic Ridge had their Christmas trees up and their front porches decorated with glistening lights and illuminated characters. Emma glided through the house as Christmas carols played softly and Caleb added an angel to the top of their freshly-cut Christmas tree. The kitties wrestled beneath the tree.

A knock sounded at the door.

"I'll get it. You be careful." She opened the door to find Opal wearing oven mitts, holding out a foil-covered loaf.

"Hi, bestie, I brought you something. I know you've been a bit queasy lately. I've missed you. I made you some pumpkin bread with cream cheese icing. It's hot and fresh from the oven."

Emma stepped aside. "Oh, thank you so much. Please come in."

"I can't—Murphy's wrapping gifts, and I need to get back and fix him dinner."

"Well, thank you so much for the treat. It smells wonderful."

"You are so welcome. Good luck with decorating. It's going to be the best Christmas ever." Her voice was giddy and cheerful. "Murphy and I have been so blessed this year. And hey, you're never going to believe this. A few days ago, we were in town, and he insisted on going into that musty antique shop. They had comics and aluminum lunch boxes in the window and a cute little desk. Anyway, he found a green necklace, and swore he had to have it. He literally begged me to buy it. He said it was all he wanted for Christmas and practically cried."

She threw her hands up. "I didn't want him to have a meltdown right there in public. It wasn't terribly expensive, way underpriced, if you ask me. So, I bought it for him. I thought maybe it was for Grandma or Nana. He was overjoyed. Crazy, right?

"He took it home and wrapped it in gold foil paper and put it in his dresser drawer. When I asked him why, he said he was going to save it for many years, and that it was for someone very special." She ran her hand across her chin. "Isn't that the weirdest thing you've ever heard?"

Emma stood frozen.

"Last night when I tucked him in, he said that a friend he knew a long time ago came to him in a dream and begged him to find it." She laughed openly. "He said she wanted it really bad. Cuckoo, right? I think he's been watching way too much television. It's so bizarre."

"Yeah," Emma managed.

"Anyway, I better get home. My, my, that Murphy." She giggled as she made her way down the front steps. "Motherhood is a learning experience. Just you wait and see. I bet someday that sweet baby of yours will throw you for a loop."

"Someday," Emma breathed.

"Well, you have a good evening."

Speechless, Emma closed the door, turned, and leaned against it. The rhythm of "Hark the Herald Angels Sing" filled the air around her.

"Food?" Caleb questioned.

For a moment, Emma felt like she would unravel right there in the foyer. But the three cats circled her and rubbed softly against her ankles, and she felt calmed. She steadied herself on her feet as Opal's words replayed over and over in her mind.

"What's wrong, honey?" Caleb asked as he wrestled with a strand of blinking lights.

She took several deep breaths, cleared her throat, and swallowed hard.

"I underestimated the forces of Mystic Ridge and fate and destiny and Violet and..." She stopped, bewildered, and then whispered, "I underestimated Everly."

# THE CHRISTMAS WISH

MARIAH ADDED A BLANKET TO HER TOTE BAG. "IT'S JUST A MID-night movie, Stuart. Daisy says all of her friends are going to be there. Thankfully, I get to come along."

He pouted. "But tomorrow is Christmas Eve. I was thinking we could make a huge pot of stew and check out a few manger scenes here in town."

"We can still do that," Mariah insisted.

"You guys will be all pooped out." Stuart's lower lip puckered.

Daisy breezed into the room wearing black yoga pants, a pink shirt, and hiking boots.

"Dad, this movie is going to be epic. Vampire loves girl. Girl loves rock star. And it's a musical!" she gushed. "You can come if you want."

His lips turned upward. "That's really okay. You ladies have a fun time."

Mariah kissed him on the cheek and grabbed a jacket and gloves. She also handed a set to Daisy.

"Don't wait up—with all the extra movie previews it will be super-late when we get back."

"Tilly says we should get breakfast after," Daisy added. Stuart's brows rose, so she hugged him swiftly. "Later, Dad."

They hurried out to the car and proceeded down the street. After several minutes had passed, Mariah murmured "I hate lying to him."

"What were we supposed to tell him? The truth—that we're helping a time-traveling nun disappear forever?" Daisy propped her feet against the glove compartment in front of her.

Mariah briefly glared at her. Her daughter was way too *good* at lying.

"It does sound rather preposterous. I'm not sure we should even be helping her. She's getting up in years. I have to wonder if she's thought this through. Everyone in town adores her. She has a life here."

"Mom, it's her wish. After all she's taught us, we owe her."

"I don't want to make a mistake I can't undo."

"Mom, you're being such a wimp. If Sister Crystal Grace wants to go hang out with Jesus, who are we to stop her?" After several seconds passed, she continued. "She's been there before. She knows what she's doing."

"But this time, she's going to stay," Mariah pointed out. "And we are going to be accessories in her disappearance." She pulled up in front of the Sisters of Southern Mercy Convent and turned off the car's headlights. "I feel uneasy about all of this."

The ornate iron gates were dimly lit by two small lampposts. It was extremely dark out. She climbed out and stretched a sock over her license plate, then returned to the car.

"Better safe than sorry." It was growing cold quickly. She handed Daisy a blanket.

Suddenly, she saw someone scaling the tall gates. "It can't be."

Sister Crystal Grace ran up to the car wearing black pants, a black shirt and a stocking hat. Only a few strands of her blond hair were visible. She carried a small vintage suitcase. She opened the door to the back seat and scooted in.

"That was freaking awesome," Daisy gushed.

"Thank you," Sister Crystal Grace said, situating the suitcase beside her.

Mariah was beyond flabbergasted. She turned toward the back seat.

Sister Crystal Grace waved a hand in the air. "The wheelchair thing was just for show. I *am* ninety-something. I had to act it." She cackled openly, excitedly. "I haven't aged in years, another reason I have to go."

"You are a dang superhero, I swear." Daisy laughed.

"Nah," she said, buckling her seatbelt. She gazed at Mariah. "Darling, stop worrying. I've been able to feel your anxiety for hours. Like I told you, I can't leave a body here, stuck in a coma, stuck in limbo. I have to disappear. I have to physically go back through that crevice. It ends where it began. This is my last wish."

"A Christmas wish," Daisy mused.

"Yes."

Mariah just stared. She wanted to bawl.

Sister Crystal Grace touched her shoulder. "It's all going to be okay. I took every trace of me from the convent. There may be a couple of group photos, but everything else is coming with me. In a few years, I'll be a cryptic rumor, mostly forgotten."

"A legend," Daisy suggested.

"Are you sure this is the best idea? I mean, disappearing?" Mariah asked her.

"People disappear all the time. Haven't you heard of the Mayans, the people of Easter Island, the Cahokia in Illinois, and the people at Angkor Wat in Cambodia? They all vanished in some way or another. Much of the world is beyond our comprehension. I'll be a memory soon enough."

"I don't think so, Sister." Mariah shook her head.

"Trust me. Now, start the engine before we're discovered."

Mariah faced the front. "Did you give me your calming hocus-pocus when you touched my shoulder?"

"No, but heaven forgive me, I was tempted," she admitted.

Daisy giggled.

Mariah began driving toward the famous caverns, full of misgivings, full of doubts, feeling sad and disturbed and a bit panicked.

"So," Daisy began, facing Sister Crystal Grace in the back seat, "you're going to Bethlehem. Gonna hang with Mary and Joseph and see Jesus get born? The real manger scene. Righteous!"

"I'm looking forward to it immensely. I've looked forward to this day for many, many years. Did you find any new information on the paths through the caverns? Did you find any restricted caves? It's been so long since this whole thing began, since I first disappeared. You'd think I would have gone back to the cave, but I haven't. I always felt like it might take me away again." She exhaled. "Let's pray I'm right. I'm ready."

"There are several partially collapsed caves," Daisy told her. "Our neighbor Caleb Parsons is a geologist, and he had a full map of all the caverns, even the ones that have been closed off to the public. I took a photo with my phone."

"Wonderful!"

Mariah exhaled. "I read over every single newspaper clipping on your disappearance and eventual discovery. I think I know where to start. But it's quite a hike, especially in the dark."

"We have to find the right one, the exact one, or I don't know what I'll do."

"You can leave your body at our house," Daisy told her.

Mariah felt her hands begin to perspire.

Sister Crystal Grace groaned softly. "No. But thank you kindly for the offer. This is all uncharted territory."

"How does it work?" Daisy asked.

"When I travel, I lie down and envision where I want to go. Pictures help. I concentrate on a specific place and time. My body stays at the convent, but my psyche goes. It's quite mysterious, even to me.

"After several days my body is exhausted. I physically give out, even if I eat. I assume it's because my real body is at the convent, unnourished. Whenever I began to feel weary, I would close my eyes, pray, and return to my body. I never stayed past that spent feeling.

"Once, at an outdoor festival I passed out, but I still woke up at the convent. Which was a miracle in itself. Our Lord is a forgiving deity."

Mariah chuckled.

"I was careful. I knew my window. And I couldn't travel again until my body had completely recovered, usually a month or so. I don't know what will happen in the cave, but I can't stay in Mystic Ridge any longer. The answer to my future lies there, so I must find it. I must." Her voice was shaky. "When I was a child, I traveled for weeks, so it must be possible." She sniffed several times and wiped her eyes with the sleeve of her jacket.

"We'll locate it," Mariah promised. "Don't you worry, Sister Crystal Grace. We got this."

Daisy touched her elbow and relayed a proud feeling. Mariah was grateful. She pulled into the Crystal Caverns Park and turned off the headlights.

"Kind of cool that you have a whole park named after you," Daisy remarked.

"Kind of awkward, if you ask me," Sister Crystal Grace replied. "I've never desired any attention. It's the last thing I wanted."

Mariah wrapped a scarf around her neck and handed one to Daisy. "We need to cover up—there are probably surveillance cameras." She added gloves and a thick coat. Daisy and Sister Crystal Grace followed suit. They all climbed out of the car, flashlights in hand.

"Oh, no." Mariah pointed to a video camera atop a restroom. It was pointed directly at them, and a green light on the device was blinking.

Daisy quipped, "I can disable that." She closed her eyes for several seconds, and then opened them with a laugh. "Done-zo. It's offline, and any others in the area as well."

Mariah saw that the light was now off.

"You're very talented," Sister Crystal Grace said. "Remember with great power comes great responsibility."

Daisy howled with laughter. "Sister-girl, I am not Spiderman."

Mariah and Sister Crystal Grace both cackled, and the seriousness of the mood was lifted. A cool breeze surrounded them, and the clouds seemed to dissipate. A full moon lit the entire mountain range.

"Wow," Daisy said. "Purple mountains' majesty."

"Oh, my Lord," Mariah breathed. "I feel like we're being watched."

"I'm taking that as a good sign." Sister Crystal Grace turned on a battery-operated lantern. "We need Him on our side."

Mariah took the small suitcase, still conflicted.

"He started my journey. Hopefully, He will bless and assist my resolution and understand my need for refuge." Her voice was unsteady. "Please, don't misunderstand. I am grateful for all that I have experienced. But the time has come for a permanent sanctuary."

"We got your back." Daisy pointed to the full moon. "Girls, we need to bounce before that goes away." She held her phone out to Sister Crystal Grace. "Here's the pic I took of the layout and the restricted caves."

Sister Crystal Grace studied it, zooming in and out and then doing it again. "Let's just head up that ridge." She pointed. "I can remember it was a challenging climb." She put one arm around Daisy and the other around Mariah and closed her eyes. "Heavenly Father, protect our fragile bodies, and guide our steps with Your celestial wisdom."

❦

Vines and thicket and rocks and bushes made the journey proceed very slowly. After thirty minutes or so of walking up a clear path, they came upon the first cave. It was marked by a plaque with geological facts, and several iron benches.

"This is definitely not the one we're looking for," Sister Crystal Grace told them.

"Then no need to venture inside," Mariah said, concerned about what wild animals might be lurking in there. "There's two more up on that ridge." She pointed. "It's a long way from here, though."

They exchanged glances and set off up the path.

"Can I time travel?" Daisy asked Sister Crystal Grace.

"Not that I know of."

"Do you know anyone else who can?"

"Not yet."

"Is there such a thing as a curse?"

Sister Crystal Grace stopped walking and turned around. "Why do you ask?"

"A palm reader at the state fair said she cursed me and my family."

"That's troubling. Why would she curse you?"

"She abandoned her son Rahul and lied to her husband Ramir about it. I told the big guy where to find his kid."

"Is there anything in your way, blocking your daily journey?"

Daisy shrugged. "I don't think so."

Sister Crystal Grace exhaled very slowly and rubbed her forehead. "This woman is alone now. I can feel her anger. Certain instances can affect the future. Some actions can even prevent a person from existing altogether."

Mariah sighed. "I didn't feel that woman had any real powers, especially something that intricate."

"Yeah, she was just an ugly-ass witch." Daisy chuckled.

Sister Crystal Grace touched her elbow. "Keep your eyes open, Daisy." Her tone grew serious. "Watch for anything unusual in your home, or anything that seems out of place. Be aware. Don't take chances."

Mariah felt deeply concerned but refused to focus on another outlandish situation. "Lord have mercy. One problem at a time, ladies, that's all I can deal with. We must keep moving. Come on, you two. I'll think about that witch later."

As they climbed, a million questions jumbled through Mariah's mind, but the cool chill of the air and her respect for Sister Crystal Grace steadied her. Tonight had its purpose. She couldn't get distracted.

Oh, how she would miss the old nun. She knew it was selfish, but she really liked having her around to answer questions about when to intervene and when to leave things alone. Circumstances were never clear. Managing the townsfolk and keeping lives on track was going to be harder than she had initially imagined.

It was also confusing, and coping with confusion was not her strong suit. She wondered if Sister Crystal Grace was some kind of angel, somehow transported to Mystic Ridge.

Her brow furrowed as she stepped over branches and rocks. Did each town have a designated protector? Was Daisy like Sister Crystal Grace? Would Daisy disappear? Fears and misgivings consumed her, but she forged forward.

When they reached the next cave, there was a no-admittance sign.

"That's good," she remarked.

Sister Crystal Grace shone a flashlight into the opening, past a net intended to keep thrill seekers out. "I don't think this is it.

The opening is way too large. It's been years, but I feel quite certain this is not it."

Daisy looked up from her phone. "The next one is just a few feet away." She pointed.

They passed several large pine trees and scooted over a rocky area before spying a four-foot gap in the hillside. "Holy crap. We'd have to crawl to get in this one."

"Not it." Sister Crystal Grace said. "Too small."

Mariah took the phone. "There's one on the other side of the ridge about midway up. It's not a cave per se. We'd have to circle the mountain. And there's no pathway."

Sister Crystal Grace looked down the mountain. "This view is all wrong. I think we need to be on the other side, and it was more of a crevice. I'm sorry."

"Not sorry," Daisy spoke up. "No biggie." Her flashlight went out. "Give me the lantern, I'll lead the way."

A few clouds blocked the ivory glow of the moon, and the temperature seemed to drop even more. Sister Crystal Grace pulled Daisy into an embrace and began to sob loudly.

"Oh, sweet Daisy, you're so young and brave. I'm so sorry to put you through all this."

"Stop, Sister, you can't lose it now. We've gotta find your cave before the sun comes up. We can't get busted up here with you. The *Mystic Gazette* would blow the story off the hook."

"I hadn't thought of that." She dried her cheeks.

Mariah touched Sister Crystal Grace's shoulder and passed on a feeling of safeness and calm.

"Thanks, you're getting it. I feel better."

"No time for a meltdown, believe me. I've been suppressing one all night." Mariah shook her flashlight as it flickered and went out. "Let's go."

They tramped through the thick woods with only the small glimmer of light the lantern provided. After an hour they had only traveled halfway to the other side of the mountain. Mariah handed each of them a bottle of water and a granola bar. After a brief snack, they continued in silence.

The temperature continued to drop, and they all began shivering as they trudged through the dense forest. When they came to a small clearing with several flat rocks, Sister Crystal Grace sat.

"I must sit down. My knees and my back are aching, and my heart rate is extremely fast."

"I need a break, too," Mariah said as she found a smooth rock and sat. She took out her phone. It was dead. "Daisy, how much farther?"

Daisy looked at her phone. "It's..."

She looked at the trees around them, then toward the mountaintop. She moaned and handed the phone to Mariah.

"I'm not sure where we are. I may have taken us off-track." She plopped down with a thud. "My legs weigh a thousand pounds."

Mariah looked at the screen. The battery was at three percent. Crap. She pulled up the photo of the area and was also perplexed.

"I think we should head upward, but I'm not sure."

"It was high, but not the top of the mountain," Sister Crystal Grace said shakily. "I was young, but I remember that much."

Moisture filled Daisy's eyes. Mariah wrapped her arms around her daughter's waist, feeling her anxiety, suppressing her own.

Sister Crystal Grace's chin lowered, and she began to cry softly.

They were hopelessly lost.

Mariah rubbed her sore calves. She knew they needed a miracle, a real biblical miracle. *Please, God, help us! Jesus, Mithra, Mary—anyone?*

The chirping of the crickets and sounds of the wildlife around them seemed to quiet. Mariah looked at Daisy and Sister Crystal Grace, the soft glow of the moonlight on their tender faces. Stillness set in around them. Love poured from her heart, and sadness as well. Sister Crystal Grace's sobs tore at her, and now Daisy was weeping as well. What was she to do? How was she to help this lovely, giving pillar of the community find closure and peace?

Without so much as the crackle of a crinkling leaf, a solid white cat sauntered into the middle of their circle. No one moved. It greeted Sister Crystal Grace, wanting its head and chin rubbed, purring loudly as she obliged.

"Oh, my," she said. "At first, I thought this was Sterling, but it's not." She rubbed its head. "This boy has green eyes, and he's much thinner." She chuckled. "Sterling's eyes are like sapphires. But he is one of Sterling's offspring. I feel that."

Daisy wiped her face and pulled her knees up to her chest. "He's handsome."

Sister Crystal Grace continued. "When I was just a child, I rescued Sterling from a despicable man. He was a terrifying, soul-sucking devil from New Orleans, Eraste LeBlanc. He said he would return one day to retrieve him, but thankfully, he never came back.

"Sterling lived with me at my home, then at the convent, looking out for my body as I traveled. When Sister Mary Jean Stevenson began questioning his age, I took him to Senior Smiles Retirement Home. I wanted him settled before I left. He's slowed down a bit and fits in perfectly. He has way more than nine lives, that's for sure."

Mariah suddenly saw a tall, thin man wearing a tall hat, black tuxedo jacket, and soiled jeans strolling into downtown Mystic Ridge in a deluge of rain. Her breath became erratic. The kitty moved to Mariah and captured her gaze. The visions disappeared, and her body settled. She petted him and felt her remaining tension dissipate.

"Are you okay, Mom?" Daisy asked.

"I'm fine. How old is Sterling?" Mariah inquired.

"Crazy old—more than seventy, but he still gives off bountiful good vibes. They adore him at the home."

Mariah rubbed the kitty's chin as he purred loudly. "I think this guy is making me feel a tad less hysterical."

When the cat moved to Daisy, she stood and ran her hand down the length of its soft spine. "He's taking pity on us, that's for sure. He's here to help, I know it."

The cat headed into the forest, and she motioned for the others to get up. "Come on. I think we should follow him."

"You took the words right out of my mouth," Sister Crystal Grace said, stumbling to her feet. "We must trust and be obedient."

"Let's do it," Mariah added, rising and grabbing the suitcase. "For heaven's sake, he's almost glowing."

The cat walked purposefully into the woods, Daisy following. "Even in the pitch-dark, I can make him out. This is righteous!"

Sister Crystal Grace moved behind her.

Several minutes passed, and they kept a steady pace.

"Sister, is this normal? I mean, we're following a feline," Mariah pointed out.

"Sometimes we must trust in the unknown. It's weird, allright, but no stranger than my entire life. He could be an angel, for all we know. Angels come in all shapes, sizes, and species. Mystical occurrences are never far from me. Sometimes, there's just not a plausible explanation for things that happen."

Mariah stepped carefully but purposefully. "You sound like a grocery store quote book. You should be an author."

"Maybe I am," Sister Crystal Grace joked. "Well, I did help translate and copy a scroll or two."

"The world will never know what a rock star you are," Daisy pointed out.

"That's okay with me. I took vows of poverty, chastity, and obedience." She was quiet for a few seconds. "But I didn't vow to have a boring life."

Mariah laughed. "You're fearless, Sister. I'm always so unsure and frightened—like now."

"You just need to accept that the world is not all about you. There are forces bigger than us, and we have to follow our instincts and be the best person we can. Trust your path."

"I wish I had a path right now." Daisy giggled.

"My good friend John used to say 'You don't need anybody to tell you who you are or what you are. You are who and what you are!'"

"John? John Lennon?" Mariah chewed her lower lip as she carefully stepped through the dark pine branches. "So, Sister, were you always meant to be a time traveler?"

"I guess."

"You think the Lord sent that cat?"

Sister Crystal Grace turned and looked at her through the darkness. "He could have. Or maybe Sterling knew I was in danger. Maybe it's just forces of nature, like us, pitching in to make everything the way it has to be."

"Like you do? Like we do?" Mariah questioned.

"Sure. Good must prevail. We help out whenever we can. Maybe they're doing the same thing.".

For the first time in many hours, Mariah felt hopeful. Someone or something wanted Sister Crystal Grace to reach her destination. Someone with power.

❧❧

After an hour or so, Daisy stopped. Sister Crystal Grace and Mariah moved beside her to see what was going on. They watched as the cat scooted up a tiny path over several sharp rocks to a ridge. It gazed down at them.

"I guess it's up we go," Mariah remarked.

"I'll go first," Daisy said, securing her feet on the slick rocks.

Mariah stepped beneath her. "I'll catch you if you fall. Be careful."

Daisy easily scaled the steep area then disappeared. Sister Crystal Grace placed her palms together. As the lantern went out, Mariah exhaled and dropped it.

Daisy appeared again, peeking over the ridge.

"There's a cave up here, all right. It's covered by branches, and it's small, but there is a cave. Come on, ladies."

She reached down and grasped Sister Crystal Grace's outstretched hand then carefully helped her up. Together, they pulled Mariah to join them as she struggled to hold on to the suitcase.

When all three were atop the ledge, Sister Crystal Grace knelt facing the cave as the cat situated itself beside her. The two sat stoically. It was a sight to see.

Mariah was suddenly overwhelmed with emotion, and her knees wobbled. Once again, the clouds parted, and the alabaster moonlight illuminated the area. She pulled Daisy into her arms and wasn't surprised to find her crying.

"I'm scared," she confessed.

"Me, too," Daisy whispered. They held each other tightly watching...waiting.

"Amen," Sister Crystal Grace said, and then stood and faced them. Tears covered her face. "We...We've found the portal."

Mariah rushed to her, and Daisy followed. The three of them cried tears of relief, tears of joy.

Daisy was the first to speak. "What are you gonna do?"

Suddenly, a teeny glimmer of crimson appeared on the horizon. Sister Crystal Grace's face twisted in a wave of realization.

"That's it. That's what happened last time I was lost. He gave me light. The light is the key. It was a combination of worlds. I have to go. I have to go now."

She released them, lifted her suitcase, and hurried to the opening of the cave. An amethyst light appeared in its depths.

"Look." Mariah pointed.

Sister Crystal Grave turned and gazed at them once more, a slow smile spreading across her face.

"It's for my return. I love you both more than you will ever know.' She pointed to the cat. "Take care of Gabriel."

"Wait!" Daisy shouted. "I promise to help everyone I can, but I'm never going to be a nun. I'm so sorry."

Sister Crystal Grace giggled. "I know that, darling. Merry Christmas." She blew them a kiss, turned, and ran into the cave and into the light. An indigo blast of color illuminated the interior.

Mariah grabbed Daisy's hand and squeezed and tried to catch her breath. They watched as the light grew brighter for a few seconds and then faded to indigo and then disappeared altogether. The sun peeked over the horizon and bathed them in a warm orange glow. The cat rubbed against their calves as their heartbeats calmed and steadied.

Mariah took a deep breath and looked downward. "You're good, Gabriel."

Daisy released her mother's hand and chuckled. "That cat passes on better mojo than me." She went to the entrance of the cave and peeked in. "I don't see her."

Mariah went all the way to the back. There was a plain unremarkable wall of rock, and no Sister Crystal Grace.

"It's pretty small. It ends right here."

"Yeah," Daisy said, joining her and touching the dirt walls. "It's not very deep at all. It's kind of boring."

"She is really gone." Mariah said. "Hopefully, she's found her rightful place in the universe. Oh, Lord, let her be safe."

"Are you praying?"

"Yes, I am. Definitely, yes."

"Me, too." Daisy put an arm around her. "There is a higher power. I feel it."

Back outside, Mariah turned to take in the lovely horizon. Tiny snow flurries swirled magically through the rays of sunshine. Miles and miles of amethyst mountains were awakening to a fresh terracotta sky. A slight fog lay over the scene, blanketing it in a loving embrace.

"Epic," Daisy whispered, then cleared her throat. "I don't know if we can maneuver our way back. We came a really long way."

Mariah looked for the cat and found him waiting patiently by the rocky edge they had initially come up.

"I think we can," she said softly. "Gabriel is waiting." Her smile slowly turned to a thin line. "Your father is going to be worried sick." She took her phone out and glanced at it. "It's dead."

Daisy checked. "Mine, too."

"Hopefully, he hasn't called the authorities. You know your dad—he's probably at the theater right now, discovering there is no vampire musical. He knows we lied. When we get home, I'm telling him everything."

"Everything?" Daisy questioned.

"Yes, about me and you and all of this. He can't be in the dark anymore. Your powers of persuasion are astute. He's your parent, and he's my husband. He deserves to know."

Daisy thought for a second. "I'm not sure that's such a good idea, but you're the boss."

"We should get going."

Daisy went over to Gabriel and stroked his soft fur. "I wanted a cat for Christmas."

Mariah laughed. "He is a miraculous gift." She thought for a second. "And he might be with us for many, many, many Christmases to come. Merry Christmas, darling."

"Merry Christmas, Mom."

# EPILOGUE

D OLLY SLID INTO THE CORNER BOOTH, COFFEE AND NEWSPA-per in hand. "Oh, my word, I am exhausted. That was a long, long shift."

Eve sat across from her with a plate of hash browns doused in ketchup and pepper, and a large Coke. "I never got a chance to eat. So..." She pointed to the newspaper. "What nuttiness is going on this week in good ol' Mystic Ridge?"

Dolly opened the paper. "Hmmmm. Not too much. They're bragging about spring being here, like someone did something special to make it happen, like the folks here have a hand in the rotation of the earth."

"Ya never know," Eve drawled.

Dolly continued. "Looks like the winner of the Mystic Ridge Garden Club award for prize azaleas this year was Sally Jacobs. She's good people. Oh, hallelujah, Charlene and Emmet Huff are going to open a new pub and call it *Bubba's.*"

"Bubba's Honky-Tonk?" Eve asked. "Like the old one?"

"Na, just Bubba's. And they're going to have live entertainment. Lorraine Priscus is going to sing the ballads of Patsy Cline at the grand opening."

"I'm glad to hear it. I heard her sing at church. Heavenly. But Bubba's sounds like a blast. We need some action around here. I refuse to do that online dating thing. Anything else?"

"Seems like Josephine Evans just signed a book deal with a publisher in Charleston for a trio of books on southern families of the Civil War."

"Good for her. Sounds interesting. I remember her husband was quite the battle buff. I guess it rubbed off on her. Ain't that just like a man? Anything else?"

"Remember Millie from Enchanted Treasures?"

"Yes."

"Well, her cat Snowbell Two had a trio of white kittens, and they will be available for adoption soon."

"What? Ninety-nine percent of the kittens that I foster are white. There ain't a person in town without white cat hair on their clothing. It's cray-cray."

Dolly laughed. "Just the profound weirdness of our community, I guess. Somewhere we have a busy tom cat. The Gilberts have a new white feline. Or it could be that big ol' white male at The Senior Smiles Retirement Home—Sterling. He's been there, well—forever, and they probably never got him fixed."

"He was there when my great-grandmother was there," Eve told her. "And I saw him a few weeks ago when I took kittens there for a little pet therapy. Those blue eyes are just too heavenly. He was sitting in the lobby on that old blue children's desk, staring out the window, looking protective and ethereal at the same time. My great-grandmother used to say he was looking out for a dangerous man—the man who left him behind—praying he would never return. But my great-grandmother was several biscuits short of a dozen."

"It must be a different cat." Dolly pressed her lips together then spoke in a concerned tone. "I did see a huge black cat the other day."

"Really, a black cat? In our town?"

"Yes, it was clearly following Daisy Gilbert as she left Mountain Bagels."

"Hmm, that can't be good," Eve said. "Has Daisy offended anyone recently?"

"I dunno. It had hazy purple eyes. I almost called you, but it didn't look lost. It walked with purpose, and it appeared well-fed."

"You should have called me, pronto! I rescue any and all cats, and I could have assessed his motives."

"Sorry, my bad." After a few more minutes of reading, Dolly spoke in a surprised tone. "Well, Lord have mercy, I'm in shock. Lucinda Smith bought one of those tiny houses on Smokey Lane and is opening a charity boutique to help outfit needy women. She's gonna gather upscale clothing donations and sell them at extremely low prices. It's gonna be a non-profit organization."

"Wait." Eve held up her palm. "Lucinda? Black coffee-and-dry toast Lucinda?"

"Yep,"

"One-dollar tip Lucinda?"

"Yep. Says here she's turned over a new leaf and wants to help women succeed in the workplace." Dolly lowered the paper a tad. "She got some kind of inheritance and decided to use it for the greater good."

"Holy cow, I'm not gonna lie. I'm shocked. But I have seen her in church lately, staring at her daughter as she sings with the choir."

"I think Lorraine avoids her. No judgment, but mama-daughter drama is a pity," Dolly mused.

"Maybe one day they can work it out. I heard Simon moved out and even took the dog. Apparently, loneliness has been a good thing for Lucinda." Eve nodded.

Dolly ground her teeth together. "If someone took my dog it would be cause for war. That Lucinda just needs a hug. She does." She turned another page. "Looks like we're finally getting our own veterinarian—Leo Moses. It says he was a popular television personality on several African safari specials. He purchased a barn and some land near the mall."

"I saw one of those specials. He has a keen sensitivity to animals. It's astounding," Eve's eyes grew wide. "I mean it. He really talks to the animals, and they understand." She crossed her arms.

"That's just ridiculous. Well, he's moving to the right town. Maybe he can crack the case of the immortal cat at the old folk's home or the black stalker cat. Anyhoo, I'm looking for the weekly Sister Crystal Grace update." She paused as she scanned the columns. "Here it is." She paused once more. "Dang, still no sign of her? I mean, how does a elderly nun just vanish in the dead of night? It's so messed up."

Eve shrugged. "It's bizarre, allright. But they've searched every inch of town and that convent. She gone!"

Dolly glared at her. "Where does a woman of that age go? I mean, I just can't picture her cavorting around Atlanta or Vegas."

"Don't start again. We go through this same conversation every single Sunday. I don't know. No one knows. It's a dang mystery, just like when she disappeared as a child. History is repeating itself. Maybe they should call a ghostbuster or the FBI."

"I heard they did," Dolly said. "Both." She lifted the newspaper again. "Oh, thank heavens, some good news, at last. That sweet elementary schoolteacher Emma Parsons had a little girl."

"Hallelujah. What did they name the precious baby?" Eve inquired.

"They named her Evelyn."

END

# ABOUT THE AUTHOR

**SHELLY GAIL MORRIS** was born in Atlanta, Georgia, and attended the University of West Georgia in Carrollton. She has been married to her soul mate, David, for over thirty years. They have two sons, Keith and Mitchell. They lived in Chicago for eight years and now reside in Tennessee. She has had five books published and several short stories.

In the sixth-grade while walking home from school, Shelly found a white cat in a sewer. She scooped her up and took her home. She kept and adored that white cat for sixteen years. Today, she has three white cats and a cocker spaniel. She assists with two different rescue groups in fostering kittens and helping with adoptions.

# MORE FROM
# SHELLY GALE MORRIS

*For thirty-eight years Dandy James has only known farm life in Grady, Tennessee, her marriage, her children and her future arranged by her father. Daily, she endures the wrath of a man who stays with her for the sole purpose of acquiring her land.*

*Colin has led a rich, swinging life, enjoying all the vices wealth has to offer. He barely knows his children, and has no emotional connection to his wife. His job as a land developer is the only thing keeping him sane.*

*The two meet on a stormy night when Colin crashes his car into a ditch. Dandy breathes life back into him, and he knows she's an angel sent to change his ways, save his soul and love him for eternity. As he speaks tender words to her, words like she has never heard before, Dandy knows she is irrevocably in love with him.*

*Life is worth living again—worth fighting for. Dandy quickly repairs her distant relationship with her son and begins to investigate her property and why it had been listed as potentially available. Colin and his wife separate, and he learns his teenage daughter is pregnant.*

*Together, Colin and Dandy sort through the lies, and the evil Dandy's husband has been hiding. She remembers a painful detail of her past and begins searching for answers. For the first time in her life she has a friend, a real friend she can trust. Colin is there for her through the discoveries, and realizations too painful for her to bear alone. Will she ever be free? Can anyone save Dandy James?*

# CHAPTER 1

D andy gripped the steering wheel as her heart pounded. This did
*not* look good.

Why? Why did she decide to run to the market for a silly magazine? She'd seen the dark clouds drifting toward her neck of the woods,
and heard the deep rumbling of the storm approaching. In springtime, when the rains were heavy, thick patches of slick mud coated
the worn concrete roads—she knew this well.

But with Patsy Cline crooning on the truck's old cassette player
she'd sung along, enjoying the beginnings of the downpour. Running
into Adele's Mart, the cool rain had felt delightful on her skin. She'd
actually giggled.

Nothing was amusing now. Tennessee rains could be dangerous,
and as the seven-mile journey home loomed before her, she started to
sweat. It seemed like she'd driven directly into a typhoon.

The windshield wipers had little effect as heavy rain pounded the
glass. The skies were a deep gray and it was only four o'clock. She bit
her lip hard. It had been utterly foolish of her to leave the comfort of
home with the impending storm and for such a ridiculous reason. Had
she lost her mind completely?

She noticed two red taillights ahead of her in the distance. Thank
heavens. She could follow them and hope the driver could see the road
a little more clearly and guide her in the right direction.

She sped up, thankful for the coincidence. Although she'd lived
here all her life, she'd lost track of exactly where she was, and there
were ravines all along the edges of this tiny two-lane road that led
nowhere. And what in the world was such a puny car doing way out
here?

Suddenly, lightning flashed. A tree to the left of the road went up in flames, and the tiny car plummeted into a ditch. Dandy stiffened and slammed her foot on the brake. The back of the truck spun around on the slick surface, completely out of control. She kept her foot on the brake and prayed the old piece of shit would just stop.

The tires squealed. A scream burned her ears, and her throat dried out in an instant. Her stomach knotted as terror coursed through her. Finally, the world stopped spinning, and the steering wheel was the only thing she could focus on.

Glancing up, she saw that an oak tree had split in two, although only a few flames now trickled upward as the heavy downpour extinguished the blaze. Her heart shook her chest and she exhaled, struggling to catch her breath. She leaned back in the seat, put the truck into park and began to cry. *Thank you, Lord.*

She closed her eyes then opened them again. Through her tears, she saw the taillights in the ditch beside her. *Oh, my God, the puny car.* Someone was trapped, probably injured. *What should I do?* She had to get down there—and fast.

Inching the truck out of the middle of the road and over onto the far edge of the shoulder, she tried to be calm and think clearly. Thunder boomed. She turned off the engine and stared through the rain at the vehicle in the ditch. What was she going to find?

She'd never been brave, and the sight of blood made her sick, even when it belonged to the livestock. Ben had called her a pathetic coward too many times for her not to believe it.

She wiped the fog off the windshield and looked up and down the winding road. No one was coming. It wasn't a well-traveled road, and especially not on a day like today. It was purely up to her to help whoever was in that car.

She grasped the door handle. This was going to change her. She could feel it. At thirty-eight, Dandy James was finally going to grow up.

She took one final breath and darted out into the storm. Her feet were unsteady as the immense downpour drenched her. Flashes of alabaster lightning lit her way as she headed down the embankment. Suddenly, her feet slipped out from under her, and she fell hard on her backside, sliding right up to the passenger's side of the car.

Ignoring the pain, she stood and confronted a fancy Mercedes. The airbag was inflated, filling up the interior and coating it with white powder. She rushed to the driver's side and pounded on the window. There was a spattering of blood on the glass.

"Hello!" she shouted. "Are you okay?"

There was no movement. She tried to open the door, but it was jammed, so she dashed to the passenger's side, flung the door open and climbed in. There was a man, unconscious, still belted in, his head resting on the airbag as it slowly deflated. Dandy took his face in her hands. He opened his eyes, and despite the darkness, she could see he was struggling for breath.

Leaning over, she placed her mouth on his and started giving him mouth-to-mouth-resuscitation. His emerald eyes were red and swollen, and she could almost feel his agony.

She blew air into his mouth and prayed. After a few minutes, when she pulled her mouth away, he gasped, and she watched with relief as the color returned to his pale face.

"Are ya hurt bad?"

He gripped her hand. "Don't leave me," he whispered, and then his chin slowly sank to his chest and he passed out.

A clap of thunder shook the small car. Dandy felt tears of fright flowing down her cheeks. What was she supposed to do now? She glanced out the window as flashes of lightning lit up the dark countryside. *I should go get help. I should.*

Pain centered in her chest. He'd told her to stay. She did what she was told—always. She studied him. He seemed to be breathing with ease now, but his legs looked crammed up under the steering wheel and she wondered if he was trapped. She turned so her back was toward the windshield and sat on the center console. Blood oozed from his nose. She swallowed the lump in her throat and wiped the blood away with the sleeve of her jean jacket.

She touched his dark hair. It was tousled and slightly long. The strands were soft beneath her fingers. She ran her hand over his cheek. It was smooth, clean-shaven. He was a pampered man, for sure. His neck was thick and muscular. He was wearing a suit and tie. She loosened the tie and the top few buttons of his shirt. She caught a sweet musky scent, unlike anything she'd ever smelled on Ben. If she'd been standing, it would have made her knees weak.

He was good-looking, like one of the celebrities she watched on television or one of the cowboys she saw on the Rodeo Channel, but he looked more like the executive type than the rugged type. She didn't want him to die, not now.

Not ever.

Suddenly, he squeezed her other hand, and she remembered he was still holding on to her. She stared at their entwined fingers. They looked so comfortable and natural that way. She didn't know him at all, but for some reason, she liked him.

She caressed his hand. "Don't die," she cried.

With the rain beating down and her body growing cold, she found herself trying to remember when was the last time anyone had held her hand. Ben didn't hold her hand, never had. They hadn't even made love in many years. She'd given him a son and a farm—her job was done. Perry was eighteen now and probably hadn't held her hand since he was six.

She pressed her lips together. Her mother had held her hand four years ago, as she died in the cottage. Yep, that was it—the last time anyone had grasped her hand. Yet, this stranger's touch provided her with a feeling of warmth, like maybe everything would be alright, like maybe people still held one another for support and comfort. She prayed her hand gave him the same assurance.

Suddenly, she heard a crashing sound and turned to see her truck rolling down the hill behind them, landing on its side then flipping over, the wheels spinning.

"What?" the man said, lifting his head. "What happened?"

"My truck," Dandy began. "It just slipped down the embankment 'cause of the mud."

"Shit, my legs," he groaned, squeezing her hand tighter as lightning and thunder cracked the sky.

"What can I do to help you?" she asked, feeling that all-too-familiar uselessness. "I have to get you out."

He turned to her and spoke, his voice soft. "You breathed life into me. You're my angel."

Dandy was stunned. She'd never had a man speak so tenderly to her. His words warmed her, and unconsciously, she squeezed his hand.

He smiled weakly. "There's a cell phone in the briefcase in my trunk. It's coming down too hard right now, but when it eases up, you could get that."

"I'll get it now."

"No. It's too dangerous."

Dandy tilted her head and smiled a bit. "You hush up. You need medical attention pronto." With regret, she released his hand. "How do you get your trunk open?"

"There's a latch on my left, but I think my left arm is broken."

Dandy leaned across him and pressed the button his window down, grateful that the accident hadn't damaged the electrical system. She jumped out, dashed around the car and leaned in the window, located the trunk latch and pulled it. Nothing happened.

The front of the car was at such an awkward slant it was difficult to get back out of the window. Her feet sank into the mud as she took in the man's battered face. The wretched pain on it tore at her heart.

*I have to get him out.*

She leaned in again and fumbled beneath the airbag. Her hands were slippery, and the muscles in her arms tensed as she pulled and yanked at the latch. Her feet were unsteady. She felt clumsy and useless. With horror, she realized the dashboard practically rested on his lap.

His eyes met hers. "It's no use."

She heard the despair in his voice. "Don't worry. Maybe I can pry the trunk open." She straightened and looked around for a stick. All she could see was water, more water and mud. She hurried back around the car and climbed inside. "Can I get into the trunk from here?"

"Not that I know of," he said, turning his head slightly.

She dove into the back seat and checked for a way to gain entrance to the truck, but there wasn't any. She crawled back to the passenger's seat, pulled her jacket off and wiped the rain from his face. The deflated air bag covered the steering wheel. She laid her jacket over it.

"Oh, my legs," he groaned. "I can't stand it. Talk to me. What's your name?"

"Dandy," she murmured.

"That's a nice name. Different."

"When I was born, my daddy saw me in my mama's arms and declared I was a fine and dandy young'un. My mama said she knew right then that I was meant to be called Dandy." She pressed her lips together, trying not to think about her father.

The man winced in pain.

"I'm sorry. I didn't mean to run on."

He let out a slow moan. "No, you have a lovely voice. I could almost picture that happy scene. I'm pleased to meet you, Dandy. I'm Colin Kessler. How..." He took a slow breath and continued. "How did I get so lucky as to have an angel like you find me?"

"Lucky?" Dandy repeated. "You've gotta be kidding. What are you doing out in this neck of the woods?"

"I'm a builder, and my corporation is always looking for scenic spots for new developments and golf courses. An agent contacted us about some land that was going on the market this fall." He pressed his lips together. "I was just checking out the view."

"Not a good day for that. Me and my husband own a farm nearby."

"Were you on your way somewhere important?"

She felt a tinge of embarrassment. "It's stupid," she replied, shaking her head.

He grasped her hand again. "Distract me from this misery, or I think I'll start screaming," he told her in a shaky voice.

"Oh, you poor thing. I'm so sorry for you."

"Tell me about yourself, Dandy. Why were you out on such a night?"

"Well..." She paused. "The new *People* magazine comes to Adele's Mart on Saturdays. I like to pick one up every now and then. Sometimes I get to feeling a little out of touch. I like to read about all the exciting things that happen in the rest of the world." She gazed at him, and he smiled. "Nothing much ever happens out here." He coughed a few times, and her heart ached for him. "Let me try and get to the Harrison's place. I know it's near."

His eyes locked on hers with an intense urgency. "Don't leave me."

"Are you sure?" she asked, caressing their entwined hands again with her free one. "I need to get help."

"Don't go. I need you. I need your voice," he said in a broken whisper.

Her chin began to quiver. "I'm frightened," she admitted.

He tried to lean his head back on the head rest, closed his eyes and tightened his fingers around hers. "Me, too. You can't drive in that."

"My truck slid down the hill," she reminded him.

"Oh, yeah. I think I remember that. Well, you most definitely are not going out on foot."

Dandy exhaled. "I wish I had a cell phone. My son has one."

"Tell me about your son," Colin suggested, without opening his eyes.

"Perry's a good boy, helps Ben a lot." She racked her brain. They weren't close. "He travels around competing in rodeos—he wins the blue ribbon in calf-roping almost every time."

"Do you go with him?"

Dandy shook her head. "Oh, no. They don't want me around. I'd just be in the way. I stay home and tend to Lilly Bell and the other horses we board. I keep up the yard around the house and do a little gardening."

"Lilly Bell?" he asked.

"She's my old mare. A gentle sweetheart."

"What do you grow in your garden?"

"Tomatoes, peppers, pumpkins and stuff. I make a mean hot salsa."

"I'd like to try it someday. Will your husband come looking for you?" he asked, sounding hopeful.

"They're both in Texas right now—another big rodeo. I'm afraid I won't be missed by anyone. What about you? Will your wife call out the authorities?"

He raised his head and opened his eyes. "I'm up from Chattanooga, and I was planning to stay the night. Bridgett is probably whooping it up with her friends."

She detected a twinge of sorrow in his voice. A man with such a compassionate voice should be missed, cherished. "Do you have any children?"

"Two girls. Megan is fourteen and Celia is seventeen."

"Little girls are so precious."

"Just one son?" Colin asked.

She took a slow, deep breath and thought hard about her answer. Colin was a stranger to these parts.

"No. A long time ago..." She stopped mid-sentence, rubbed her forehead and changed direction. "It's been a joy raising Perry. When I had him it was the best day of my life. Three days after he was born, I spiked a temperature of one hundred and five degrees and had to be rushed to Grady General for an emergency hysterectomy. I'd always dreamed of a house full of children. That was the worst day of my life." She gave a little snort. "And believe me the Worst Day of My Life Award had a lot of competition.

"I think Doc Wallace caused the infection. He was three sheets to the wind when he delivered Perry. Anyhow, what's done is done."

Colin caressed her fingers. "I'm so sorry."

Dandy was wholeheartedly embarrassed. "Oh, I don't know why I gave you that whole sob story. It must be this storm. It's thrown me for a loop."

"You have every right to be upset about that. You should have sued the pants off that guy. What did your husband do? Wasn't he furious?"

"He and Doc go way back. He'd never admit his good buddy did anything wrong. It would be my fault before his."

"You didn't deserve..." He broke off, and his eyes began to flutter. He fell gently forward onto the steering wheel to rest on her jacket.

Tears choked Dandy, and she sobbed uncontrollably. She released his hand, crossed her arms over her stomach and rocked back and forth. He'd fainted.

"Oh, Jesus," she cried. *He has to be okay. He's so kind and considerate, and he asks thoughtful questions. Why am I telling him my life story? Why am I burdening him with old painful memories? He's a stranger, yet it doesn't feel that way. Am I that desperate for companionship? What the hell is wrong with me? And how—how—am I ever going to get us out of this nightmare?*

# CHAPTER 2

After weeping for what seemed like an eternity, Dandy forced herself to stop. Ben always said crying was for losers and fools. She cried a lot, sometimes for no reason at all. Simple television shows reduced her to tears, and even a glowing sunset could bring on sobs. She was unsure if it was sensitivity...or the sadness that never quite left her.

The ferocity of the rain slowed just a bit. She concentrated on Colin's breathing. The interior of the car grew darker by the second. She struggled to study his profile in the dim light and grasped his right hand again. He was warm. That was good, wasn't it? Again she moved onto the center console to be closer to him. She wanted to touch him, and began stroking his forehead gently.

He let out a soft sigh, and his eyes slowly opened.

Dandy's face was only inches from his. "Oh, I'm so sorry. I didn't mean to wake you." She started to move back to the seat.

"No, stay," he said, releasing her hand, and slid his arm around her waist. She leaned toward him and combed his hair back with her fingers, longing to provide comfort as he suffered.

"I want to help you. What can I do? Is there any way I can pry you out?"

He nuzzled his face into her arm. "I don't think so. I know my left arm is broken and my left shoulder may be dislocated. And my legs..." He groaned.

"Oh, Jesus!" she cried. She couldn't even imagine the pain he must be suffering. She could feel his breath warm on her neck. This was no time to fall apart. "Can you move them? Can you feel them?"

He let out a sharp cry. "I...I think I'm moving my toes. But my legs are immobile, trapped, probably broken." Lightning lit up the interior of the car. He pulled her close. "Your body warms me."

She threw both of her arms around his neck. "This can't be happening!"

"If I die, tell my girls I love them," he pleaded.

Dandy felt a chill rise up her spine. "Don't talk that way. You're going to be fine."

"I haven't set a good example for my daughters." His chin rose, and his eyes filled with moisture. "You're my angel. You'll tell them for me. Won't you?"

His words stabbed her heart. She wanted to kiss him and beg him not to speak of last wishes and dying.

"Colin, just relax. Put your head on my shoulder and sleep. I know you're in a lot of pain. This rain is going to stop sooner or later, and when it does I'm going to go get help. I'll make sure you're taken to Vanderbilt. The best doctors are there—no local yokel will get a-hold of you. You're going to be fine, darlin'."

She sounded reassuring, but she didn't feel that way.

His lips parted, but no words came out. She eased his head onto her left breast..

"Sleep. Things will be better when you wake up."

"I'm sorry for a lot of things," he whispered.

"Aren't we all," Dandy said, trying to keep an even tone as panic erupted inside her. If he was losing blood, getting all riled up would be the worst thing he could do. "I don't have much to talk about. If I tell you a little story, will you relax?"

His rested his head on her chest and exhaled. "I want to hear your voice, in any capacity."

"Alrighty. No one knows it, but I write fairy tales sometimes. I started writing them for my little girl, to tell them to her someday. It made me feel like we were together. I daydreamed for years and years about holding her in my arms and telling her my little stories. It brought me some peace."

He gazed up at her, his green eyes narrowed. She paused and wiped the moisture from her eyes.

"Anyhow, I never got to share them with her. It wasn't meant to be. Perry was only interested in cowboys and Indians, wolf legends and stuff like that. I've never told my stories to a living soul. They're probably stupid as all get out."

"I'd like to hear your tales," Colin said, relaxing on her shoulder.

"It might distract you from your suffering for a spell." She took a deep breath. "Once upon a time there was a tiny fairy named Rinka.

She was the tiniest, sweetest, most sincere fairy in all the Floating Daffodil Tribe. She gave off a soft lavender glow wherever she flew.

"Rinka loved adventure, and too often left the comforts of her soft flower home searching for excitement. One afternoon as she explored, she came upon children playing in a schoolyard. Since no one could see her but other fairies, fireflies and butterflies, she decided to investigate.

"She soared over the children, enjoying their laughter, dancing in their games, weaving through their arms and legs, having the time of her life, until a tiny handicapped child named Melissa spoke directly to her, and Rinka's teeny world changed forever."

❀❀❀

Dandy leaned forward and gazed through the windshield and up at the onyx sky. She could see stars now. Hours had passed, and the rain had finally stopped. Colin had fallen asleep about thirty minutes into Rinka's dilemma.

She chewed on her lower lip. He probably thought she was ridiculous, telling him silly stories while he suffered. Maybe he wouldn't remember anything at all. Was it too much to hope for? Maybe the pain would wipe away his memories of their frightening ordeal together. At least, at this point, she felt like he was not going to die. God had decided he could wait another day for Colin Kessler.

She felt an odd connection as she looked at him. She always took an instant liking to kittens and puppies or any creatures that needed her. This was probably just the same situation. She'd never had feelings for a man before, except Perry, and even they had become distant. He'd be graduating from high school soon, and if they weren't discussing a meal, they had little to talk about. Men were scary and pushy and had always treated her disrespectfully.

She thought that Colin was somehow different—and, oh, so beautiful. It was deeply odd to find him so enchanting.

"Colin," she whispered, "let me go get help now. I won't go without your blessing."

His head moved, and he made a short coughing sound. "My life has been a joke. I'm sorry. I'm sorry I haven't been the kind of person I should have been." His eyes met hers. "Will you forgive me?"

"I'm just Dandy, plain and simple, no one at all. I need to get to the Harrisons' and call for an ambulance."

"I want to die. I do," he cried. "Fucking take me to heaven or hell. I can't do this anymore." He bit his lip, and even in the darkness, she could see blood trickle down his chin. "Where's my laptop? I didn't

organize that foreclosure. Where's Jenkins? Is Phil here? It was un-
ethical to fire him. Did I miss the meeting?"

A knot formed in Dandy's stomach.

"It was Bridgett's idea," he bellowed. "I never wanted to sleep with
those women. They're just a bunch of bored, sex-starved, bitchy house-
wives."

Dandy perched on the center console and brought his hand to
her mouth and kissed it. "You're in Grady, Tennessee, and you're hurt.
I have to get to a phone. I have to leave you just for a minute."

"*No!*" he shouted, clawing at her.

"Yes," she insisted, shifting back toward the door, trying to be
strong, stronger than she'd ever been before. "I don't want to leave
you, but it's for *you*. I have to get help." She opened the car door.

"Don't leave me. I love you. You're good and pure. I can see that."

She climbed out, her feet sinking into the thick mud. *If he knew
the truth about me, he'd never say those precious things.*

"Colin..." She leaned in. "I'll be right back. I promise you."

"What about Rinka?" he shouted. "You can't lock her away forever."

Dandy was taken aback. "Please. Close your eyes and relax—you're
going to hurt yourself even worse. I'll be back." She closed the door,
and closed her ears to his yelling.

She took in her surroundings. Nothing looked familiar. *All my
damned life in the same crappy town, and when I need to know where I
am, I don't.*

She rushed up the hill, slowed as her feet sank into the wet muck.
As she reached the top, she saw lights up the road in the distance.
Harrison's Homestead.

She took off her mud-covered shoes and started running. As the
thick clouds disbursed, a silver moon lit her way as she raced down
the deserted road. The cool air soothed her mind and brought her soul
strength. The moisture in it filled her lungs as she reached the Harrisons' gravel drive and dashed up to the house. She stumbled onto
the porch and pounded her fists on the wooden door.

Joe Harrison opened it, gun in hand. "What in tarnation...?"

"Call an ambulance," Dandy screamed. "A man's run off the road
down there..." She pointed. "...at the curve over yonder. He's hurt
bad, trapped. Call the fire department, too." Her report made, she
took off again back toward Colin. He was delirious, and he needed
her like no one had ever needed her. She wouldn't let him down.

Her bare feet pounded the uneven pavement, and all she could think about was seeing him pulled from that death trap of a car and his pain relieved. When she reached the scene of the accident, she slid down the hill and flung the passenger-side door open.

"Help is on the way," she shouted. "Joe is calling an ambulance." There was no response. She leaned toward him. "Are you okay? Can you hear me? Colin?"

His eyes were closed, and he didn't react. She kissed him on the cheek once and then again and again, his soft flesh tender against her lips.

"You can't die. I have a feeling about you. You're a good man, a *real* man, with a soul and feelings you aren't afraid to share. I want to know everything about you. I *have* to know you." The sound of approaching sirens filled her heart with joy and relief. "Hold on, Colin, honey. Jesus is coming."

**SAVING DANDY JAMES,** by Shelly Gail Morris, from Zumaya Embraces; Trade paperback, $17.99, ISBN 978-1-93484-124-2, 244 pp.; Ebook, $5.00, ISBN 978-1-93484-125–9 (Kindle), 978-1-61271-431-8 (epub) Available wherever fine books and ebooks are sold

Printed in the USA
CPSIA information can be obtained
at www.ICGtesting.com
JSHW022132090124
55120JS00001B/32